T0204717

Killing Williamsburg

Bradley Spinelli

Copyright 2013 by Bradley Spinelli.
All rights reserved.
No part of this book may be reproduced, stored in a retrieval system, or transmitted in any form, by any means, including mechanical, electronic, photocopying, recording, or otherwise, without prior written permission of the publisher.

Le Chat Noir
www.lechatnoir.us
www.killingwilliamsburg.com

This is a work of fiction. Names, characters, places, and incidents are either products of the author's imagination or are used fictitiously. Any resemblance to actual events or locales or persons, living or dead, is entirely coincidental.

The author would like to thank Will Kenton, a sounding board since the beginning of this project, and Mike DeCapite, who shoved it over the edge.

First Printing, 2013
ISBN-13: 978-0615801414
ISBN-10: 0615801412

Cover design by Meghan Carey.
Printed in the United States of America.

To another He said, "Follow me." But he said, "Lord, let me first go and bury my father." But He said to him, "Leave the dead to bury their own dead; but as for you, go and proclaim the kingdom of God."
—Luke 9:59–60

"This is where I get off."
—Harold Wobber, the first suicide jumper from the Golden Gate Bridge

Killing Williamsburg

I. $100 Bar Tab

RUMORS

It started like a whisper... the gentle hum of a fall breeze whistling through the drying leaves of September's trees, gracefully spaced on concrete lawns. We overheard words dropped subtly, like cigarette butts and taxi receipts ground forgotten into the asphalt, snippets of clandestine conversation intercepted while standing in a deli line or crowded onto the morning L train. A whispered word to a close friend or colleague would fall strangely out of the corner of a skewed mouth, out of context and Day-Glo against an otherwise monochromatic montage, and an open, idle ear would pick it up like a torn scrap of newsprint and walk away curious.

I wondered if people in the neighborhood were doing more drugs than usual, because at first, the underlying buzz of the streets took on a feeling of energetic excitement. People seemed more on their toes, a little more likely to step back when jumped at. The distant attitude I had come to expect seemed to slacken, replaced by an alacrity hidden by raised coat collars. I thought everyone was suddenly looking to score. Or perhaps the slight drop in the temperature had brought about a reverse vernal effect, and the darting eyes of the street belied an eagerness to go home with somebody new.

Even Veracruz, on Bedford, was changing. I never went there. I wasn't cool or tattooed enough for the mobbing slew of hipsters lining up to slurp frozen 'ritas at happy hour, peeking out the open French doors with glances of undeserved superiority. But now, as I walked by, the eyes spooled out to me, trying to reel me in to tell them something. All the cool cats, dying of curiosity.

There were more sirens than usual, whining in the distance at all hours, singing their sad song, bouncing their incandescent tone off the buildings and down resonant sidewalks, blaring by with twisting light, splattering our wonder-struck faces with crimson and cerulean aptitude. Something strange and mildly sinister was afoot, but there was no answer forthcoming, so we tried to tune out or turn down the din and incorporate it into our lives as background music, like an Indian summer in suburbia peppered with the drone of chittering cicadas and staccato sprinklers oscillating over expansive green lawns.

The papers gave us no clue. We checked the metro section and found nothing out of the ordinary, and the obits were no help either. But we knew. Somehow we all knew. Something was happening. Our world was changing around us, and it was bigger than the influx of yuppies and trustifarians, bigger than the impending grand opening of the mini-mall down on 5th in the old Real Form Girdle Factory, bigger than Plan Eat Thai moving to a larger space, bigger than the shadow of the Empire State Building which never quite seemed to reach us. There was a darker shadow falling over us, a shadow not of New York, not of King Kong's body falling, riddled with bullets, not of Boss Tweed's fleeting shape running down the tarmac to catch a flight to Spain… a shadow of uncertainty. We could feel it in our bones and in our boots, in our carrot juice and our bagels, in our 3:55 final shot and our four-in-the-morning slice, in the *Village Voice* ink sticking to our fingers, in our American Spirits. Our eyes chased each other away, our ears begged to be bent.

This is the way we learn in the city, through innuendo and rumor, a pieced-together patchwork of seemingly useless information. Soon it seemed that anecdotes were traded by sheer osmosis. Sitting next to someone at a bar or coffee shop became a nonverbal education, as if we had learned to smell each other's thoughts, and each unfinished story became urban legend—and urban law—overnight.

An ambulance arrives at a residence, and a hysterical woman is seen on the street writhing, shrieking. Passersby see the gurney, the shrouded figure... but no one, not even the next-door neighbors, knows how or why. We wonder aloud, our voices carried in the wind and sucked off the street by hungry ears blocks away... "He was only thirty, maybe younger." "The girl went back home, out West somewhere." Nothing more... just dangling empty morsels, as tantalizing and tasty as petit fours.

Still, strangers were never pumped for information. The buzz rose to a deafening yet somehow muted collision of opinions. At Veracruz, the big French doors were shut, the blame placed on the stultifying September humidity, and through the glass, bathed in air conditioning, one could see small huddles of hipster heads pressed together in rapid-fire consultation, like the planning of a revolution. The L Café and the Deli Mart and Anna Maria's, the cornerstone businesses of our wampeter street corner, became hushed rush zones, express libraries; get in and get out. The neighborhood had the aroma of a conspiracy—the chthonic stench of competing conspiracies.

We dismissed the perpetual whine in the night as mere white noise of the New York soundscape, but the scream of the siren was a signifier of something more grave, like a pachuco teardrop tattoo. Half-swallowed anecdotes and rumors became fact, stepping the transubstantiating boundary between the ephemeral, ghostly vapor and the realm of the solid, the undeniable. Some people witnessed. Others attended funerals of friends or accomplices. Others heard, and believed. Sirens led to quick steps and bent heads. Quick looks on the street evolved into hardened stares. People quickened their pace, moving as fast as their counterparts on the island to the west, and went about their daily business with deadly precision. The scene at Veracruz, the litmus test of the neighborhood, morphed again, becoming a quiet, terse huddle of slackers staring downwards into their two-dollar margaritas and stubbornly refusing to speak except in monosyllabic heaves, like a diaphragmatic bellows blast, the squawk of an organist hitting a sour note.

Olive and I, no different than any other couple in the 'hood living in sin, bent towards each other over the kitchen table night after night as the light faded, the sun setting earlier and earlier. We spoke in hushed tones of what no one would say in public.

"Supposedly she took pills."

"I hear he stabbed himself, somehow. A kitchen knife or something."

"Gas. The oven, I think."

"A light socket? I don't buy it. There's not enough juice in these old buildings to kill."

"It sounded crazy, but you should have seen the look on her face."

It wasn't anyone we knew. Not yet, anyway.

LIFE IN THE 'BURG

Summer of '99. I lean out our bedroom window and take in the smells of the garden next door, the fecund scum on the tiny pool with its koi, hundreds of roses scaling the chain-link fence, the scent of the vegetable world laced with the pungency of cat piss. There are voices in the courtyard, so I step out to be introduced to Jamie, who came to visit Everett, and it isn't long before the entire Rear Gang gathers, sipping canned beer and settling into plastic patio chairs that Olive and I pulled out of an East Village dumpster at three a.m.

I thought that was it for me when I met Olive. That was love—all I knew of it, anyway. She was a Bay Area actress with a following and a reputation, and I was nobody, filling in at a playwright's festival. At the after-party in the Mission she was impossible to miss—sexy, tall, and brunette, flaunting her mad actress energy, with a French nose and eyes that disappeared when she smiled. I stayed late and drank, and when we were the last of our crowd left at the bar, sitting close and drunk at a table, she turned to me and said, "What am I going to do with you?"

"What do you mean?"

"You've been coming on to me all night."

"Wow… I thought I was being cool."

"You're not being cool at all."

I followed her into the lady's room and pushed her against the wall with a kiss and slid my fingers into her already-wet pussy. It was too fast, it was dirty—it was hopelessly romantic.

When we got to my place she wouldn't let me go down on her because she was having a herpes outbreak. STDs, and the threat of them, are the crux of sexual entanglement to my generation. We made out and groped, falling all over each other in the drunken bliss that poses as suspended animation.

I thought she was out of my league and figured I'd been played for a one-night, not-quite stand, but she came back that afternoon and we stood on my hardwood floor and smooched in sobriety. She was a good three inches taller than me even in her Chuck Taylors. We had protected sex, got stoned, and went to the Mission for tapas, staring at each other over tiny plates of delicacies like moon-eyed teenage lovers. The whole scene was embarrassing, but so was my lazy life in a town better suited to instant-millionaire dot-commers. She wanted to try her luck in New York, and I was an easy sell.

In May 1999, after a few weeks of couch surfing and frenetic apartment hunting, a thirteen-hundred-dollar broker fee got us into an apartment in the hip, hopping, happening Williamsburg neighborhood of Brooklyn. We joined the displaced East Village artists and the new wave of immigrants—not Eastern Europeans or Puerto Ricans, but cool kids and hipsters migrating to the cultural nexus of the world from Lansing, Denver, Austin, Des Moines. Twelve-fifty a month for five hundred square feet in a back building on North 6th Street, just off Driggs. The selling point was the courtyard between the eight-unit building in front—packed with aging Poles—and our three-unit building in the rear.

The rear building is a reno, so we all moved in at the same time. The downstairs is two early-twenties guys; Everett, a graphic designer from D.C., and Sam, a low-level government employee from Queens. The middle floor is ours, and the top floor is Scarlet, a gay girl from Texas, and Belle, a straight girl from North Carolina. New people, new place, the instant camaraderie in the miasma of change. Like the first week of college, cocktailing it up in the courtyard.

Belle has some mid-level management job and works insane hours, so she isn't inclined to hang out too long. She has a nasal twang to her voice, so I'm never sad to see her go. Scarlet doesn't stick around either; she wants to pick up girls, and it's hard for a girl to pick up girls with a straight girl, a straight couple, and two fraternity-minded guys in tow. But a few beers into the evening Everett stands and yells, "Black Betty!" I pick up the chorus with him: "Blam ba dam, oh Black Betty, blam ba dam, oooooh Black Betty…"

The undisputed hot spot of the neighborhood, on the dicey corner of Metropolitan and Havemeyer, recognized only by the crapped-out awning in front advertising the Don Diego Dance School. The kids are hyped, swinging with a DJ spinning dance tunes and the glamorous, gilded sine-curve ceiling winking down at us, convincing us to ignore that the joint is just a dive with a pseudo-Arabic face lift. All the tables in the front room are filled with late-twentieth-century beats in black drag and seventies butterfly collars, eyeing each other whole-heartedly and hoping for the last-call hook-up.

Jamie buys the first round of cosmopolitans in celebration of her cat's homecoming after three days on the prowl. She's an old friend of an old friend of Everett's, some crazy D.C. connection that I don't understand and don't aim to, but she's cute and knows how to drink.

Ty is happy to see us, his large frame held in place by a sports coat as always, his long hair threatening to dip in the drinks. "How are you guys? Good to see you," with handshakes all around. Ty sets up five glasses to chill and takes his time, slowly mixing the cosmos with the perfect ratio of vodka, Cointreau, lime, and cranberry, leaning over the bar to pour the pink. When the glasses are full we do the giraffe—slurping them down a half-inch without picking them up—so Ty can pour out what's left in the shaker. "There's a little more in here," he says, grinning, knowing that we love him precisely because we always get more than we pay for.

Everett dips into the dance floor, gettin' jiggy with the resident go-go, a sexy blonde, prone to wearing skintight spaghetti-strap tops. She's always here, and she's always on the floor.

Reeling into me, Everett's clearly drunk, as the primer of beers generally guarantees that one cosmo will put him over the edge. "Where's Sam?" I ask.

"He's over there." I follow his pointing hand and see Sam at the end of the bar, with an uncomfortable look on his face, clinking glasses with a black guy about six foot eight and weighing in at a cool ton. Sam laughs nervously and gives Ty his money.

"What's that all about?"

"I don't know." Everett downs his cosmo. "I think he accidentally ordered in front of that guy, and now he's buying him drinks."

"Better him than me."

Everett puts his arm around me with the confidentiality and congeniality that only the inebriated can muster. "I love you guys. I really do. You and Olive are so great. I'm so glad you're my neighbors."

"I love you too, Everett."

"Whoa, look at that," and he's gone, back on the dance floor doing the bump-and-grind with a Puerto Rican girl in a tight skirt.

Jamie snuggles up next to Olive on a shared barstool. It looks promising. After all, Black Betty is the dirty bar, where last call can lead you to a coke-sniffing Metrocard party or a wild ride to Brighton Beach to decipher Cyrillic billboards. Why not a threesome?

Sam comes lurching over, one hundred percent frat boy. "Oh my god, did you see that guy? That guy is huuuuuuuge. Whoo hoo! Yeah!" and he does an embarrassing little cabbage patch move, bumping into a girl in a white dress that looks like it was painted on. She casts him the evil eye. He turns to me in confidence. "See her lookin' at us? Yeah… I saw that."

"So why are you buying that guy drinks?"

"When you see someone that big, it's better to stay on their good side."

"Fuck that asshole. I've seen him in here before—he was giving me shit because Liv is taller than me. I wouldn't buy him a body bag."

"It would be expensive!" We laugh and Sam moves on to "take a leak" and I don't see him again for the rest of the night.

I get on the dance floor with Jamie and Olive, and end up

doing most of my dancing with Everett and the go-go. Jamie and Olive square off, digging each other. Jamie is training to run a marathon and has the ass to prove it. She can't be taller than five one or five two, which I admit to finding alluring since my girlfriend is taller than me. But Olive is the dancer in this scene, Olive and the go-go. They move like gypsies. Everett and I watch like hyenas.

Sex is always in the air at Black Betty. It hangs so thick you could cut it with sarcasm, smelling the steamy underside of the boys' balls as they sweat on the dance floor or lean over the bar trying to get Ty's attention. The women fan themselves, trying to look fresh, but it's hot as Death Valley in here and those skimpy clothes are getting wetter and wetter, from the plunging necklines to the hiked-up hems. It's hot and the cosmos are getting to me in the best possible way.

It's four a.m., the ugly lights come up and Ty, still smiling, yells in his booming bouncer voice, "Drink up! You don't have to go home but you can't stay here!"

We pour out into the throng of partiers accumulated on the sidewalk, arguing about where to go next. Summer has opened its arms to us, and no one who's made it this far has any interest in sleeping.

Everett speaks German to some brunette cutie. He's half black, half white, and grew up in Germany. He has no accent whatsoever and it's easy to forget that he's bilingual. "She knows of a party on 3rd," he says, and moves off with her out of the oasis of streetlight.

"I'd invite you over," Jamie offers, "but there aren't any drinks at my house. Nothing."

Olive and I share a look.

Jamie's apartment is a dingy old storefront with graffiti on the outside walls, but the inside is a cozy little hideaway. Jamie sits in the corner of her eight-foot vinyl couch, and Olive side-saddle on the floor. The talk winds its way into slow comfortable chatter, and I close my eyes to it all and let the girls while away the morning, letting my head fall into Jamie's lap, as I rub one of her tiny feet and Olive rubs the other. She succumbs to the moment and bends over me in submission to relaxation, and Olive asks, "Will you kiss Benson?" She does, leaning over me and kissing me with little birdlike kisses, her tiny tongue delicately darting into my mouth. Olive leans in and kisses her, and I lie underneath and between them, watching, nibbling and caressing Jamie's breasts through her shirt. Olive keeps stopping and asking, "Are you okay? Is this all right?" But all three of us are relaxed, lovely, caressing, kissing… I say nothing and take the opportunity to rub Jamie's quim through her black capris as she kisses Olive.

But it's five-thirty in the morning. Olive has early plans and Jamie has to be up at Seasons to work brunch—how typical that an art historian would be reduced to waiting tables.

"But I don't want to miss an opportunity," Jamie complains, but there, in the wee hours of the morning at the start of a seemingly endless summer, her regret falls softly without meaning. We have the whole summer, we have all the time in the world.

Of course, back then, none of us knew.

RAINY DAYS

Wasting away in Williamsburg, watching the teeming masses streaming in from their lucrative Manhattan occupations, milling past ancient Polish ladies toothlessly gumming their macaroni and cheese.

The women are beautiful. The weather is muggy but dry, overcast without rain, warm without sunshine. The people are inscrutable, preoccupied, surrounded by the myth of skyscrapers and persistent notions of greed. The unspoken boastful nature of the successful is continuously in our faces, flattening our noses as if pressed against panes of glass. The dedicated fail, and the witless and lucky become millionaires.

I have too much time on my hands and can't stop my mind from revolving it all. I'm not working, I don't know enough people in this dirty, sweaty city, and I'm beginning to wonder if this is going to pan out. The impending dread is starting to get to me, and not nearly as bad as the overwhelming sense of whatever.

Even with Liv in the next room, I am waiting for the phone to ring from a distant land with a familiar voice begging me to come back. Or waiting for the front-door buzzer, the arrival of the girl next door, who watched me through the window touching myself and wants to help me out. I am waiting for something to happen. I am waiting to walk to the corner for cigarettes or coffee or toilet paper and find myself face to face with my destiny, the love of my life, my soul mate, my perfect match, my one in a million. But with six billion people in the world, even if you're one in a million, there are six thousand people just… like… you.

I see computer geeks. You know, that kid who got his lunch money stolen in elementary school, got beat up all through high school, never went to college but stayed home jacking off to porno mags? That guy launched an internet start-up and is now a millionaire hiring thousand-dollar-a-night hookers and thinking about buying something nice, like the Bahamas.

The polarities have been completely reversed. The shady deal is now the standard. Production is bunk; ideas are commodities. The industrial revolution is over. Steel has been replaced by software, and the sweatshop is now a mid-town skyscraper filled with cubicles.

It's the birthright of the white man. Work in an office, sell your soul, and learn to dig white guilt and emasculation. The nuclear family has detonated, and all those petty functions it used to serve are merely services that can be easily bought. If you have a psychological problem, talk to your therapist. If you have a money problem, talk to your financial advisor. If you have an emotional problem, talk to your hairdresser or your bartender. You work with peers, celebrate with your cronies, fuck your lovers. You live with a stranger who is never home but always pays the rent on time. As near as I can tell, that's the New Yorker's ultimate dream.

And the hobby, the ultimate pastime, is bitching. Bitching is the fashionable form of expression. It connects us across racial and religious boundaries—we all love to bitch.

But why bitch when you can leave? The exit door is clearly marked, and handguns are widely available in America. And for many of us, the Prozac life we're living is worse than death. Hopelessness, loneliness, and depression are rampant, our occupations and relationships are unsatisfying, and the struggle for validation is seldom won.

The only thing that might keep Americans going is the chance at fame. All interesting humans are famous. They have money, they have prestige, they are recognized everywhere they go, and you're not one of them. Which means you want to be.

And the famous exemplify the lure of death. The ones we love the most have seen the exit sign and run right towards it. Kurt Cobain is a legend, and Hemingway set the shotgun precedent. Half our heroes in the entertainment industry have killed themselves with self-medication—River Phoenix, John Belushi, Jimi Hendrix. Our heroes—suicides, all. Unconsciously, we know. This is the life. A life leading to death, a slow, regulated suicide. Last I heard the mortality rate was a hundred percent. Life causes death, more at eleven.

I know I can't be special. I know I won't be famous. And I know I can't kill myself—I'm too vain for that—but I know I'll be dead tomorrow. I think that's what tomorrow really is: death. Every day tomorrow is still out of reach. But the exit sign is clearly marked, and it's only a heartbeat away.

THE TRACK

After surfing the subway to Penn—stopping to dig a jazz combo ripping it up—I rode the LIRR out to "The Island" and wormed into the Belmont racetrack through the maze of people and coolers and blankets, finally finding Phil and Toni near the rail. I've known Phil for a good ten years, though we're only now living in the same city. He's finishing up his PhD in literature at NYU, as is Toni. Phil's a tall, lanky genius with a square-jawed, Kentucky face, and he and Toni—a tall Wisconsin cutie with an irresistible gap between her teeth—complement each other well. It was just good to see him, like a fish dropped back in the water, suddenly able to breathe. I wanted to dump my entire existential crisis in his lap, but I didn't need to. Phil handed me a cold Tecate with lime.

Toni asked the inevitable question: "Where's Olive?"

I shamefully admitted to having ditched her. Phil shrugged, and I slouched onto a bench in the warming sun of the track. No one was winning any money and the thing to do was to talk smack.

Phil was in the middle of a conversation with an old dog in his early forties, complete with racetrack hat and the permanent fixture of a Camel between two fingers, who apparently had lived in Williamsburg in the late eighties but moved to downtown Brooklyn when the East Village artists started coming en masse.

"What was it like before?" I asked him.

"It was a great place back then. We were pioneers. It was

nothing but old Italians and Puerto Ricans. There was the L Café and nothing else out there. You'd see another white person, like, once a week, standing on the platform for the L train, and kind of wave at each other."

"Paisanos," Phil said.

"Exactly." He took a drag and reflected on the rapidly changing odds on the big board. "You used to be able to score drugs right down on South 2nd. It was sketchy, not like it is now—fucking trash bags in the cans on the street. Like it's Times Square or something." He gave a little snort. "You used to be able to walk into a bodega, ask for a pack of cigarettes, and kind of look at the guy—'And a shot of rum?'—and he'd take a bottle out from under the counter and pour you a shot."

"That's cool."

"Yeah, well, no good thing lasts forever." He tipped his hat and gave us a grin that exposed a broken tooth. "Good luck, you kids. And you—" he shot Phil a grinning gaze "—trifectas will break your heart." He disappeared into the throng, making his way to place a bet.

I was in a bit of a tight spot, as Olive had the money, and after the train ride I was down to my last two bucks.

Olive breezed in and sidled right up. "I can't believe you left without me!"

"It was the last train."

"They ran another one. There was hardly anyone on it. It was nice."

"Fuck, I'm sorry, baby. I didn't know if you were coming." I was in hot water, but she had some money, so we all hunkered down to the serious business of betting.

The ninth race was the big to-do, because a horse named Charismatic, having already taken Preakness and the Kentucky Derby, was up for the first Triple Crown in decades. Olive and I bet Charismatic to win, and I boxed a trifecta with

Charismatic, Best of Luck, and the Lemon Drop Kid—I liked the name.

This was a race that actually mattered. Big-time gamblers all over the country were watching this race on TV, listening to it on cheap transistor radios, hanging out at sleazy OTB joints to lay their money down, calling bookies and changing bets at the last possible minute. And here we were, watching it all, up close and personal. The gates blew open and the horses tore out, throwing dust. As they came around the final turn it was impossible to see what was going on. I screamed like an amateur, and we were deafened by the yelling behind us—everyone seemed to want Charismatic to take it. They roared by us with thunderous hooves, unstoppable steam engines of jockey, hide, and sweat, bearing down on the finish line in a bundled frenzy.

It was a major upset. The Lemon Drop Kid won it, a horse that we hadn't even figured on came out of nowhere to place, and Charismatic ran third, closely followed by Best of Luck. The man was right: "Trifectas will break your heart." You could come so close to winning a grand on a two-dollar bet.

I braced to get chewed out by Olive when we got home, but I was spared by three messages on the machine from Hoagy, telling us to come to a party at his place.

The second we moved to New York, a fellow actress Olive knew from Seattle came to visit and stayed with a painter ex-boyfriend. The ex-boyfriend, Hoagy, turned out to be an amiable, broad-shouldered Washington redneck in his mid-thirties.

We careened on to Hoagy's, at Bushwick and Devoe, on the other side of the BQE. Hoagy met us at the door, his boyish face smiling, tall and big and a little fat, every inch of him aching to be hugged. He promptly poured us double shots of Absolut on the rocks, then gave us a tour of his mind-bogglingly exquisite art. We were the only ones there. "My neighbor passed out already," was his explanation. "I guess it's hard to throw a last-minute party."

Then the Dick, Hoag's roommate, came home, decked out in fancy-schmancy clothes that made him look like even more of a puny little shit than he is, with those birth control glasses and that straight-line, no-lipped mouth. "I'm very upset with you about the very idea of having a party tonight. The idea!" He berated Hoag, failing to recognize that whatever was going on in the apartment could never be considered a party. Hoag came off as sufficiently ingratiating, and the Dick said he'd be back later and left.

I started to fade. I lay on Hoag's bed with a hat over my face.

I woke at four in the morning and Olive was crawling into bed. I was overcome with that just-woke-up-in-someone-else's-bed-and-desperately-need-to-go-home feeling that we drunks know all too well. I found Hoag in the kitchen. "I'm going to sleep outside tonight," he said, "so you guys go ahead and get comfortable."

"Man, I really gotta get home."

"Okay, that's fine too."

I went back to Hoag's room and tried to get Olive up but it was no go. I shook her, talked to her, kissed her, finally grabbed her bodily and sat her up. She opened her eyes but it was nothing but whites. "I can't walk," she said, and fell back out of my grasp onto the bed.

Hoag stood in the backyard looking around at the grass, mentally doing the dog's three turns before lying down.

"I can't get Liv up. Is it cool if I leave her here?"

"Oh sure. I'm gonna sleep in the yard tonight. Bye, buddy."

I stumbled home and passed out.

We're broke, we're unemployed, and it's a pretty good life.

DOG BAR HIJINKS

"I wonder why we bother, why we trouble ourselves trying to figure anything out," I said. "If the nineties taught us anything, it's that there's nothing left to learn." I was on the phone with Phil, getting dressed to meet Hoagy at the Dog Bar.

"History always offers a perspective," Phil said. "Living in a time is never as fulfilling as looking back on it with reverence and nostalgia."

"Yeah, everyone always wishes they were born in a cooler era. But were the twenties roaring for everyone?"

"And the thirties," Phil said. "Life is a shit sandwich, and the more bread you got, the less shit you gotta eat."

"Yeah, but living through it gave survivors infinite hardass points. Didn't your granddad ever call you a pansy?"

"Natch. But the forties were deliciously romantic. Men in hats, calling women dames."

"But there must have been a dark side to film noir."

"Nice," Phil laughed. "I think you mean World War II."

"What about the candy-ass fifties? Sweet cars, the novelty of TV, Mr. and Mrs. Cleaver—"

"Sheltered innocence and the quaint paranoia of nuclear holocaust."

"Bomb shelters and smiling women selling cigarettes on TV. The sixties?"

"Vietnam protests, free love and free dope."

"And the seventies were so groovy," I said, "Disco and swingers' clubs and real good drugs."

"And, oh, the eighties."

"Frankie says, 'Relax.'"

"Credit cards and cocaine. And a president who couldn't remember anything bad ever happening, and neither could we."

"Man, what are they gonna say about the nineties?"

Phil didn't blink. "AIDS and the Internet."

"I gotta go." I had my boots on.

"Cool."

I put the phone in the cradle and went out the door. On the walk over my mind was revving. The nineties are almost over, nothing in the glass but spit… but Phil missed something. AIDS, the Internet… and the seventies. Because for all the hype about a new age, the nineties utterly failed to develop a persona. Culturally, we're in a rut. So we've recycled the seventies. Everything that made the seventies has been dragged out of the closet, de-mothballed, and put back on display by Generation X—our earliest collective memories rooted in the seventies firmament of Carter and disco. We miss *Star Wars* and butterfly collars and white-boy Afros, and that lipsticky kiss our mother gave us on the way out, the kitchen still reeking of nail polish remover, somehow covering up the possibility that she and dad swing, that they're going to a discoteque to get crazy on quaaludes, or maybe they are just going out to dinner with friends. To Sizzler. In the station wagon. And maybe a movie. A drive-in movie. With Ernest Borgnine.

We're not slackers, whiners, or lazy wussies. We just don't care. And we don't care precisely because we've been given the license not to. It's the curse of freedom, finally understanding that it doesn't matter what you do. Eventually you'll die, and all you leave behind is a paper trail and maybe a couple of rugrats that have already forgotten your name. This is the freedom that our forefathers paid for, with brutal wars and marketing strategies.

The love of the seventies isn't about aesthetics, we just want to forget. We want to go back to that safe sanctuary of the Cold War, knowing who was good and who was bad and believing that divorce was a tragedy. We want a recognizable difference between the people on TV and the people on the street. We want to wake up on Saturday mornings and watch cartoons and eat cereal until mom and dad get up and cook pancakes and take us to the movies. We want to forget everything we've learned about adult situations—divorce, pregnancies, politics, unemployment. We want to wear bell-bottoms and go to the disco and have casual sex.

"We learned existentialism too young and are screaming for some Sartre-centered absolution," I said, almost getting it out without spitting. "We want a release from the responsibility of adulthood."

"Sing it, brother," Hoagy said.

"The rigors of adulthood are ridiculous to us, and we, um, we either embrace it with a stiff upper lip, y'know, doing the yuppie fandango with such commitment that we come off like carbon copies of baby boomers, somehow more shallow and sitcom-quoting in our self-mockery…"

Hoag peered at me over a pint glass. A blonde with a tattoo sleeve gave me the stinkeye from the corner of the bar.

"What does *fandango* mean?" Hoag asked. I really should have been having this conversation with Phil.

"I don't know. *Or*, we just refuse to grow up, keep calling ourselves kids, and swing temp jobs and table-waiting gigs into our thirties. And some of us waffle back and forth. 'It's time to grow up, get a real job—'"

"'Get married, get a house—'"

"'It's time to stop taking myself so seriously. I'm quitting my job. This marriage is over!'"

"'I'm getting a motorcycle and hitting the road!'"

"'I'm gonna move back in with my parents!'" My beer was empty and the hot blonde had disappeared. "My god, how we loved the seventies."

"You're so totally right. I'm buying you a shot." Hoag called out, "Oh, Dizzy!"

I knew that Hoag's buying me a shot was his way of disagreeing with me, but it wasn't the first shot and I realized that I didn't give a shit.

Alcohol is the grease that keeps our wheels lubricated, saves us from despair, and keeps us plugging. Night after night at the Dog Bar with Hoagy and Olive, none of us employed to our satisfaction, the two of them artists frustrated with their inability to make a living at it, and me an angry philosopher with no outlet but the drink.

Olive, at least, got a job at Oznot's Dish. She wanted to wait tables but they needed a hostess, and apparently they want to groom her as some kind of manager. It's only twelve bucks an hour, but it's under the table and will get her out of the house three or four nights a week and put some money in her pocket. The definite disadvantage for me is that she has to work at night. It's easy to find something to do during the day, but nights have a tendency to whittle themselves away like redwoods, making me wonder if time has stopped and the clock is only joking.

By one o'clock, Olive sits next to us at the Dog Bar slamming martinis to catch up, and as the night wanes on to early morning Hoag begins his whine: "I want to smoke some poooooooooooo…" Since Olive's friend in San Francisco sent us some nasty shit stuffed in a pound of Pete's coffee, we oblige and head home to talk smack and pull bingers and watch Hoag do impersonations.

We sneak home, chasing each other, running down the block, hiding behind cars and ducking into doorways like a bad *Starsky & Hutch* episode, playing like children—or like drunks. Olive needs to pee, and Hoag, of course, wants weed, and I must need something, because Hoag kicks up a soliloquy in a whining, four-year-old's voice: "I have to pee. I'm cold. I have to poop. I want a Popsicle. I have to wipe my butt.

I'm cold. I have to poop and pee *and* fart." We all join in and whine together, sliding down Bedford Avenue at four o'clock in the morning, and a Boar's Head truck comes rolling down 6th and Hoag and I chase after it.

"Hey, can I get a chicken sandwich?"

"Hey mister, please stop. I need a side of roast beef."

"Come on, throw us some salami!"

The truck doesn't stop but the driver waves, grinning at our inebriatic idiocy, and soon we're back at our place, puffing on a pipe and pouring bourbon, and a light rain begins to fall, cooling the air and delivering a reprieve from the crushing heat of our stagnant apartment. Olive runs outside and stands on the makeshift bar—a chest of drawers that Sam and Everett and I dragged into the courtyard for one of our parties—her arms extended above her head, face smiling brightly up into the rain, a grin bigger than the moon. I turn to say something to Hoag and hear a heavy, sharp crinkle of sound followed by the unmistakable tinkle of breaking glass. I look out and Olive has vanished. Hoag and I run down and find her behind the slippery wet bar, on top of several cases of empty beer bottles, the dead soldiers of the Brooklyn Brewery's ten-dollar Fourth of July beer sale. She's lying on a crumpled mountain of broken glass, but god bless alcoholism, her body is so perfectly gelatinous that she doesn't have a scratch on her.

We all run back upstairs laughing and Hoag discovers an old roll of gaff tape—black, cloth taped use in the theater, which Olive must have picked up somewhere with pack-rat reasoning. I do my standard routine of lying on the floor, stretched out like a corpse on the cool hardwood with my arms behind my head, and Hoag gets creative with the gaff tape, making mustaches and beards and cracking us up—the Hitler mustache, the Snidely Whiplash, the sexy French maitre d', the Elvis sideburns, the slacker goatee. Olive goes digging and comes out with some glow tape, and Hoag cuts out a mustache and turns off all the lights.

From my vantage point supine on the floor, Hoag's glowing mustache becomes my beacon in the dark, a bouncing, guffawing will-o'-the-wisp of hope, my light at the end of the tunnel: sheer, unadulterated silliness, the only defense against boredom and inevitable financial destitution.

UNDERWATER

I was out too late with Hoag and spent Sunday surfing Everett's couch. Olive came downstairs on her way to work and hassled me. "I have to go to work *all night* tonight, and you spend *all day* downstairs? You have all night to play video games. Can't you spend a little time with me?"

"I'm sorry, baby. I only came down for a minute and then…"

"Uh huh."

"I'll get a nap so I can get up when you come home."

"You better."

"I love you. And did I tell you how beautiful you look?"

"Oh, shut up."

"No really, you do." And she did, all decked out in a peach sarong and a tight black top, her hair washed and bouncing in black curls all around her lovely little face. I hate this damn restaurant job of hers, but I have to admit, the fact that she has to dress nicely is an added bonus, even if I only see her on the way out the door. This hippie from Berkeley is transforming into a stylish New York beauty, wrapping herself in long, snug skirts and tight sweaters, wearing a lot of black.

Sam and Everett flipped to live TV. A rear admiral from the Coast Guard gave updates on the missing JFK Jr. plane.

"Man, that guy looks nervous," I said.

"He oughta be. He's on every station," said Sam.

"You think?"

"Let's see." Everett started clicking through the channels. Sure enough—CBS, NBC, ABC, CNN, UPN, the WB, and Fox.

"That poor guy," I said, "he must be scared to death. That's a man with a regular job, he rides around on boats, probably does a lot of paperwork—he's in the Coast Guard, he works for a living. And he's on national TV with all these moron journalists asking him stupid questions about JFK Jr. Look, he's sweating. Wait—go back one, Everett. The other angle is better."

"The color's all wrong." Everett clicked to another station.

"Does the sound seem off?" I ask.

"Sounds bad," Sam agrees.

"Must be one of those microphones way on the left there."

"Look at all those microphones."

"Mmmm… I like the other angle better."

"Yeah, but the sound is better on—yeah, yeah, that one."

"But the color sucks."

"They set up in a hurry. Give 'em a break."

"I think that's his good side. If he wants to be a newscaster he should always make them shoot from the left."

"Go back, go back—look at that guy in the background!"

"Ha! He thinks he's out of sight. We see you!"

Everett laughed heartily, and Sam clapped his hands.

"Man, we are some sick fuckers. Everyone's all worked up about JFK Jr., and we're comparing camera angles."

"Who cares about Junior?" asks Sam. "He was always whining about how the public wouldn't leave him alone. What's he doing living in Tribeca?"

"Did he ever do anything?" I asked, genuinely ignorant.

"Made a good living off his dad's name," Everett answered.

"Had a magazine or something. Did nothing, died a

hero." Sam was antsy. "I can't believe there's nothing else on."

I knew that Sam was being callous, but it's hard to disagree. The generation above us remembers where they were when JFK was assassinated. But JFK was our president, a leader, a famous philanderer who got to fuck Marilyn, the guy with Bay of Pigs egg on his face. He did something, like him or not. But JFK Jr.? The coverage is trying to present him as some sort of victim, an innocent pilot lost at sea. But if he's dead—and he probably is—it's because he was dumb enough to fly in unsafe conditions. Or maybe he was whacked, which would make him just another Kennedy. The real tragedy is the girls who were with him, and they're not getting any play.

The rest of the week I'm fighting for the surface. I see a job lead in the paper, and there's no listing of the name of the company, an actual person to send information to; just a description of the job and a number. So I send out fax after fax, but can't follow up and don't know if they even received the damn things. It's like a lottery out here. Hustle, hope, play the odds and wait for your number to come up. I'm tattered and transparent, a losing betting slip waiting to be torn away by the slightest breeze.

I pick up a copy of the Greenpoint paper as I'm walking through Poland, see a lead for an artist's model, follow it up. I take the L way out into Brooklyn, catch the M up to Queens and walk ten blocks in a pounding rain, arriving at the house drenched. The guy takes a full five minutes to get to the door, but when he does he hands me a towel. He's your typical stay-at-home artist, with a pot belly and long, greasy black hair.

He shows me beautiful, fantastic storyboards for his version of *Where the Wild Things Are*, which basically culminates in the wild romp from the book, with the boy and the wild things running wild—and fucking each other. I get a look at a study where the model—a man-child—is fucking a chimera from behind, his hands clutching its tail, his enormous member ramming into the beast, his feet arched up, only his toes touching the ground as he gives it away with everything he's got.

But the bottom line is that he's not going to pay more than ten or fifteen an hour and it's a forty-five-minute schlep, even if I wanted to deal with the pervy way he's looking at me.

I follow up a lead on a legal proofreading gig, working bankers' hours, swing shift, or graveyard, sitting in a cubicle and proofreading confidential legal documents. It pays close to twenty an hour, and if I have to be stuck in a cubicle like a chicken expected to lay eggs, it would be nice to be left alone and have a choice about the hours that I work.

The agency looks like it opened yesterday. There are boxes all over the room and two desks with computers and some phones. A little blonde girl who looks all of seventeen takes me into the back room and hands me the test, a legal document littered with typographical, spelling, and formatting errors that I'm supposed to mark up. She calls me two days later to say, "You passed the proofreading test. So you sign up for the class, which is two hundred and fifty dollars."

I don't speak the language. I faked the test like I faked my way through high school, and, in Brooklyn parlance, fuck that.

The rules are different out here. You get what you pay for, maybe, if you drive a hard bargain and insist that you pay for only what you get, and if you're lucky with the lottery system of give and take, and if you know how to barter, and if you can swallow your pride sometimes and turn on your bitch bone other times and keep your mind fine-tuned enough to know the difference—through the smog and the panhandlers and the missed trains and the reek of garbage and the fat rats on the subway tracks and the tourists who don't know how to walk on a sidewalk and the suits shoving you out of the way and the Upper East Side blue-hairs that glare at you with their firm belief in economic Darwinism and the gutter punks and the pounding, hard, indifferent pavement.

I break out the strained credit card and take Olive to Tribeca for a decent meal. We stumble across the vigil for JFK Jr.—a screaming pile of flowers; handwritten cards all seemingly made by children; posters declaring love, admiration, and sorrow; Mexican novena candles; wreaths; photographs and newspaper clippings, both of JFK Jr. and his media-determined predecessor, Princess Di. As if the world's largest piñata had been smashed with a wrecking ball, the zesty contents spilling out over the sidewalk for a full city block, a haphazard mosaic of colorful petals and glassy-eyed people. Cops are on parade, keeping the devoted followers in strict order. I'm looking for the rice offerings before the temple, for the lamb, neck slit and gutted, bleeding upon the altar.

Our waitress at the restaurant tells us, "Yeah, John, Jr. used to come in here now and then. Nice guy. But he's certainly not worth all of this. And I don't even think he'd like it."

There are no more gods, only high-profile martyrs.

THE BRIDGE

"I wish all the yuppies would just kill themselves off," I said. I was talking to Phil at a Southside loft party, and the line would come back to haunt me. I was in a flip because *Time Out New York* had run a blurb on Black Betty, and the next weekend, when Everett and I went over for one of Ty's cosmos, we couldn't get into the bar. There was a line of people outside, and it was obvious, by the endless line of yellow cabs, that none of these people were from the neighborhood.

"It happens," Phil said, going into professor mode. "You take a bunch of undesirable real estate populated with lower- to lower-middle-class families, and the artists will discover it. The rent is cheap for lofts and studios, but artists need bars and restaurants, and they need money. So they get that entrepreneurial spirit and open up the places they need. A bar pops up, a comfortable café, or a copy shop or a bookstore, and now the neighborhood doesn't look quite so undesirable. Now it's trendy, hip, cool—besides, all those funky artsy types live there."

"So a bunch of fucking social climbers with no soul of their own move in."

"Sure." Phil was unflappable. "So they can be hip, too. And their friends follow. The real estate brokers see the trend and start making the rounds."

"I saw the same shit happen in the Mission. The hipsters I don't mind so much. I just hate the fucking YUPS, SYPS, and GYPS."

"What are GYPs?"

"Gushy Young white People."

"That's pretty funny."

"Thanks, I made it up."

"Let's get another beer."

We stumbled out of the party to score more forties. I did my highbrow impersonation. "Renovated apartment in Williamsburg? Hey, Muffy, isn't that the neighborhood you said was so... earthy?"

"Ed Koch said it best," Phil said. "'The role of the artist in New York is to make a neighborhood so desirable that artists can't afford to live there anymore.' This is just the latest round of locusts."

"Yeah. We're headed for the bottomless pit of Starbucks

and the Gap."

"You spend too much time on the Northside," Phil said. "And the only thing it's got going for it is the scenery."

He was right. Yuppies look good. Waiting for the subway in the mornings, I see some of the hottest women in New York, with their perfectly cared-for skin; their wonderful hair, exquisitely conditioned and as scented as a sorority house; their glistening toenail polish; their intoxicating eyes hidden by cat's-eye sunglasses in fashionable pastel colors; and, defying their girly-girl accoutrements, hard, well-toned bodies tuned-up by a politically correct regimen of jogging, biking, and the occasional sex session with a boy toy in a bed laced with the sticky aroma of cosmopolitans.

But, as Phil pointed out, there was still a line that the yuppies wouldn't cross—down by the bridge, where Williamsburg was still Puerto Rican and Dominican, with a sultry nightlife, the sidewalk cluttered with old men playing dominos, kids chasing each other on bikes, women chattering in quick cricket-like Spanish. Cars blared salsa and *merengue* through blown speakers as young machos in wife-beaters preened, and cute *mamacitas* in skin-tight dresses flirted back, swinging their arms to keep from sweating in the sweltering August night.

The J/M/Z still wasn't running across the Williamsburg Bridge—it had been shut down since May due to bridge repairs—so the foot traffic was rife with weekend thrill-seekers rushing to catch the free B39 bus from Marcy across the bridge to Delancey, tooling into Manhattan for the seductive allure of a wicked nightlife. Sexual conquests waiting to be negotiated, shady drug deals waiting to be completed, old and new friendships waiting to be sealed over the obligatory cold beverage, and hangovers waiting to happen in larval certainty.

We grinned at the brown-and-white parade and took our gentrified asses back upstairs. A hipster potpourri mingled in the kitchen around a makeshift bar, and in the midst of an aimless cross fire of conversation, someone produced a pad of small sticky notes, which became, in Phil's hands, a prop for mischief. We wrote ridiculous phrases and stuck them to people's backs, dumb shit, like *hot stuff*, *shy boy*, *career alcoholic*, and *recovering Catholic*, which quickly escalated to *wannabe*, *somebody's bitch*, and *future Republican*. It didn't take long for Phil to stick the word *benign* on a hotty in a sundress talking to a baseball cap-wearing frat boy. In seconds, the guy tapped Phil on the shoulder.

"What does this mean?"

"It doesn't mean anything. We're just playing a game."

"But what does it mean? What are you trying to say about her?"

"Nothing, really. Don't take it personally."

"Fucking tell me, man. What does this word mean?"

The kid didn't know what *benign* meant, and that made us feel smug.

Fuck it. At least at a dingy loft party we could get loaded with other greasy, unwashed eccentrics, even if some of them weren't so bright. It was our kind of crowd. Even the ones who could pass in Manhattan—like the guys who had actually put on button-downs over their wife-beaters—were clearly locals who had only cleaned up for the weekend chance to grab an errant yuppie chick and get her in the sack and grift her for a few free drinks, a few free lunches, a couple blowjobs and a nice sweater, whatever.

Another slow summer afternoon, I took the B39 across the bridge and Phil bought me a couple buck-fifty canned Pabst Blue Ribbons at Welcome to the Johnsons, near his place.

When my beeper started buzzing I went to find Olive in the East Village.

One of her friends worked as a carpenter for Shakespeare in the Park. Figuring rightly that I could handle myself around power tools, she told him that I needed a job, and he said he'd walk me in.

We cruised down to the Public on Lafayette and he took me downstairs and introduced me to the master carpenter, who said he had everyone he needed at the moment. But we went around the corner and I met the master electrician, who said, "What are you doing Sunday night?" So I bought a crescent wrench and a big knife and went to Central Park Sunday in the midst of the closing night festivities for *Taming of the Shrew*, and proceeded to tear things apart. They call it a "strike" in this business. Pretty simple work, really—all the lights are attached to truss with big C-clamps, and you take your crescent wrench and loosen up the clamp, unplug the light, and tear it down. The cables are a mess of spaghetti, and you start yanking on them and coil them up. The pay's pretty weak—only fifteen dollars an hour—but it's good physical work, and anyone with two brain cells to rub together can get a handle on it.

The next week I stood on a light tower above the bleachers at the Delacorte Theatre, a cool sixty feet above the man-made nature of Central Park, the lush paradise of foliage incongruously planted smack in the middle of the urban nightmare. Looking out over the trees and surrounding buildings, I tried not to singe my hair on the cigarette hanging out of the corner of my mouth as the wind whipped. I was standing tall, shirtless, the sun searing my flesh, overseeing the glory of man and nature's creation in a perverse and majestic vigil, screaming from the crow's nest in any gale that might come.

All I had to do was hang lights. It was so hot the radio

spelled out warnings: "Stay at home today. Do not stay outside for any length of time." I was outside through the entire afternoon, scalded in serenity, lifting weighty lights and sweating a tide pool and loving it.

I was invited to work out the week, underwhelmed with the routine but fascinated by the social dynamics. The crew was such a clique, such an insiders' club, it was hard to believe it represented an unenviable, mediocre blue-collar job masquerading as a role in the arts. Half the crew wouldn't talk to me, judging me correctly as an outsider, and I spent most of the week roving with a large, loud-mouthed North Carolina kid named Greg, who wore a big tool belt and smoked incessantly and never wore a shirt. He had a large flying eagle tattooed on his back and a goatee, but even so, he seemed less pretentious than the rest of them and was willing to show me a few tricks.

I had crossed the threshold into the realm of the gainfully employed, and could drink without guilt or remorse.

FURTHER HIJINKS

Olive bowed out gracefully, staying home to nurse her liver, but a solid week of actual physics-defined *work* had left me riled up and ready to go. Hoag and I sat at the Dog Bar trading nonsense with Dizzy and drinking our beers slowly, waiting for the clock to kill us. We offered each other recycled pep talks and tired words of encouragement and bland, heartfelt compliments.

As we started to tie one on, we loosened up and Hoag's tongue wagged. He spun a story of one of his solo nights at the bar, meeting a mid-forties black woman who had some coke, taking her back to his place and balling her til six o'clock in the morning. He dragged himself to his bartending job at the Northside Café at ten a.m. feeling like the underside of a chuck wagon.

"What are you doing fucking old women anyway, Hoagy? Don't you love me anymore?"

"Oh, I'm so gay for you."

"And I'm so gay for you, Hoagy."

I shot a couple games of pool with Smith, and he just made me look stupid. Smith is a friend of Dizzy's, and the Norm of the Dog Bar, maybe even the Norm of the neighborhood—I can't think of anyone else who will so predictably be found on a given barstool. I don't know what Smith does; he always comes across as some kind of artist without ever telling you exactly what he's working on. I've never seen him sober.

Yet he's a terrific shot. I can't shoot stick to save my life when I'm drunk, but with Smith, it's like the booze just fortifies him for the game. Maybe he's one of those characters that has two memories, a sober memory and a drunk memory, and he learned to play pool drunk and categorized it accordingly. He wouldn't know how to hold the cue sober.

Dizzy eventually called it and hustled the last few stragglers out of the bar. Smith stayed on his stool, and Dizzy either forgot to ask us to leave or honestly didn't give a shit. We did a shot or two on Dizzy, and he, of course, was doing shots with us, and I began to think we'd still be sitting there when the sun broke over Long Island.

Smith threw bev nap spit wads at Dizzy, and Diz grabbed the fountain gun and came at him, shooting across the bar and soaking Smith.

"What the fuck? What was that—what did you do that for?"

"Oh, so you can just throw shit at me and I can't fight back."

"You sprayed me with goddamn 7-Up. Why couldn't you use water or something? I'm all sticky."

"I'm sorry, man," he said, "I thought that was soda water." He looked at his gun. "I must have hit the wrong button."

"Oh sure, you hit the wrong button. You use that thing every night you think you'd—look, at least give me a hose down."

Dizzy looked at his gun again as if he'd never seen it before, and held it over the well and pressed a button. "Okay, that's 7-Up," his face wrinkling like Charlie Brown chewing on a pencil, "and *that's* the soda water. Sorry, man."

"Come on, give it to me already. I'm all fucking sticky."

Dizzy pressed another button. "Okay. That's the water. Come here." Smith stood on the rails of his stool and leaned over the bar, head down and arms out, and Dizzy hosed him down like a muddy kid in the front yard. Smith pulled back and shook his head like a dog, throwing water in every direction, splattering me and Hoagy. He settled back onto his barstool to pad himself down with tome-like stacks of bev naps.

I was drunk, but I'd remember this moment, months later, the calm tableau of four drunk boys at last call. It was one of the last calm nights, before the sirens started.

"So when you guys leave," Dizzy said, "just slip out the back. I don't want to unlock the front door again."

We took that as a hint and limped out the back door clutching our kidneys, weaving our way through the back hallway, tripping over Dizzy's bike, stumbling to my house, banging into the walls on the stairway, pulling bong hits, waking up Olive, facing the morning with pounding headaches and swollen livers.

This is the life. I say it to myself all the time, not with joy, but with quiet resolve. This is the life. This is the lay of the table and I have to take a shot, this is all I've got to bet on, no chalk and dead banks, even if I am behind the eight ball, even if I did wind up with solids, even though all my balls are pinned to the rail, even if I've got nothing to choose from but a long bank or a ninety-degree cut, even if English won't help, even when it turns out to be a scratch shot, this is all I've got. This is the life.

II. Law of the Land

HEADSHOT

It was a Saturday in September and the heat had finally let up, the day sunshiny, open and inviting. Olive was having a bit of a freakout, trying to get her outfits together for her headshot photo shoot. Her headshots were five years old, and showed her with luscious, long curly locks. Her hair now is not quite to her shoulders, and she's older—which might be inhibiting for ingenue parts, but she never gets those anyway. As a character actor, the age is helpful. She could still play early twenties, but can definitely play her age—thirty-three—and beyond.

Olive rummaged through her closet, pulling out alternate outfits and unnerving herself into a frenzy, her hair frizzing and her arms flapping, looking like a Ralph Steadman charcoal sketch. She'd been waiting three months to get an appointment with this photog, some big-time well-known badass, and "everybody who's anybody gets their headshots done by her." It costs a thousand bucks for a contact sheet and two eight-by-tens—a perfect scam, balanced atop the hopes and dreams of hundreds of wannabe movie stars.

I couldn't stand around to witness so I ducked out and rolled up to the Luncheonette with a paper under my arm. The sun streamed through the open door, making art-nouveau curlicues out of my trailing cigarette smoke. The Luncheonette is an old-school joint, with magazine pictures of Frank Sinatra stuck on the wall next to snapshots of Neil holding his various grandkids. It's one of these places widely rumored to be a low-level Mafia establishment, which I could buy considering its bizarre hours and low traffic. It's not a stretch to imagine it as a money-laundering operation, but for the most part I don't think about it, and find comfort in the old Italian Brooklynites hanging out at the window chewing the fat with Neil on a daily basis.

I sat at the counter and asked Neil to whip me up a cheeseburger and fries, and asked him how he felt about all these young kids moving into the neighborhood, since he'd been there his whole life.

"I like it. Nice having all you kids here."

I took it at face value and buried my face in newsprint: rehashed criticisms of Giuliani over Diallo and musings on Hillary Clinton over the upcoming Senate race. I quickly lost interest. Besides, all of Neil's cronies were stopping in. The men started talking about baseball.

"Not that Neil cares about the goddamn Mets. Whattay-agonna do."

"Fockin' Neil. A Dodgers fan all his life. Born and raised in Brooklyn."

"What a traitor."

Neil attempted to defend himself but didn't get many words out. "What, you want me to root for the Dodgers? Now?"

"That's right, that's right. Just go on to the other side."

A swarthy Sicilian in a black leather sports jacket addressed me. "Born and raised in Brooklyn, this one, a Dodgers fan his whole life. And now. Now he's a Yankee fan. The fockin' Yankees. Fuhgeddaboutit."

I realized that Neil had probably converted to the Yankees sometime around, say, 1958, and that he'd been taking a ribbing from these guys for it every Saturday since.

Neil piped up. "When I win the lottery I'm gonna take all you guys to a Yankees game, and I'm buyin'. I'll get seats behind home plate, and all the beer you want, dogs, you name it."

"I hope you can drink a lot of beer, 'coz you'll be sittin' in the stands by yourself." They all laughed, and Neil shook his head and sighed.

I thought of the way men used to hang out at the barber shop and talk ponies and gab about their wives. Being around men, especially older men, I get the feeling that I belong to a heritage, a kind of buried tradition, and that even my generation's attempt to overthrow the past can never quite wash away the coffee-stained teeth and nicotine fingers that old men have cemented into the fabric of the universe. Someday we'll all be old men, hanging around doing nothing, telling the same old fockin' stories.

The moment was shattered by the knife-point scream of a siren. Cops and an ambulance rolled into sight, cutting up 7th and parking at the corner of Bedford—Neil could see them from his window. An eerie silence passed across the counter, the men glancing about themselves without focusing their eyes.

"You think that's another someone jumped?" I asked.

They all shook their heads, not in negation, but in that Brooklyn expression that says so much without speaking. The man in the leather jacket cocked his head at Neil. "That's the third one this week."

"The train wasn't running on Wednesday," I said. "For hours."

"It ain't right," one of the other men offered.

Neil stepped away from his window and busied himself behind the counter. I pushed my polystyrene plate away from me and Neil threw it away. The other men shifted their heavy weight and said nothing. The sirens cut out and the silence grew, filling the small diner and becoming tangible. The man in the jacket said, "Ah," lit another cigarette, shook his head and said, "Whattayagonna do."

That said it all, and I stood up and walked out and cut back down to 6th, headed home, and nearly ran right into Jamie. She stared at me, taking a moment to realize who I was, and fell into my arms. I hugged her and asked her what was wrong. Obese tears perched at the corners of her eyes, and I walked her to my front stoop and sat her down.

"What's up, baby?"

"I saw someone die at the station."

She was pretty choked up, and I did my best to get the story and calm her down at the same time. The more she talked about it the more upset she got, and the more I tried to calm her down the less likely I was to get the scoop. I met her in the middle and let my brain fill in the blanks.

A young man, mid-twenties, goes down into the subway from the Bedford entrance—the Driggs entrance is closed on weekends—and walks to the far end. When the Manhattan train comes he gets on, positioned at the very back of the last car, flips the transom window open, and as the train is pulling out, he climbs up on the seat and leans his head and shoulders out the window as far as possible. The windows are narrow so he must have been a pretty skinny guy. The outcome is predictable: being at the rear of the train, his extended head would have been moving at quite a clip when it connected with the wall at the other end of the station, where the tunnel under the East River starts and the station proper ends. It was enough. His head smacked the wall, leaving a visible splatter-mark like a pumpkin-size tomato, and was ripped from his shoulders, popping off the wall and grazing an innocent bystander before rolling to a stop in the middle of the platform, the torso half dragged out the window, scraping against the inside of the tunnel and leaving a trail like the bloody smear between a boot and a smashed cockroach carcass.

Jamie had just come back from running an errand in Manhattan, and since the Brooklyn-bound and Manhattan-bound trains often cross at Bedford, she rolled into the station just after the other train had come to a screeching halt a hundred feet inside the tunnel, stepped off the train and into a circle of spooked onlookers. Jamie peeked around the other rubberneckers and got an aces view of the poor bastard's head lying on the floor of the platform, one side of the face smashed beyond recognition, a mess of blood blending with the stains on the floor, and the other side strangely calm and serene, the one discernible eye still open, glaring at the horrified spectators.

I walked Jamie home and drew her a bath and made her a cup of tea. She slipped into a bathrobe and got on the phone to her mom and swore to me she wouldn't leave the house. I told her to call me if she needed anything, and when I was fairly certain she was pulling it together—her mom seemed to be saying the right things and I knew Jamie would be in the tub as soon as I was gone—I went on home.

"Where were you? I'm done and IIIIIIII wanna drink a beeeeeeer!" Olive was excited, jumping up and down.

"Yeah, sure, we can go grab a beer."

"Where were you?"

"Got a burger at Neil's, ran into Jamie and had to walk her home. She was pretty upset."

"What's up?"

"Saw some guy get his head ripped off on the subway."

"What?"

"She saw some guy get his head ripped off on the subway. He leaned out the window and *smack!* Into the wall."

"Is Jamie all right?"

"Ah, she'll be fine. Just a little grossed out, I think."

"Was it on purpose?"

"I don't think you can lean that far out a transom window on accident."

"Oh." Her nose crinkled like a rabbit's. "That's just horrible."

"Whatever. One less yuppie in the 'hood."

"How do you know he was a yuppie?"

"Odds are."

"Odds are he was just like you."

"Liv, who fucking cares who he was? He's dead now."

"He was a person. Isn't that worth something?"

"Now he's a corpse." I shrugged. "Come on, who cares about the tragically hip in Williamsburg? Do you want to get a beer or not?"

"I do. The 'tragically hip'"—lilting her voice into the nasal register—"that's us you're talking about. You and me and Hoagy, and—"

"Liv. Please don't start on me."

"I just—" She stopped and looked at me and shook her head and slapped her hands on her thighs. "I don't understand how you can be so unaffected."

"Did I know the guy? Did I even see it?"

"Jamie saw it."

"And I took care of Jamie. I care about *her*, I took her home and drew her a bath—"

"You drew her a bath?"

"Oh, fuck, here we go."

"You drew her a bath?"

"I didn't get in with her. She didn't even get in—not before I left, anyway. I just made her some tea and talked to her, tried to calm her down, you know? Tried to be a mensch."

"That's great. I'm impressed."

"Thank you." I wasn't going to bite. I looked out the window instead and waited for her to speak.

"You know, Benson," she said finally, "sometimes I think I know you so well, better than you know yourself. And sometimes I don't know what to make of you."

"It would be pretty boring otherwise, wouldn't it?" I said

with a broad grin, and didn't wait for her to answer. "Can we get that beer now?"

UNDERGROUND

Loudmouth Greg, whom I met at Shakespeare in the Park, took a shine to me and handed my name and number to a production company that does lighting for corporate parties and events, Jewish weddings, bar mitzvahs and the like.

The routine is a breeze. Show up at the gig, sometimes as early as eight or nine but often not until noon or later. Unload the truck, rolling bins and road boxes into the event space. Take a look at the room and listen to the crew chief bark out minimalist instructions based on a thin dossier incompetently explaining the contract. Usually the paperwork specifies certain looks and the chief makes up the rest, and for the most part, the workers stand around aimlessly wondering what to do. Eventually someone makes a decision and we bang it together, and every job ends up looking the same. If there's a band, we put up some Lekos to wash the stage; if there's a dance floor, we throw in a gobo and wash the floor. Beyond that it's all rote—uplighting on the columns and other architecture, and pin spots on booms to highlight the floral arrangements on tables. Most of the day is dedicated to zip cord and add-a-taps—cheap electrical cord we run around the room and plastic taps, a male on one end to plug into the wall and females on the other end to plug in the pin spots. I'm sure any fire marshall would have a field day, but the job itself requires little or no brain activity.

The crew, for the most part, consists of a revolving door of unreliable rejects. As opposed to the Shakespeare Festival, crewed by "theater people"—spastic wannabe actors and designers grappling with the role of technician as a way to remain close to their "love" and actually get paid—this crew is a bunch of misfits who have largely accepted their fate. There are a couple of carryovers, like Greg, the loudmouth who got me the job in the first place. He considers himself an actor but will probably give up on it since he's so comfortable as a technician. There's also a cute Jewish actor/dancer type who will probably make it and sees being an electrician as a necessary and occasionally enjoyable evil. She never takes the job too seriously, much like her friend, the dead-sexy director chick who could have a career as a technician and do quite well for herself. But the rest of the people I run into at various gigs are like cartoon characters, flimsy two-dimensional figures cut out of cardboard.

There's the small gay guy with the high forehead who never speaks and never bathes. There's the slow fat guy who just moved to New York from Kentucky. There's the dark, brooding Jew with a wry sense of humor who was once in the Israeli army. There's the large, boyish man from Los Angeles who is a master at never lifting a finger. There's the tall stupid kid from Florida who never shuts up. There's the doughy girl who always wants to hear about everyone else's personal life. There's the gorgeous aspiring starlet who sucks at her job, but is cute and has a nice rack and wears flimsy tops and is happily carried by the men. There's the rangy New York kid with sideburns who seems to have the boss himself on the run, and his partner, the dope dealer who once had a small role on a soap opera. There's the prematurely bald man from New Jersey who looks twice his age, like a traveling salesman, who is really nothing more than a cleverly disguised sexual predator. And there's me, the petulant redheaded stepchild with sarcasm and bad attitude to spare.

Some people come and go, moving to other jobs and reappearing when those jobs fizzle out, and some appear on one gig and are never seen again, offended by the boys'-

club mentality or too weak to load trucks or too bored with the repetitiveness of the job. Others are a constant but still possess not a shred of loyalty; freelancers to the bone. And all of us are wanderers, lost souls who will never amount to anything and know it. People who are happy to make a decent wage, proud to not be a suit stuck behind a desk in an air-conditioned fluorescent cubicle, and never mind that we aren't paid overtime—one of many highly illegal practices in the business—that we aren't in a union, have no health insurance, no vacation or holiday pay, no chance for advancement or eventual pension, and will almost certainly ruin our bodies irreparably in this line of work. If your back doesn't give out, it will be your knees, and if you're less lucky you'll take a fall from a truss or a lift or a ladder or a scaffold, or maybe you'll catch 110 volts one day, survive, and find a desk job. Injuries are a certainty, not because the job is overly dangerous, but because all of these hungry fools work hundred-hour weeks and never sleep.

I've been pulling some pretty nice weeks myself, sixty and seventy and eighty hours. It gets me out of the 'hood and away from the sirens, usually a seven- to ten-day stretch followed by a few cushy days off, and the money is starting to roll in. I got raised to twenty an hour almost immediately, and I'm able to take Olive out to a nice dinner when we can schedule a night that we're both off. I'm finally getting a chance to live the fat-cat New York lifestyle, taking cabs and slugging cocktails instead of cheap beers, not having to worry when I want a BLT for lunch and it costs six bucks because we're working on the Upper East Side.

Cipriani 42nd Street, an old bank that's been turned into an event venue, is the center of our universe; the company has a permanent installation and we never stay away for more than a few days. It's an enormous stone room with a dozen columns, each a different variety of marble, and a ceiling detailed with wood laid in intricate geometric patterns. The house staff loads in tables and chairs, the florists come in with stunning arrangements, a stage goes up at one end, and we hang our lights on a truss high above the floor, focusing them from a Genie Lift.

When the gig starts we dress in black and hang out by the control board, making trips to the bar for free cocktails, watching the endless stream of caterers in identical black tuxedos walking upstairs bearing plates, dropping them on tables and plodding back downstairs for more, eventually coming upstairs empty-handed and making another round to collect plates littered with half-eaten gourmet foods—a steady onslaught of inscrutable penguins like a nightmarish scene from Disney's *Fantasia*. And some of the bands. At a fund-raising dinner for a not-for-profit organization made up of the richest businessmen in New York, the entertainment was the Beach Boys. Another night, KC and the Sunshine Band. At an annual meeting of food allergists, Neil Sedaka.

It's all pretty painless for a worthless day job. Loading and unloading trucks, pushing bins and lugging lights and cables is keeping my body in aces shape, and after getting the hang of putting up booms and screwing down pin spots and bashing add-a-taps, the mind is free to wander. We blow much of the day talking smack and cracking jokes and watching out for sexy rich guests and the occasional cute straight florist or the more-common hot, but bitchy, party planner. The big boss himself will pay an extra four hours to anyone who gets laid on the job—no mean feat for blue-collar stiffs dropped in among the beautiful people.

I showed up at Cipriani 42nd Street at one in the morning prepared to babysit a union crew all night as they put in the rigging for a big event. It turned out to be a bait and switch; only three union guys showed, and before I knew it, I was stuck up in the attic playing second man to a beer-bellied union Joe twenty years my senior. We were sixty feet above the floor, and I spent all night crawling through the grated trenches that provide access to the removable panels in the ceiling. Installing chain motors involved lowering a line to the ground and pulling up the hook and sixty feet of chain, securing the rigging to a cradle of shackles and high-gauge aircraft cable wrapped around the I-beams.

The work was rough enough, but there was no light to speak of and I was swimming through tangled noodles of wiring, ducts and hidden infrastructure, and I was so sleep-deprived by the end of the night I was convinced I had stepped through a dimensional portal into the film *Brazil*. The union guy kept bragging to me about the king's treatment he receives every year when he goes down to Atlantic City, conveniently allowing him to forget that he's an underground fringe member of society. I just wanted to go home and wash off the dust and fiberglass.

I finally stumbled out around nine in the morning, covered with sweat and grime, bumping into well-dressed suits on their way to the office, which made me feel as itchy on the inside as I felt on the outside: a second-class citizen, completely invisible. I was strangely lucid as I entered Grand Central Station and descended into the bowels of the city, the subway tunnel another stunning example of the vast, sprawling, secret infrastructure of the city—hidden from view, sequestered deep underground, boggling the imagination, an architect's blueprint for a nightmare.

The 5 blasted me from Grand Central Station to Union Square, screeching to a halt and spilling me onto the dreaded Lex platform that is strangely a hundred degrees year-round.

I bolted upstairs and cut across the mezzanine in a daze, down the winding stairwell to the L platform, which was empty. The packed morning train I'm accustomed to is Manhattan-bound; no one goes to Brooklyn at nine a.m. I was grateful that the L was running. It was delayed more often these days, and as usual, if one asked the cops why, they would declare "police emergency" and urge us to take the J/M/Z which was running again since construction on the bridge had been completed. I had gotten used to the fifteen-minute walk through Puerto Rico to the J/M/Z, the stunning ride across the bridge, the domineering Xs of steel speeding past, midtown and downtown pasted across the train's windows, the descent from the bridge onto the island and into the gaping maw of the city, and the wet, dank transfer to an uptown train at Canal, fifty feet below Chinatown.

Riding to Brooklyn on an empty train, I experienced the brief glimpse of infinity that the four-minute crossing under the East River afforded me, the strange bend in time that spreads those four silent minutes into an eternity—horizontal freefall, a weightless push in the dark—propelling me back to my troubled neighborhood and the concerns that would meet me even in my sleep-deprived state.

At one of our bar mitzvah gigs, a crusty old photographer told me a zinger about following a writer on a story about subway musicians. The two had gone topside for a bite in the West Village when a convoy of fire trucks and ambulances appeared, paramedics pulling a man out of the subway on a gurney. He had jumped in front of a 9 train at 14th and lived, walking the tracks down to the Christopher stop. The photog caught some snaps and sent them to the *New York Times*, who called him back to say, "It's a confirmed suicide attempt, so we won't be running it. The *New York Times* does not run stories on suicide."

"All the news that's fit to print." Every homicide gets a byline in the metro section—why isn't suicide newsworthy? Why won't anyone talk about what happens all the time? Is it indecent, like describing a bowel movement? And the subway system, the archaic, medieval monstrosity of it all… how many ways to die there must be… the third rail, jumping in front of a train, lying on the rails, stepping between cars and slipping down to the tracks….

The subway system itself is a work of insane genius, a maze of 722 miles of working track making up only a fraction of the MTA—2,038 track miles covering a four-thousand-square-mile area. Its tangled history and collected ghosts invade me on a daily basis, stepping into the Bedford L station, a seventy-five-year-old orifice that is my portal to the city's underbelly. The L speeds me down the tracks of the BMT to Union Square, where I can climb up a level for the N/R with its seventies cars—their age highlighted by the quirky seats painted varying shades of shocking orange—or go up two levels and over and back down to the IRT's 4/5/6, the speeding sixties Redbirds, hulking beasts of painted carbon steel now obsolete and in line to be taken from the tracks—a disappointment, since their blurring red hue is a welcome color in an otherwise submerged, monochromatic world.

I've learned to navigate this Stygian system, teaching myself how to think in three dimensions. Times Square is the worst—five levels of tracks sixty feet deep, a modern-day Troy, each level built on the remains of the last, an endless labyrinth of stairs and escalators and ramps, the true locus of pandemonium that Midwesterners envision when they imagine New York City, a sprawling mess of teeming bodies, backed-up stairwells, claustrophobia, loud musicians adding to the chaos—entropy in action in a hole over a hundred years old. Working definition of a deathtrap.

The train drew to a halt and I was sure, for an instant, that I was being delayed under the East River, but Bedford was coming in for a landing before my bleary eyes, and my four-minute slice of infinity was over and I was only a block away from my bed.

I caught Everett coming out of the building on his way to work.

"Benson, whassup?"

"Just getting in from an overnight. Fuckin' beat."

"Hey, some kid killed himself at the Stinger last night."

"In the bar?"

"In the middle of the bar. It was packed, too. People were freaking out."

"What, did he shoot himself or something?"

"No, worse. He grabbed the fire extinguisher off the wall and set it off."

"What?"

"He, like, tried to drink it."

"Bullshit."

"No. He put the hose in his mouth, and—it was one of those foam kinds? He just held down the lever and inhaled it. I think he asphyxiated."

"Damn, that's ugly. That stuff's poison."

"It was nasty. Everyone cleared out."

"So what'd you do?"

"Went to Black Betty."

Everett and I laughed.

"Were you blasted?"

"Oh, man... I drank so many cosmos."

"That helps."

"Yeah. The bartender told us not to tell anyone."

"What?"

"When we were all clearing out, she's like up on a barstool

screaming, 'Please come back tomorrow, we'll reopen, please don't tell anybody about this little incident.'"

"'Keep our little secret,' huh?"

"Yeah. So don't tell anyone."

"Tell anyone what?"

"Exactly."

I went upstairs and took my clothes off, grabbed a quick shower and climbed into bed with Olive and kissed her naked shoulder. She squirmed and snuggled into me and I was out in seconds. I wouldn't tell her what had happened at the Stinger. Don't tell anyone, let's keep our dirty little secret to ourselves, bury it deep in the morgue of unfit-to-print stories, underground by the banks of the river of sin that carries New York from one day to the next.

WIRED

I broke down and joined the cell-phone club. I kept missing gigs—by the time I'd get paged, get to a pay phone and put a call in, the job would already be booked. Time is money.

Ray has taught me the virtue of the cell phone as a time saving device: you're in a cab, you can't do anything anyway, so you put out all those calls that you haven't had a chance to make all day. You call the girl you want to hook up with, you call the people who offered you work. Of course, this is the gospel according to Ray, who doesn't even know that there's a subway system in New York. "What? Trains, underground? You're kidding me." He takes cabs everywhere. I've seen him take a cab two blocks. "We're in a different part of the city every day," Ray says, "and for hustlers like us, the cell phone is the only ticket."

I'm a believer. I love my cell phone like I love my brain tumor, and I nurture it daily. I love the entire culture surrounding cell phones. The protocol and manners of traditional phone use are tossed completely out the window. None of this, "Hello," "May I please speak to…." Your caller ID tells you who it is. "Hello" has been replaced, because there is only one piece of information you don't have: "Where are you?" And none of that old-fashioned "Let me drop everything." No one exemplifies this better than Ray. For a call he drops exactly nothing; the phone is a permanent growth on the side of his face, like a goiter. He could be up on a ladder, pushing a bin in the rain—anything—and carry on a conversation without missing a beat.

It speeds up your life like nobody's business, and in New York, we like nothing more than speed.

I had a gig at Le Cirque 2000, a hoity-toity restaurant in the New York Palace hotel, midtown, which was a welcome gig since Olive always works Sunday brunch at Oznot's. Sunday has always been a strange day for me. As a kid it meant church and homework—a guaranteed drag—and once I got old enough to ditch them both I never had a replacement. Sundays are a day of waste, a lonely contemplation of nothing, so I was happy for the chance to make some money.

I got a call the night before from Ray, the crew chief, whom I'd never met. I was supposed to meet him at the lot, way up in Harlem, and he called to tell me that he had the van and I should meet him at his place, on 14th and 6th, and cruise to the gig from there.

I rode the L to 6th and rang his buzzer, and a girl's voice told me he wasn't there, but buzzed me up. A stocky platinum blonde met me on the tenth floor and told me she had tried Ray's cell but didn't get an answer. She was obviously in last night's clothes, and confessed that she had stayed over since she and Ray's roommate had been out late and she lived in the Bronx.

I sat on the couch and waited for Ray to call back, noticing a rolled-up dollar bill on the table in front of me, stealing glances at this siren perched over a cigarette in a black cocktail dress on a Sunday morning. An evil thought moved through my mind. *Hey, why don't you bust me out a line? And how about a fuck while we're at it?* It was all there.

Instead I said nothing and went up to the fifties to wait on Ray. My phone went off as I was pacing by MoMa.

"Sorry. I was going to call you this morning and come by and pick you up, but I slept late. I'm in Brooklyn. On my way."

Ray showed up in clothes that had clearly spent the night on someone else's floor. Little carpet fuzzies stuck to his sweater, his face was puffy yet cadaverous, his pores releasing noxious vapors. He hadn't slept.

We surveyed the room. We were lighting a small private dinner, a half dozen tables with flowers. Two booms, six pin spots each, two runs of zip cord and a console. Ray asked me if I wanted a line, so we went into the bathroom and he racked up a couple fat rails on his cigarette case and we snorted them through rolled-up bills. We rolled in one bin and set up the gig in under a half hour, my hands shaking and my brain percolating pleasantly.

"Listen, man. I gotta go home and get a shower. I'm supposed to meet a friend of mine later and I have to get cleaned up first." I was to learn that "friend," to Ray, meant "one of the girls I'm fucking." I would also learn that this one was married. "So you mind hanging out for a half hour or so and making sure the client is happy? I'll set you up."

So Ray left me with a dime of coke, and I waited until I saw our client, refocused a pin spot for him, threw an extra one in for the piano player, and rolled over to loudmouth Greg's place and shared my coke and smoked some of his pot and watched *The Simpsons* and rolled back to Le Cirque and met Ray, who had spent the last three hours making out with a married woman in some darkened bar.

We get paid a minimum of four hours for the strikes, even if they take less, and it took us all of fifteen minutes to empty the room.

"Thanks a lot for watching my back today," Ray said before he drove off. "I owe you one."

I had clocked ten hours, making it a two-hundred-dollar day. I was wired to the gills and had worked a grand total of… maybe an hour. Not bad, I thought. Now I'm starting to live the Manhattan life, wheeling and dealing and rolling with it, making the jack and making the rounds. Cocaine and cell phones, baby, I am hardwired into the system, tapped in to the core and electric.

I took a cab home and found Olive on the couch in the kitchen—the love seat that we found on the street over by Black Betty—with a martini in her hand.

"You're home early," I said. "Was it dead over there?"

"Someone was dead, you could say that."

"What happened?"

"One of the cooks poured—I don't know—something all over himself and lit himself on fire."

"You're kidding."

She knocked her glass back and got up to make herself another. "He ran screaming into the dining room in flames."

"Holy shit. Was anyone else hurt?"

"No, he ran out into the street. But everyone was freaked out and we had to shut down for the night."

"That's fucking hilarious. Some hipster is eating dinner with a date, saying, 'So I says to Bill, I says, if this record contract doesn't go through, I'm quitting the band and I don't care if I burn this bridge,' and the chef comes running in on fire."

"It wasn't funny, Benson." She had stopped rattling her martini shaker and leaned with one hand on the kitchen sink, her eyes like fire. "It scared the hell out of me. It scared the hell out of everybody. And now we're missing a cook."

"Is he dead?"

"I think so. He was still breathing when I left, but the ambulance hadn't come yet. He was burned pretty bad."

"Probably a goner."

"Try to be sympathetic for once."

"I'm sorry, babe." I gave her a hug and she squeezed me tight. "I had a really great day and I'm pretty lit. I'm sorry about all this. I'm sorry you had to see that and I'm sorry you're out a cook and I'm sorry that I keep making jokes out of everything and I'm sorry… I'm just sorry. But don't be scared. I got you. I got you."

"I don't know how much more of this I can take." She had her head buried in the crook of my neck and talked into my shoulder.

"So fucking quit already. If you hate the job—"

"I don't hate the job. It's fine. I hate seeing… all this."

"So ditch it. I'm starting to make some cash. We'll skate by for a while. Get out there and land yourself some acting gigs. You don't have to be a hostess, Liv, you're an actress. Why do you want to waste your time at that stupid restaurant anyway?"

She pulled away. "It gets me out of the house. It'll be worse if I'm cooped up here every day, listening to sirens."

"Then get a job in Manhattan. It's normal over there. No crazy suicides."

She picked up her shaker and gave it a vigorous rattle, pulling off the lid and pouring the foggy, syrupy elixir into her glass, thick with bits of ice.

"I don't know what to do. I just don't want to see anyone else die."

"I can't do anything about that, babe."

"I know." She looked as sad as I've ever seen her. "I don't think anybody can."

DIZZY'S HOT SHOT

The little red light on the machine was blinking: "My message is: the crow flies low tonight. This is Secret Agent Hoag. Over."

We had our usual spots at the Dog Bar. As usual, Hoag talked about painting. He's a true painter in the traditional sense, actually interested in being able to produce images—in archaic oil paints, no less—that look like what they represent—a novel notion for a late-twentieth-century painter, considering that most "painters" these days are counting on, and trying to cash in on, conceptual art.

"I scraped a hundred and twenty dollars' worth of paint onto the floor of my studio today."

"You just blew the whole thing?"

"Scraped the whole canvas. Five feet by six feet."

"Man, you should do a mock-up first. Like an eight-by-ten or something."

"I did. I went in there and thought I knew what I was doing, but it sucked. I just… lost it. Had to go. All of it. Scrape, scrape, see ya."

"I'm sorry, bro. That's a drag. Don't be too bummed out about it—"

"No, it's not like I'm, 'Oh, I can't make a painting,' it just wasn't coming out like I wanted it. It's a fire truck. When I was a kid I won a contest at school and got picked up in the morning and taken to school in a fire truck."

"That is so cool."

"I know, it was great. But I want it to look like a fire truck. Not a—red bulldozer, or one of those limos that looks like a stretched-out SUV."

"Yeah, those ugly-ass things look like a Silly Putty imprint—or a minivan on acid, you know, one big long tracer."

"It's all right. I'm not really bummed, just frustrated. My model bailed on me again tonight—I can't keep a model. They all flake. I get one decent sitting and then they cancel on me. I'm trying to do this, I got a studio, I'm paying them—"

"You're paying your models?"

"Ten bucks an hour. It's not much, but I'm paying them. And I have to know the person, you know, I can't spend twenty hours looking at someone and trying to paint what I see if I don't know them a little. I'd better want to hang out with them if they're gonna hang in my studio all day… but it's so fucking hard just trying to schedule a sitting. Fuck it. Oh, Dizzy!" Hoag broke into his routine song. "Who's the best bartender in the world? It's Dizzy! It's Dizzy!"

"Yes, my fine friend," Dizzy said, in a *Gilligan's Island* English accent, "What can I get you?"

"I'll take a lager," Hoag asked, and then shot me a pointing finger.

"Yeah, another Pennant would sure be nice."

Dizzy poured the Brooklyn beers, and Hoag started up about the inevitable shot.

"Why are we teasing ourselves?" I asked. "We know we're going to have the shot, it's just a question of when. Why not get it over with and do the shot now?"

"All right," Hoag growled, "whiskey it is. Oh, Dizzy… add a Jim Beam and a Maker's to our bar tab, please, suh."

Dizzy reached behind him and poured a stiff shot of Beam, reached for the bottle of Maker's and tried to pour it, only then realizing the bottle was empty.

"Did I do that?"

"I think you did," said Hoag, poking me in the arm like a little kid.

Dizzy tossed the empty Maker's. "I have to go downstairs and get another bottle. Just let me run to the bathroom real quick."

Dizzy ducked under the bar and Hoag went into his tired routine of taking a sip from his beer glass and banging it against his teeth. The trick is concealing a quarter in his hand and clicking it against the glass as he brings it to his mouth, which sounds painful as hell. "I love you guys," he says, holding up his beer, "you're the greatest. Really. Cheers." Clink. "Owwww." The joke is weak, but Hoag is so unflagging in his repeated efforts to get a laugh, I can't help but oblige.

"Comin' through, comin' through." The crowd surged and swelled in the narrow path between the bar and the tables against the wall, making way for our hero, the bartender. Dizzy's head towered above most of the customers, even though he was walking a little stooped over with his arms clutching himself. He ducked back under the bar, swooped around, and leaned forward over it with his face inches from Hoag's. "It has to be behind the bar," he said.

"Damn straight, Dizzy. Who's the best bartender in the world? It's..." Hoagy trailed off. All the color had gone out of Dizzy's face, and he looked at Hoag with a glassy stare. An eerily serene smile moved across his face, and he exhaled heavily, with a mild aroma of blissful dreams, before slumping forward, driving his nose into the stack of bev naps, sending them spilling and careening in jumbo confetti squares across the bar, fluttering like doves gone to ground. He fell backwards into the shelf of poison bottles, upsetting several and sending a bottle of Jose Cuervo to the floor with a crash, immediately followed by the heavy tremor of Dizzy's body falling, half prone and half doubled over, onto the trap door that leads to the basement.

The room hushed and everyone looked to the bar, empty and absent without the familiar Dizzy leering behind it. Hoag stood up. I stood on my barstool and we both peered over. A syringe hung out of the crook of Dizzy's left arm like a forgotten casual cigarette in the hand of the distracted. "Fuck…" Hoag sighed. He wasn't behind the bar long enough to fix— he must have applied the tourniquet and hit a vein in the bathroom and slumped back out with the spike in him. The way the shot hit him, he wouldn't have made it back to his rightful place if he'd fixed in the head.

Smith vaulted from his Norm position over the bar, knocking over drinks. He slapped Dizzy in the face, saying "Diz, Diz, are you all right? What's up, man, what are you doing?" Dizzy grew whiter by the moment, and the only success Smith had at getting him to move was disturbing his delicate lean against the beer coolers and tipping his upper body over and onto the floor, his eyes falling open and his lips developing a bluish tinge. Dizzy's large body appeared to grow, gaining weight and magnitude, exuding a gravitational force.

"I don't think that was just heroin, man," I murmured to Hoagy.

"I thought he was clean," he hissed.

Smith looked up at us with a worried countenance. He looked back to Diz, did a double take, started to stand up, leaned back over and held his face near Dizzy's, finally placing his fingers to the carotid, coldly and with great trepidation. "Fuck, he's not breathing." He sighed under his breath, and we all held ours while he waited, his fingers waiting for a sign, his brow under its tousled red hair waiting to receive, waiting for that signal, that echo of our favorite muscle, that

divine pounding rhythm that separates the quick from the—
"Dead. He's fucking dead, man. *He's fucking dead!*"

"Fuck," I mumbled. "I wanted another drink."

Smith looked up at me with blind fury. For a moment I considered my comment—it was true, I did want another drink, and the only Maker's in the house was downstairs, through the trap door that was now barricaded by two hundred and fifty pounds of Dizzy, who would not only be difficult to move in that tiny space but who was now inconveniently placed in a crime scene. But I only had a moment before Smith jumped, crawling over the bar and wrapping his hands around my throat, snarling, "You cold-hearted son of a bitch! Motherfucker, I'll fucking kill you!"

Hoag jumped between us and held him back and I stepped away from the bar, the other customers clearing a path.

"The hell's the matter with you? Think that's funny? Make a little joke?"

"I loved Dizzy as much as anyone, but fuck, I'm next. You're next. One of us is next," waving my hand at the bar in general.

"The fuck you mean?"

"It's going around, Smith. It's going around like a wicked case of the flu." There was a general muttering, and the crowd started to thin in a hurry as drunks squeezed past us and the door flapped open, letting in a cold breeze that served as a sound excuse to shiver. "God damn," I mumbled to Hoag, "am I the only fucking person in this neighborhood who's noticed?"

Smith backed off and slumped onto a barstool. I looked out and saw a cruiser at the corner. "Man, I got weed on me."

Hoag concurred. "Let's hop. Smith, come on, we'll get you a car."

"No, no," he said, defeated. "I want to talk to them. Someone has to. Dizzy would have wanted me to."

Dizzy certainly didn't give a rat's ass at this particular moment, but I kept that thought to myself. Hoag and I hustled outside, muscling through the throng, trying to be invisible and avoid the cops. They were having a hard time getting in the door with so many people pouring out of it, the sidewalk a sullen assembly. We got a dozen steps away from the bar when a hipster stopped me, grabbed me by the arm and shoved his hatchet face into mine, saying, "Is it true? Is there nothing we can do?"

"Fuck if I know. Just don't kill yourself."

We slid into my kitchen and cracked a couple beers. We were trying to be quiet, but Olive poked her sleepy head out as I was loading the bong. "What's up, kids?" she asked, scratching herself and blinking in the light. We sat her down and told her the story, and then she needed a shot and a bong hit herself, and soon we were all drinking straight shots of bourbon, trying to humor ourselves out of the bleak reality that someone we knew and loved had fallen. Olive was disturbed but seemed to take it well, slipping right into the bottle.

"A really hot shot of dope," I said, "not such a bad way to go, I guess. He didn't seem to be in a whole lot of pain."

"Oh, poor Dizzy," Olive said. "He's been so good to us. He made such great martinis. We'll miss him. I wonder if it was too much heroin or if he got something bad on accident."

Hoag and I looked at each other. "It seemed pretty deliberate," I said.

"Those last words seemed a little too much like last words," Hoag said, doing his Robert De Niro impression. "I think he did it on purpose."

"So how would you do it, Mr. De Niro? I mean, your public would kill you if you actually killed yourself, but if you did, how would you go?"

"I'd hang myself, so they'd find me with a boner and a butt full of poop."

I had to laugh.

THE L

The L train was packed as usual. I was sandwiched between a cute girl and Everett from downstairs, whom I had run into on the platform. I was on my way to light a fashion show for Weber Grills, hosted by Al Roker himself, who unsurprisingly confessed at the dress rehearsal to owning several Webers. I told Everett and the girl, an eavesdropper whether she wanted to be or not, about the models hired to show off the features of the grills, Vanna White–style. One black guy, a total Oreo, practiced his moves during a break, pulling out the flavor grates and passing his hand delicately in front of the grill, lifting and lowering the lid with attempted precision. I tried to demonstrate in the cramped quarters and almost cracked a guy across the face, quickly apologized and felt the heat from everyone in the car who wished I'd shut up. Everett just laughed. The cute girl was stranded too far from the vertical poles, too short to reach the railing above, stretching in vain with nothing to hold on to, bumping into us and cracking up.

"Don't worry about it," I said to her. "You couldn't fall down if you tried—there's nowhere to fall."

And almost on cue, I was proved wrong when the quiet of the car shattered in a deafening gunshot, and the scene erupted in a cacophony of flurried movement, bodies shifting like flesh Tetris, swiveling and twisting and pressing against each other in a desperate effort to let the person fall and get as far away as possible, all of us wondering what had really happened and whether there were any more shots coming. The horrific roar of the shot echoed in the metal car, ringing shrapnel in our minds.

It was the first gunshot I'd heard in New York. I never saw the victim, but the whispered words "shot himself" were carried on the stifled air like a virus, and the train pulled into the First Avenue station and promptly went out of service. Everett and I, shocked and delirious in our respective states of hangover and from the sudden, panicked exertion of bodies straining to get out, fell out into the station, relieved amidst a mob of frenetic bodies making a break for the stairs. We broke into stifled peals of laughter and decided that we had the god-given right to be as late to work as we damn well pleased, and cantered off to grab breakfast and a Bloody Mary. Everett invited the cute girl to join us, but she just crossed 14th Street, clinically pale, and went back underground to catch a Brooklyn-bound L back home. I got to the Weber gig late and worked with the detachment of a vodka buzz.

Surfing the L train home, I saw an early-twenties Dominican standing near the door with an aluminum junior Louisville Slugger. I couldn't shake a nagging feeling of dread. I always hated baseball as a kid, and later, when I lived in a sketchy neighborhood, those bats were associated with gangs and beatings. But the guy looked nice enough and I tried to convince myself that it was for his kid brother's Little League game in McCarren Park.

He got off the train ahead of me and I followed him up the stairs and out onto Driggs. He made it about seven steps away from the corner, right in front of the Luncheonette where Neil sits at his window, and began to beat himself with the bat. It was ludicrous. You could hit someone else with one of those child-portion atrocities, hard enough to kill, but to hit yourself? The human arm just isn't designed that way. You can't get enough of a swing to inflict real damage.

The Dominican was learning this the hard way. He swung

once, hard and leaning to drive it over the fence, and connected just above his left eyebrow; he was a righty. The bat made that hollow, unmistakable sound of tubular metal meeting resistance, not unlike the sound we might have heard had the bat hit a fast ball. He bellowed loudly and reeled on his feet. Across the street, at the bus stop in front of Tony's Trattoria, were a half dozen people, including a couple of Hasids in full black regalia, who turned away as the others chimed out, "Ohhh." As the Dominican swung a second time I took a step back to avoid being hit, as he was dizzy and missed himself completely. The third strike and he was out—he swung upwards, gripping the thing low and hard, like a lumberjack about to split a log. The bat arced up and nailed the very crown of his head, the moment halting in respect for the idiocy of the situation and then starting up again, the film rolling in the projector and picking up speed as the bat bounced off his head, leading the rest of the six-foot frame with it, teetering to the sidewalk and crashing with a dull surrender, followed by the metallic ring of the bat clanging on the cement.

Neil leaned out his window. "Mary, Mother of God," he whistled under his breath. From the gang at the bus stop came cheering and subdued laments. The Hasids slowly turned to look.

I caught the bat as it rolled into the gutter and slung it over my shoulder, as if I were on my way to the dugout. I glanced at Neil, who gave me the nod, and walked around the Dominican's unconscious body and headed home.

You just can't off yourself with a blunt object like that. I don't think it can be done, and I didn't want the poor bastard to wake up and try it again. It's just too embarrassing.

It's impossible not to think of the L, sitting out in the garden in a rare moment of peace, where I can hear it pulling into the station two doors down and just underground. The L Café was one of the first signs that the hipsters were coming, an unconscious celebration of a day in '31 when the 8th Avenue station opened up and gave us a straight shot from home all the way across the two-mile island of Manhattan. Olive and I used to call it the Swell Train, and no matter how often we got bagged in the summer with the train running on one track late at night, no matter how long we had to sit stewing in our drunkenness waiting for the ride home, we refused to speak ill of the L, as it was ours. Nowadays we call it the Hell Train.

The white glare reflecting off the table pierces my eyes with a calm serenity… it's a deliciously charming fall morning, and the L Café has opened up the back due to the surprisingly clement weather. Olive is working brunch and I have the day off, and while I could get a discount at Oznot's, I can't resist the garden at the L.

Everyone is here, sparkling and popping with conversation, blooming in the spirit of a warm if overcast day, as if the recent sorrows of the neighborhood were temporarily suspended, an island of peace in an ocean of violence, a quietly bursting moment of relative calm. Bustling cute waitresses serve tattooed cool kids in shades and vinyl leather jackets, and the diagonal shafts of light cutting through the cloud cover make everyone look lovely, like dashing cutouts in contrast to the long, brooding shadows. It's warm enough to rock thrift store skirts and fancy hose, cool enough to show off suede jackets and butterfly collars. We're so cool. We're so cool we don't even talk to one another, even if casually connected. We still act surprised when friends walk in and join us, ordering food though the rest of the group was waiting on the check. Service in the 'hood is dodgy enough to play this game for hours. But cell phone use is lower than it would be at any such café in Manhattan, and my peers look happy and content, not pressured to wear angst on their sleeves, cynical as they may be.

The girl next to me with the pert ass and the young polished face beaming in the glaring sun speaks with an uncharacteristic grate in her voice, a low sexy growl that can only be the result of a heavy smoking habit.

I can relate. The one thing I crave these days is a smoke. I'm well past a pack a day, craving the next one even as I'm taking a drag. I have to fill my Zippo every other day, and I'm burning through flints like a teenage girl through boyfriends. My lungs are black and sluggish as molasses. I wake in the morning greeted by the foul yellow odor of the overflowing ashtray next to the bed, the scent of lingering fumes in my matted hair, and wipe the gritty residue from the corners of my eyes with fingertips painted in Spring Nicotine Ocher. I've got a habit. It's as if this mild form of slow, self-imposed death ingestion is inoculating me against our little epidemic, our pet neighborhood disease. The self-destructive impulse, taken in small, measured doses administered in the form of coffin nails and chased with a steady liquid diet of a favorite poison appears to be effective in the prevention of suicidal attacks.

But from what I remember of Smith, the mascot of the Dog Bar, he smoked and drank more than me, and it didn't help him any.

I call over to Jamie's to see what she's up to, and her roommate tells me that she's gone up to Pete's Candy Store to meet Everett and his new girlfriend for a drink. Olive is at work, and I've been meaning to check out the new bar, so I walk over to Lorimer and duck in. Everett and his girlfriend have just gone, so I chat with Jamie for a few uncomfortable minutes until she leaves.

It's been weird with her for some time now. She thinks

that I go back and forth between behaving angelically towards her and basically being a prick. I think that she wants to fuck me but keeps coming up with reasons why she shouldn't, and she's so overly analytical in her neurotic intellectualizing about everything that talking about it is basically bullshit. It doesn't seem to matter that I'm not planning on fucking her anyway, despite our little intrigue with Olive over the summer. Olive thinks I still have a crush on her, which makes it weird all around.

Pete's looks like a seedy old metal shop that has been transformed into a bar, with a layout that could almost be a shotgun apartment if it weren't for the odd L-shaped room that seems to spell the architect's plan for a kitchen. I move to the back room and catch about three and a half minutes of a cheezy band—two guys noodling on guitars while a drummer taps along to a different beat on a snare and a ride. I suck a couple slugs of bourbon from my flask and go back to the front room and sit at a table alone with my beer.

I notice Smith at the bar and realize I haven't seen him since Dizzy exited. He always looks a little dirty, always in a black leather vest over a dingy T-shirt, with his unkempt goatee and his unruly red hair, but tonight he looks even more disheveled, stains on his trousers and on the once-white long-underwear shirt under his vest. His eyes seem unfocused, and I want to ascribe it to drunkenness, but I know that this man has beaten the pants off me at pool with more belts under him than I could even endure.

I'm draining the last of my beer and wondering where to go next when I see Smith putting on his coat. He's in the middle of the bar and he has to nudge a few people out of the way, slipping into a black motorcycle jacket. He looks to the bartender with a nod of thanks, stumbles through the crowd to the door, pushes it open, steps out, reaches into his jacket, pulls out a small handgun, puts the barrel into his mouth, pulls the trigger, and blows out the back of his head as the door closes behind him, the bullet shattering the top of the door glass, covering everyone close by with glass snowflakes. Smith's body slumps back into the red-stained remains of the door into a seated position on the sidewalk.

Screams peal through the air, people duck, people lie on the floor, expecting more shots, and a gentle snow of plaster falls serenely from the ceiling, exposing the bullet's final resting place. The people in the front room try to move to the back room, and the people in the back room, wondering what's going on, try to move to the front room. The bar is a chaotic conundrum of nervous, frightened energy with no destination and no outlet. The bartender picks up the phone to call the cops, and I stand up, brushing glass from my leather jacket, and pull the door handle.

But, per fire code, the door opens out. I try to shove it but Smith is firmly planted, and when I try again three people pull me away.

"Wait for the police."

"An ambulance is coming, you might kill him if you move the body."

I snap, "He's dead already, sweetheart, don't fool yourself."

The bottom half of the glass door is a candy-apple waterfall seen from behind, a black smudge of life on a glass slide. All that remains of Smith is a cirrhotic liver and a black leather jacket, a final fingerprint on the trigger of a gun.

I can't make a break for it with all the fuss and worry, and I catch a couple of threats that I don't want to cash in on, so I sit there for an hour looking at the inside of the back of Smith's head, waiting for the cops to come and let us all out. It's the first gun I've seen in New York, and only the second gunshot

I've heard. I remember the warnings from people—friends, strangers—when I announced I was moving here, words of caution about how dangerous New York really is, and how I secretly fantasized about getting mugged or beat up in a bad neighborhood, caught on the business end of a Saturday night special, and I can't believe that my closest encounter with a gun was watching a veritable demigod of pool—an amazing shot—take himself out of the game.

And there I am, sitting out in the garden behind the L Café, looking up at the fire escape of the apartments above us and the overcast sky as Mr. Sun makes periodic appearances of stunning, serotonin-giving splendor, thinking of Smith and thanking my stars for this reprieve in the pattern, when the quiet-looking dark-haired boy in the jean jacket and hoodie, who slouched in carrying a bag and joined his friends at the center table, squeezes his fists tightly around a pair of stain-less-steel forks and drives them into his eyes with a fierce Oedipal intensity. He screams out yet twists the implements in still further, a slick river appearing behind his hands, quickly turning to a raging torrent of crimson. In a final par-oxysm of conviction he slams his head downwards, the ends of the forks clicking forcefully as they meet the tabletop. His friends recoil in knee-jerk horror as his body lurches forward, upsetting the table, falling sideways out of the chair and onto the concrete floor. A wave of shock breaks, tables emptying and chairs overturning amid squeals of disgust and screams of surprise.

At the table next to me, the guy rising and calmly pulling money out of his billfold to cover the tab mutters to his date, "I hoped we could get through an afternoon without any of this." It's not just me anymore; we're hardening. I suppose you can get used to anything. The kid made a hell of a mess and everyone is clearing out, a few filtering inside the restaurant in the hopes of getting a seat, picking their way past the crumpled body. Only two courageous souls try to help out, the kid's friends sticking around for the unpleasant formalities, and a pair of stubborn girls in the corner call out for more coffee.

I can't help but wonder, in that fatalistic vein of unsupported self-importance, a delusion of grandeur, of sorts: am I making this happen? Is there a connection between thinking about Smith and this inventive bastard following suit? Or is the exit sign just too brightly lit, too much like a star over Bethlehem, too vivid an offer of release from expectation and disappointment, too neon an image to shake from the mind once it has truly been seen. I see it all around me, snarling in red LED:

"EXIT."

STATUS QUO ANTE

Suicide is shameful: Judas. Suicide is stupid: Kurt Cobain. Suicide is dramatic, ironic: the actress Peg Entwistle jumped from the *H* of the "Hollywood" sign. Suicide is difficult: Sylvia Plath, at least three attempts. Suicide is painful: Virginia Woolf drowned herself. Suicide is political: Bobby Sands of the IRA starved to death after a sixty-six day hunger strike. Suicide is epic: Thich Quang Duc, a Buddhist monk, performed self-immolation in a busy intersection of Saigon in protest of the Vietnam War, the flaming image reproduced hauntingly all over the world. Suicide is catching: in 1933, after a nineteen-year-old Japanese student jumped into the thousand-foot crater of a volcano on the island of Oshima, the act became fashionable and three hundred others followed his lead. Suicide is revealing, shocking, and all too real: Budd Dwyer, convicted in federal court of bribery and conspiracy in

'87, called a press conference and offed himself in full view of spectators and television cameras. And beating him out with the best last line: in 1970, Chris Hubbock, a Florida prime time newscaster, said, "And now, in keeping with Channel 40's policy of always bringing you the latest in blood and guts, in living color, you're about to see another first—an attempted suicide." She successfully shot herself in the head.

All of these are rarities, strange and peculiar incidents, strange and uncommon for one reason only—we heard about them. No one talks about suicide in America. The subject is taboo. The only suicides we ever hear about are celebrities.

Thirty thousand people commit suicide in America every year. As the world goes, we're sitting at about the median rate. Thirty thousand people. That's a football stadium full of screaming fans, exiting the universe by their own hands. That's how many people run the New York marathon every year. That's an entire small town, wiped off the face of the map. Jackson, Mississippi; Monterey, California; Saratoga Springs, New York.

In 1997, there were 30,535 suicides in America. That's about eighty-four suicides a day. Somebody checked themselves out every seventeen minutes. So if you're watching *The Simpsons*, by the time you get to that commercial break before the third act, someone else has caught the bus.

Suicide is the eighth leading cause of death in the United States.

Homicide is thirteen.

More people kill themselves than are killed by others. Yet homicide is the national pastime, the preoccupation of every book on the *New York Times'* best-seller list, the subject of almost every TV drama—we love it. We can't get enough homicide, we breathe it as part of our national identity. We worry about our friends walking home alone late at night ending up in a bad neighborhood, but odds are better that the one you love would be both victim and aggressor.

Guns are, of course, the leading method of suicide in the U.S., constituting 57% of all suicides nationwide. Overall, the crown belongs to the white man. Of the 30,535 suicides in 1997, white people accounted for 27,513 of them, and 22,042 were white men.

New York City, for all its angst-ridden PR, is not the hotbed of suicide one might expect. In a ranking of the fifty largest U.S. metropolitan areas, New York–Northern New Jersey–Long Island ranks forty-nine with a suicide rate of 7.4 (per 100,000). Topping the list is Denver–Boulder, with a suicide rate of 17.6. It makes you wonder if the altitude really does do something to the brain.

Our statistics are a little different from those of the West. We have stricter laws on handguns, and we have taller buildings. In 1998, 524 people died of suicide and self-inflicted injuries in New York City. The number-1 method was hanging. Number 2 was jumping from a high place, with firearms coming in at number 3.

If 122 Brooklyn residents killed themselves in one year, it's a conservative bet that in an average year, a half dozen people would kill themselves in Williamsburg. It's not a crushing number, but an appalling number of people I've been crammed up against on the L train for their names not to appear in the paper.

If pressed, the *New York Times* would probably claim that their policy of refusing to run stories on suicide is to prevent copycats, and the explanation does carry some weight. But the steady if slight decline in New York suicide rates over the last fifty years (the last big peak being during the Depression) can probably be attributed more to rising economic trends and the popularity of antidepressant drugs than to the fact that no one talks about it. No one ever talked about suicide in America. It's an embarrassment here, having none of the nobility of foreign traditions, like the notorious seppuku of Japanese samurai—an honorable death. And yet people continue to do it, thirty thousand a year.

Murder we understand. We all know the feeling of wanting to kill someone. We are animals. The confession of a willingness to take another's life is an admired strength, an outdated yet romantic allusion to our tangled roots. But the admission of so much as the contemplation of suicide is a weakness, admitted only to therapists in stuffy confines.

The suicidal impulse goes against the law of the jungle, spits in the eyes of God and man alike, a furtive, desperate molestation of all that is decent to a Judeo-Christian mindset. A coldhearted murder is an offense against mankind in general, but a suicide is a crime against every man and woman specifically. It reminds us that we are all connected, that we are all to blame for any failure to support our fellows. A murder can bring us together in anger, but a suicide makes us feel guilty and alone.

No one wants to talk about that.

HOTLINE

Olive, in her bleeding-heart-liberal, Berkeley-hippie-shit way, started a suicide hotline. She printed up these flyers saying, "Feel sad? Depressed? Think suicide is the only way out? Someone cares. Someone can help." She stuck them up on all the bulletin boards on Bedford, the ones that used to boast sublets and studios and guitars for sale and man-with-a-van and job opportunities, but are now cluttered with nothing but apartment-available signs.

The opportunists are arriving in droves, picking at newly vacated apartments like vultures, the brokers still making nightmarish profits and still touting Billburg as the hip, hot, happening 'hood it was before the killings began. Economically, it can't last. Even an outside observer's eye ought to see that the turnover is unusual for such a popular neighborhood, and the prices can't stay so high when the supply is so abundant.

The speed of our mad influx of fresh meat is accelerating—the newbies to the neighborhood kill themselves off disturbingly quickly. When an immigrant moves into an apartment vacated by a suicide, the new tenant tends to follow suit. The defeated wander here, through some uncanny homing mechanism, to die. It's not enough that we've become the scourge of New York City, that we unconsciously avoid mentioning where we live on the off chance that someone will ask us an embarrassing question, that we fear riding our beloved L train, that we endure sirens day and night, that we stifle friendships so as to reduce the propensity for mourning—now we have the added pleasure of importing meat for the slaughter. We're living in the fucking *Bell Jar*.

Olive thought I would be upset because our phone would ring off the hook, but nothing could be further from the truth. I was convinced the phone wouldn't ring at all, that the whole idea was a joke, but I couldn't dissuade her.

The first week, the phone didn't ring once. That week, there were six suicides by L train at the Bedford stop, and three or four at the Lorimer stop. That's just the ones I know about. There were half a dozen attempts on Bedford by people jumping in front of cars, but I think most of them failed—no one drives fast enough on Bedford to be fatal. On top of all that there were half a dozen self-shootings, a couple of bathtub wrist-slicings, and one really impressive hanging from a telephone pole near the bus stop on Driggs. It was pretty stunning. I went out in the morning and saw a woman, probably in her early thirties, hanging from the pole by her panty hose, wearing a short skirt and, of course, nothing else below the waist. It was hard not to look. She had great gams and a pretty pussy for a corpse.

I tried again to talk Olive out of it.

"Take them down, will you? No one's going to call."

"People will call. These people need help, they need someone to talk to."

"If they need any help, what they need is a handgun."

"Just stop it."

"We're not talking about people who have thought about suicide for years, or even weeks. We're talking about a spontaneous idea that enacts itself immediately."

"Do you know all these people?"

"Well, you should have been on the platform with me Monday morning. That blond kid I told you about, the suit?"

"What about him?"

"He was on the pay phone planning a lunch date. He was all excited about this presentation he was going to make—some kind of software or something. He was talking to some chick and was stoked about his day, dying to see her at lunch so he could tell her how it went."

"So?"

"So, he hurried his conversation because the train was pulling in, he hung up the phone with a big smile on his face, and he stepped to the edge of the platform and took a dive just as the train came into view. It didn't even look like he was going to jump—I mean, he didn't telegraph it at all. He took half a step and that was it. He didn't plan that shit in advance, I'd bet my life on it."

"I'm not going to take them down. If no one calls, then no one calls, but I think they will."

She proved her point and I had to drop it. A Puerto Rican

from the Southside called to say that his mother, who must have been in her sixties, had offed herself and he was thinking that it wasn't such a bad idea. I only heard Olive's half of the conversation.

"Just because someone else did it, even someone close to you, is no reason to do it yourself. Think of all you have to live for. If everyone else jumped off a bridge, would you?"

A short pause.

"Yes, it probably would kill you. That's my point."

I laughed. She had given him an idea without even meaning to.

The next day I was on the phone when the other line beeped. I clicked over, and a laconic female voice asked for the suicide expert. "Hang on a minute," I said, and yelled for Olive to pick up the extension, but stayed on the line.

"Hi, this is Olive. Can I help you? Are you okay?"

"No… I'm really not okay… I just don't understand."

"What is it, sweetie? What's the problem."

"Well, I'm in the tub… and I cut my wrists about twenty minutes ago and I'm still not dead."

I wanted to ask if she'd cut them horizontally or vertically. It makes a difference.

"You already did?" Olive asked. "Where are you? I'll call an ambulance."

"No, no… just help me… is the water not hot enough? Do I need to stand on my head or something? How come I'm not dead yet?"

"Look, tell me where you are, all right? I'll get someone over there right away to help."

"You'll help me die?"

"Yes, I'll make sure you die right away." Olive was no fool, you had to hand it to her.

The girl gave her the address, and Olive went tearing

out of the house and told me to call 911. I did, even though I knew it was useless. A cab, a pizza—a pot dealer would come quicker than an ambulance these days.

Olive was back within a half hour looking like she'd swallowed a golf ball. "She was dead when I got there. The ambulance never even came."

"Aw, I'm sure they'll get there in the next week or so. You know. Backlog."

"I don't see how you can be so cavalier about it." She slammed the bathroom door and I heard the shower running.

The phone rang again and I answered. It was a guy with a nasal voice calling from Greenpoint.

"I don't have a reason to live."

"Yeah," I said, "I bet you don't. I mean, there's not really much of a reason to live. Never has been."

"I just want to die."

"Yeah, me too. But I think if you wait long enough it kind of happens naturally."

"But I want to die right now. I really do."

"Well, what have you got, bud? Got a gun?"

"No."

"Got a piece of rope? A razor blade? It doesn't take much."

There was a long pause on the line. "Aren't you going to talk me out of it?" he asked. He sounded close to tears.

"No," I said. "If you want to off yourself so bad then just quit your whining and do it. What the fuck do you want from me?"

Olive came out of the shower just as that line was coming out of my mouth. She had a towel wrapped around her and looked as lovely and surprised as a goddess climbing out of the river with dripping hair and a mouth wide open in shock. She snatched the phone out of my hand.

"Are you going to kill yourself?" she demanded, and

after a brief pause she put down the phone. "What the hell did you say to him?"

"Not much. What did he say? Is he going to or what?"

"No. He said he wouldn't."

I licked a drop of water from the crevice of her clavicle. "Come on, baby," I crooned, "let me make sweet love to you."

"I… I can't. I mean, really."

"What, we just saved a life. Isn't that what you want?"

She was already in the bedroom with the door closed.

OVERTIME

I settled into a groove with the electrician gig. We looked like a gang, all dressed in black—the universal color that makes you invisible, by mutual consent of technician and civilian—with our pockets bulging with tools. I never left the house without my leather satchel packed with a crescent wrench, big serrated knife, mini-Maglite, handkerchief, water bottle, cell phone, cigarettes, weed, and cocaine, wearing black jeans and big boots and my battered leather jacket, and a decent shirt for the stay-through.

We hustled gear in and out of the Chrysler building, dodging union crews, jostling each other for a place in the puny, ineffective service elevator maintained by a grouchy, pouchy man with a cigar stub crammed in the corner of his mouth. We rode to the sixty-seventh floor and carried gear up to the sixty-eighth, and I fantasized about old man Chrysler looking out over a mahogany desk through these standard glass panes unceremoniously lit from behind by fluorescent tubes, arranged in such radiating splendor as to appear a beacon of beauty over the Manhattan skyline atop this towering shaft of seeming chrome. When the window washer opened a window and leaned out, one leg outside the building, his head on the other side of the glass and the rag in his hand working at the grime, I held my breath and prayed for him not to fall.

We pulled a gig on Ellis Island and I imagined I could still smell the stink of thousands of immigrants standing in line in the Grand Hall, reeking of the sea and cramped quarters, praying to myriad gods they would not be declared insane or criminal and shipped back to their own miserable countries. I imagined my own ancestors standing in such lines, amazed by the immense history that dwarfed the actual size of this tiny island, half of it landfill and belonging to New Jersey.

We pulled a gig at a swanky restaurant under the Queensboro bridge for the opening of the new season of *Sex and the City*, and I stood next to Sarah Jessica Parker, a butt-ugly little thing. During a break, we loped up a couple blocks and got on the Swiss-designed tram to Roosevelt Island, a clunky car hanging delicately from a thick taut cable, rising up above the midtown skyline that shimmered in tandem to the reaching towers of the magnificent bridge. We looked down godlike upon the crawling traffic, tiny armored beetles beeping each other along. Roosevelt Island seemed quiet and unassuming, and we found it impossible to believe that anyone lived there, surrounded by the unstoppable slow sweep of the East River, between bustling midtown Manhattan and the humble promise of Queens. It seemed as likely a place as any for a lunatic asylum.

We pulled a gig on the USS *Intrepid*, a massive aircraft carrier permanently docked on the Hudson off the end of 46th Street, a ship with a history of service in World War II, Vietnam, and Korea, and the recovery of astronauts after splashdown. It was a USO convention, and we crowded around the boss and asked him how much extra money he'd give us if we slept with Miss America. "She's not that hot," he said, "but it's Miss America. Hell, I'll pay you for eight hours and give you a case of champagne." More impressive to me was the appearance of Senator John Glenn. "That guy's been in outer space," I said, "lucky enough to have gotten off this stinking planet." I hit him with a spotlight and wished I could shake his hand.

We pulled endless gigs in hotel ballrooms, marveling at the idea of spending a quarter of a million dollars on a party for a twelve year-old. At midtown venues with stunning views, I learned that you can pay to have the Empire State Building lit in colors that coordinate with your party's decor.

We pulled a gig at the Metropolitan Pavilion in Chelsea, for the launch of Oprah Winfrey's new magazine, O. The entertainment was Tina Turner. When she did her sound check, the entire room of hustling caterers and electricians and designers and cooks and sound and AV guys stopped dead in blatant admiration. She ran the rehearsal, and it was an efficient machine. When she came out for performance, decked out like her dancers in tight-fitting black leather, shaking her hips remorselessly and craning back her head to let the tumult of emotion pour out of her, I was torn between wanting to listen to her sing and wanting to bang her mercilessly. "Fuck," I said to Ray, "that woman's in her sixties at least."

He nodded. "And she's *hot*."

When the DJs took over we lost ourselves in a river of cocktails, waiting for the party to wind down so we could strike our truss towers and booms. Ray was there, as was Luz—a sweetheart, butch as hell, who could hold her own against any of the men, but with sexy, swaying hips, full lips and a sultry voice, making her a delightful contradiction. We hit the dance floor with a vengeance—unlikely, uninvited guests dressed in black. Ray's face seemed to light up for a moment with insane glee, and I realized that the light came from a camera poised just over my shoulder, and that the body cavorting next to me was none other than Oprah herself, a celebrity to end all celebrities, one of the few people on the planet who will always and forever be known by one name. Oprah joined in on our little dance circle of electricians, and we shook it with her and laughed about it for the rest of the night.

Everything was starting to heat up. I had always been fascinated and amazed by the presence of "dancing girls" and "dancing boys" at many of our bar mitzvah gigs. These rich fucks hire young, good-looking girls and boys to come to the party and dance with the twelve-year-old boys and girls. The sick upper-crust culture compels party hosts to hire beautiful people to dance with their ugly ducklings, to encourage dancing in a venue that might otherwise turn into a classic junior high dance. Even at weddings it was common practice, especially if the reception was made up of mostly single men or single women. Ray and I got kicks out of flirting with the hired dancing girls, who, for the most part, were only one nice outfit above the rank of common trash.

At a gig at the New York Palace, out of sheer boredom, I flirted with the party planner, the only cool party planner ever. She was mellow and always tipped us—she'd kick all the electricians twenty bucks—so we always gave her everything she wanted. She wasn't the uptight, bitchy type we were used to, and she wasn't bad-looking.

I pulled a cable out from under some chairs, breaking down a room that was no longer being used, and I had to ask the party planner, relaxing with a glass of wine, if she would move out of the way.

"Fuck you," she said, obviously joking.

"Now or later?"

"Later. I have to have a few more drinks before I start feeling amorous."

A few minutes later I was coiling cable silently in the corner while she listened to a greasy little guy—apparently an agent for dancing boys and girls—vent about someone who had failed to show up.

Ray walked in and overheard the conversation. "Hey, Benson, you still want to be dancing boys?"

"Hell yes," I said. "How easy would that be? We look good in suits, we could bust a move."

The man looked us over. "I don't know about him, but Ray could do it."

The party planner came to my defense. "Come on, he's gorgeous. He's got a great bod."

The guy looked me over again, and before I knew it, Ray and I were in the next room in our stay-through shirts, boogying down on the dance floor with the rest of the dancing boys and the scads of single young wedding guests. We proved our moves, because when it was over the greasy little man kicked us fifty bucks each, "a starting-off tip," and told us he'd hire us for future events.

We continued our electrician stints and worked in dancing-boy gigs, double stacking them whenever possible. Load in a gig, change clothes, dance during the party, change out of our nice clothes, strike the gig, load up the truck, and collect two paychecks.

New York is a good place to be, I thought, and then got off the L train at Bedford to see a girl who'd kissed the third rail and had no face left, just a black stain. She looked like an upside-down exclamation point on an advertisement in Spanish.

Yeah. New York is a good place to be.

TIME OUT

Time Out New York ran a ten-page spread on Williamsburg. The cover was a candid shot of the Stinger club with a group of hipsters clustered around a table, with a chick in a stocking cap and Tyler Durden–orange shades, one arm raised in victory. The picture was too well-lit and phony, and splayed out under the headline "The Ultimate Party Guide to Williamsburg."

They listed all our bars, our hot spots and our dives; all our restaurants, old and new; all our galleries; all our good shops and all our stupid little boutiques, including that tacky-ass mini mall that finally opened between 4th and 5th. They even gave up the taqueria at Matamoros, having the balls to insert a quote from a customer actually telling the *TONY* writer, "Don't tell anyone about this place." There is no cure for journalists. They gave up everything but Kokie's, the bar on Berry that sells laundry detergent coke out of the DJ booth and has a tiny curtained-off closet for consumption.

And they printed a map—a map!—charting exactly where everything was in the neighborhood, with subway directions so that all the bridge-and-tunnel people could be assured of not getting lost, mugged, or killed while following the trail of locusts.

I went on a rampage and Olive handed me a shot of bourbon and made me go sit in the living room and smoke pot until I calmed down. "Benson, I'm not talking to you until you're stoned enough to be reasonable." And when I was, and we were sitting at the bar at the L Café, waiting on lattes, she took the other side. "It's good for business. Those ladies at Matamoros need to make money."

"So it can expand to a huge warehouse of machine-made *sopes*? That taste like shit and cost five bucks?"

"That's not going to happen."

"But it could! It happened with Plan Eat Thai!" It only moved two blocks, but grew from a quaint eatery to a roomy barn obviously set up to attract Manhattanites.

"Go home and smoke some more pot, will you?"

"Fuck, I can barely see straight as it is."

"I'm sure all the businesses are glad to have the publicity."

"Liiiiiiiv," I whined, my pimply eyes squinting, "this place will be crawwwwling with yuppies."

"People are dropping like flies and you're still bitching about yuppies? Get over it. When are you going to realize that yuppies were not put on the planet as the scapegoat for everything you hate."

"I just can't deal with gentrification."

"I'm so tired of hearing that." The forty-something man sitting next to us, hunched over an espresso in a baseball cap, stepped right into the conversation and quickly began steering. "I don't want to hear it anymore."

"Why do you say that?"

"You think you're any different from anyone who ever lived in this neighborhood?" he asked.

"Come on," I said, waving him along. "Let's have it." I was just high enough to be curious, if not amiable.

He put his elbow on the bar. "You think the Canarsie were happy when they finally realized the Dutch weren't going away? If you spoke Algonquin, you'd be standing around your hometown of Cripplebush, knee-deep in swamp mud, bitching about the Dutch. And if you spoke Dutch, you'd be bitching about the English."

"He would be," Olive mumbled, lighting a cigarette, but the man was at a full rolling boil and didn't acknowledge her.

"Bet you the French and Scandinavians were happy enough until Hazard came in with his goddamned ferry boat. Then you got people from Manhattan coming across the East River to North 2nd—it's Metropolitan now, but it's always been the line between rich and poor. Then Mayor Berry makes Billburg part of Brooklyn to get out of a scandal, and there's your ancestors bitching about how they don't wanna live in no Brooklyn. Or maybe you're one of the last Dutch, bitching about how goddamned fashionable the neighborhood's gotten now that all these Germans and Austrians and Irish have moved in and turned it into suburbia. And I can just see you, some German kid, frothing at the mouth when the Williamsburg Bridge opens up and all these stinking Eastern European Jews, all poor as hell, come swarming into your neighborhood. Or if you live farther west, you can bitch about all the Italians coming in with their loud-ass *giglio*. So they build the BQE and cut the neighborhood in half, and if you're poor you lose your house and join the riots. And if you're Jewish, you can start oy vey–ing about all the dirty Puerto Ricans and Dominicans flocking in to work in the Domino Sugar factory. Nothing's changed, kid. *Gentrification* is just the latest term. People in Williamsburg have always been pissed when strangers come in and start changing the demographics. Besides, you're white, you're young—you're the latest wave. You're part of the problem."

I took it all in for a moment, and Olive asked the guy questions about the 'hood—he was a walking encyclopedia. He told her how Williamsburg was named after the guy who surveyed the area, but who never actually lived here. He thought there was a historic trend of strangers leaving their mark, making the rules that the locals would end up following.

"Some things," the man said, "don't change. You know, they say the name Bedford comes from an old Dutch word meaning a place where old men meet, because the Manhattan and Nyack Indians met here. Just take a walk on a Saturday afternoon—look at all the old men standing around saying 'whattayagonna do,' all the old ladies on the street in folding chairs."

"Haven't seen much of that lately," I said. "All I see is

people offing themselves left and right. What do you make of that?"

The man shook his head, knocked back his espresso, threw a five-dollar bill on the bar, and walked out without answering.

"Lot of help he was," I muttered. "Guess we're stuck between the yuppies and the dead."

Olive sighed heavily. "There's nothing anyone can say to you when you're like this. Look, *Time Out* comes out every week. *Every week.* New York's got too much going on for this to be that big of a deal. So this weekend, Williamsburg will be crawling with yuppies. Next weekend, it'll be somewhere else."

She was dead right. Friday night the 'hood was yuppie heaven, but by Saturday there were fewer and by Sunday the Manhattan siege on Billburg was cut off in its tracks by the mere fact that so many were taken back to Manhattan in body bags. It was as if they became infected the moment they set foot on our turf, and without the proper inoculation, they fell instantly.

And it was only then that it truly dawned on me, the sprawling scope of the irony, that such great press on our neighborhood would be released right in the middle of an ensuing crisis of unusual disease. It seemed almost magnanimous of *TONY* to throw us a bone in a time of need, and it backfired wickedly.

The *New York Times* ran an article the following Monday, briefly citing the "strange and inexplicable deaths" of visitors to Brooklyn. No mention of suicide. It was beyond the pale. Williamsburg was an island, untouchable.

The next week *Time Out* had something else on the cover, and everything went back to normal. Our normal, anyway.

SANGRIA

The double duty of electrician/dancing boy kept accelerating, and I was spending more time in Manhattan and less time with Olive, Phil, or any of the Rear Gang. I wandered the rat-maze underground crawling with caterers in the underbellies of the finest Manhattan hotels, and I put on a flashy smile and cavorted topside with the rich old ladies and the sparkling JAPs.

We loaded in a wedding at the Hotel Pierre up on 5th Avenue, but as soon as we got the truck spilled and the bins dragged inside, down to the basement, over to another elevator, and up to the ballroom, the mother of the bride called the party planner to announce that the bride had jilted the groom. We were pissed about tipping a truck just to load it again, but ultimately we laughed, packed it in quick, took our four-hour pay and shut up.

Ray and Luz and I took a walk in the park by the zoo, smoking a bowl and enjoying the icy blue sky and our shadows as long as the trees were tall. I split a cab with Luz to the Lower East Side, rode on across the bridge and surprised Olive and jumped her bones. My eyes were slits but my passion was genuine, and I suggested we go out to dinner.

We did our usual thing of being disorganized and indecisive about where to eat. We walked by Tony's Trattoria, tempted by the cozy checkered tables in the back room, but Liv wanted something a little more upscale. From the corner we saw flashing lights down by the subway entrance and knew what that meant. We kept walking. It was almost sundown and there was a sticky feeling in the air.

We walked by Wasabi on Bedford, but I wasn't in the mood for sushi, so we decided to go up to a little Italian place where they served sangria. As we turned up 6th an older woman came running out of her apartment, crying and wringing her hands. We kept walking.

"It's getting out of control, Benson."

"I know it, baby, but it's not us." I took her cold hand and squeezed it.

We walked on, and as we approached Berry, we could see our destination and I licked my lips, thinking about sangria. I was in the mood to tie on a light wine buzz and get a belly full of pasta and go home and make love to my girl again. Olive had a strange look in her eye and I couldn't tell what she was thinking. Her hand felt even colder. "Come on."

We stepped across the street towards the restaurant, and we heard a muffled pop from inside followed by a blood-curdling scream, and the lovely brunette who usually serves us dashed out of the restaurant, her face all screwed up, and disappeared around the corner. We turned away, and I knew I wasn't going to get to drink any sangria.

We passed the sushi place across the street and could see through the window two sushi chefs sprawled out on a table, one with his arms extended in front of him, the other slumped in a chair. The first had his forearms filleted, the pieces on the table before him like extra large servings of salmon sashimi in search of a big bowl of rice; the second had committed hara-kiri and had his innards falling before him like so much flotsam and jetsam thrown to the beach by an angry sea.

I stared until I heard pounding footsteps receding, and looking up, I realized Olive was gone. She was half a block away already, running down 6th at full tilt, her long legs a blur.

"Liv!" I yelled after her but she didn't look back. I ran after her, pushing myself full bore, but couldn't gain. Sirens whined in the distance, and the sun stubbornly refused to go away. The woman we had seen by Bedford was still in front of her house, still moaning and wringing her hands, hanging her grief out to dry. I ran past Bedford and lost Olive, seeing her again on the opposite side of the street, a blaze of white calves showing in the breaks of her skirt, her hair bouncing behind her. She had me beat on stride—and a head start—and I couldn't catch her.

I hit the stairs at a sprint and blew into our apartment panting. Olive was at the kitchen sink with a glass of water at her elbow, leaning on the counter with her head down. I came up behind her and stood on tiptoe and put my chin on her shoulder, slowly reaching around to caress her with a hug. She turned to face me, pushing me back from her, and leveled a piercing gaze.

"Why is it?" she demanded. "What is it? What—what is it, Benson? What did we do? What are we supposed to do?"

"I don't know, Olive. I don't think we're supposed to do anything. Whatever it is, it will have to work itself out."

"What is it with you." Her tone was acrid.

"What do you mean?"

"Everyone in our neighborhood is killing themselves, I'm falling to pieces, and you don't even care."

"Of course I care."

"No, you don't. You've told me fifty times."

"Okay, so I don't care so much if people are dying. But I care if you're really falling apart."

"That's not enough."

"Why not?"

"Because it's not enough." She was snarling now. "You watched your friend Dizzy die and it didn't even faze you."

"It was a drag. But if he wants to die so badly, what's it to me?"

"Exactly. What's it to you? The only reason you cared about Smith dying is because you'd never get to play pool with him again."

I shrugged lamely.

"And that guy at the L Café? You came by the restaurant all cheerful, and when I got off you brought me home and fucked me like nothing happened at all."

"Wait, I never—"

"Everett told me about it. That's right, you never even told me."

"I thought it would upset you."

"It *would* upset me! It's normal to be upset! A normal person would be *very* upset if he saw someone drive a fucking fork into his eye!"

"Well, it was pretty nasty…"

"But you don't care. It doesn't bother you at all to see all this… and it's everywhere now. We can't even go out to dinner because half the neighborhood's dead. And it doesn't bother you at all."

"It bothers me—"

"It bothers you now because you're hungry."

"I—I wanted to drink some sangria."

"How can you be so selfish?"

"I'm selfish? Suicide is the most selfish deed I can imagine, Liv. Do you see me jumping in front of the L train?"

"No, but—"

"I'm just trying to get by, babe. I'm sorry you're taking it so hard, but I refuse to have my whole world detonated just because of a little weirdness in my neighborhood."

"This is way beyond a little weirdness. It's tragic. If you had a heart—"

"Don't tell me I don't have a heart. My heart's breaking right now, listening to this. Watching you get so worked up. You're not mad at me, you're mad at all those dead people."

She held her tongue for a minute.

"Babe…" I approached her cautiously, as one would

approach a wild animal. "Come on…" I touched her arm gently, and when she didn't flinch I put my arms around her. "I don't want us to fight about this. This is dumb. This isn't us… this is everyone else. We're bigger than all of this. If the whole fucking city goes up in flames we'll still have each other."

She was crying. It was no use.

I wanted to pick her up and carry her away, far away to some tropical place where the brown natives served pineapple juice all day and cold sangria all night, where we could listen to the gentle lap of a crystal turquoise ocean against white sand and stroke each other softly in moonlight unsullied by smog, where death is a legend and suicide an unimaginable fantasy, a parlor trick performed only in jest. I wanted to take her in my arms and fly away, high above the city and east over Brooklyn, far out past Montauk and on over the Atlantic, finally setting down on a forgotten, hidden island where no one would ever disturb us. I wanted to smack her, to snap her back to her senses, but more than that I wanted to lay down my insensitivity, my coarse soul and my callous demeanor, lay my very will at her feet and let her kick it under the refrigerator. I knew in my heart there was only room in the house for one set of values, and mine were flawed beyond repair.

All I wanted was to drink the red wine of her tears and eat the fruit of her sorrow, but I didn't have the faintest idea how to do it.

THE QUICK

I've always hated Christmas, but I'd never experienced the onslaught of New York City Christmas parties, and the discovery of this exciting new delicacy brought me to appreciate the decadent celebration of the decadent celebration itself, an open license to inflate oneself with excess food, drink, and intoxicants and write it all off as the holiday season. The spent dregs of the year, designed to be wasted.

I spent weeks working my ass off at a mad frenzy of corporate Christmas parties, watching monochrome suits slap each other on the back while their dim, black-attired wives teetered around on high heels, getting sloppy drunk in celebration of another record-breaking year of wealth and prosperity. I watched from the sidelines, humping gear and running ragged from one gig to another, barely managing to make it home long enough to curl up next to Olive for a couple hours of dreamless, exhausted sleep before dragging my beaten body back onto the island for more abuse.

Winter was upon us now, and on late-night strikes we slipped on ice, pushing bins onto the steep lift gates of trucks, visibly huffing steam. I had taken to regarding my leather jacket as home, and I lived in it fully, pockets loaded with the bare necessities—cigarettes, fingerless gloves—and with my black watchcap I could almost pass as an underfed longshoreman. I had conformed to the blue-collar aesthetic and been absorbed by the working man's persona, my hands callused and my back aging by dog years.

By mid-December the season was over and my bank account was as spry as I was beat, and I was looking forward to a couple weeks off with the jack to enjoy it.

Everett designed and distributed invitations to his girlfriend's annual party at her lovely apartment on Berry, just across the street from Oznot's. The invite said, holiday attire, but I had no idea what *holiday attire* meant. Dress up like Santa Claus? Red and green only? I put on a blood-red butterfly-collar shirt and a deep-red-and-blue tie, a pair of vintage 1960s Levi's, low-riding hiphuggers with black and mustard stripes and a slight bell bottom. I put on steel-toed oxblood wingtips and painted my fingernails bright sunflower yellow, and I traded my leather jacket for a long, black overcoat.

Olive would join me when she got off work, but first I had another party to catch, around the corner from Phil's place. We hadn't seen much of each other, since he'd been slammed with school and I with work. I grabbed Ray and the obligatory shitload of cocaine, and we blew in like a couple of peacocks too cool to preen.

No one would talk to us for fifteen minutes. Ray was all decked out in high-class, high-profile black, and both of us were so grossly overdressed for the nondescript party in a cramped tenement apartment on the Lower East Side that everyone thought we were somebody. Ray systematically flirted his way from room to room. Phil and Toni came in right after us, and soon we were all taking turns in the bathroom.

I spent most of my time in the smoking room, sipping cheap bourbon from a plastic cup and chatting up a lovely young girl from upstate, and every time I tried to get off the couch, saying, "I need to make this party in Brooklyn," Phil piped up and said, "What you *need* is another shot of bourbon, and I'll get it for you. What you *need* is to sit right there on that couch and talk to that girl. What you *need* is another cigarette, and while you're at it, give me one of those cigarettes."

Ray just looked at me and said, "Brooklyn? Whattaya wanna go to Brooklyn for?"

By the time I arrived at Everett's girl's party it was after three in the morning and I was amped into overdrive. Olive danced in the center of the living room, looking more relaxed than I'd seen her in some time, the way she used to look before all the madness started, and when I caught her eye she just shook her head, amused by my outfit and unimpressed by my tardiness. Sam from downstairs was shitfaced, and stood off to the side pointing out busty Polish girls. Everett careened into the room mumbling, waved me dimly to the appetizer table and disappeared again, camouflaged in vapors thick as kerosene. I felt surprisingly sober by comparison.

I was perusing the dips when a girl in the bathroom drew herself a bath, and for a bath buddy, chose a running blow-dryer. Everett forced the door with his heavy, drunken body, and his girl broke the party's alcoholic sheen with her screams. The girl had slid under the water wearing a contorted death-mask that contrasted sharply with her buoyant naked body, and the water sparkled steadily with electric current, casting lovely rippling arcs across the surface that were still visible after the draw tripped the breaker and killed the lights.

Olive and I walked home in silence and I secretly wished I had stayed on in Manhattan, being served bourbon and cocaine, doling out cigarettes and sitting comfortably on a couch flirting with a girl who knew nothing of this.

The next night was the company Christmas party, and the crew rallied at 1st and 1st with the promise of an open bar. Everything was free from seven to ten, and when the boss showed up he extended it to eleven, and before he left he extended it to midnight. I picked out the finest bourbon on the shelf, Baker's, and stuck to it faithfully, until the bartender tapped me and said, "You're drinking Knob Creek. I'm all out of Baker's. You drank it all."

We had all worked the season together, and it was refresh-ing to socialize with kids I had been forced to hang with out of economic necessity. Without exception, they were consum-ing well beyond their natural limits, stepping into the bath-room in twos and threes, stepping into the street to smoke weed, and slamming cocktails back with abandon, paw-ing each other in a wickedly shameful pretense of dancing. Girlfriends, boyfriends—all were forgotten in a happy pile of workers who had spent the season eyeing each other, suf-fering together through long days and nights of incomplete instructions, overbearing bosses, incompetent crew chiefs, frustrating clients, asshole designers, bitchy party planners, troublesome caterers, lack of food and lack of coffee and lack of cigarettes and most of all, lack of sleep. But we'd made it, and everyone was in lust and intoxicated with the fever of the season's end.

Ray gave a whole new meaning to his catchphrase, "And you don't stop." It had been ringing in my ears, every time we were given another task at the last minute, every time anyone yawned or moaned or merely hitched up their trousers to dive back into the fray, sighing and lighting a cigarette and cradling a deli cup of tepid coffee. "And you don't stop." He had always said it as if he were at a party. We all picked up the refrain, toasting each other and racing to the bathroom— "And you don't stop."

I grabbed a shot with one hand and Luz with the other, and we tumbled into the bathroom to make out, groping at each other drunkenly, and I nibbled her full breasts as she gripped my cock—and even then, before I came on the tiled floor, I was thinking, *Liv just doesn't need to hear about any of this.*

I was tanked when I arrived at Jamie's party around one. I waited for Olive to get off work and come around, and when she did she took one look at me and begged me not to have another drink.

"It doesn't matter."

"Please, please, don't drink anything else." I was already walking to the makeshift bar on the dining room table.

"Please, Benson, don't have another drink."

I was pouring it. "Liv, it doesn't matter. If I were going to puke, pass out, or start a fight, it would have happened by now."

"Please…" She leaned forward, whispering in my ear, her

breath hot and steamy. "Let's get out of here before somebody dies." I remembered where I was and decided that it wasn't a bad idea. I let her lead me out.

Y2K

We avoided wallowing in the rampant commercialism of Christmas. We did our shopping the previous week and stocked the house up with food, alcohol, and weed so we didn't have to leave the house on Christmas day, and gave each other books and CDs and a couple new sex toys. We stayed in, cooked, cultivated a steady daytime buzz and listened to music and watched *It's a Wonderful Life*, which I had, miraculously, never seen before. We made love and smoked a joint and turned up the new Flaming Lips album to drown the drone of sirens.

But on New Year's Eve we had to go out. There was such hype, such overwhelming hysteria concerning "the new millennium," that I had begun to genuinely hope the entire world would explode at midnight. "It's optimistic pessimism," I told people. "I want the whole world to explode, so it's a sure thing that nothing will happen."

Phil and Toni came over for a cocktail, and we walked past McCarren Park and hit a house party. It was a fairly quiet scene, with a lot of families and kids, but it was still early. A little after eleven a girl smashed the punchbowl and picked up a large shard of glass and commenced shredding herself. The kids started bawling and people scattered. Phil and Toni stuck around since they were friends of the host, but I had already put in a call to Ray, hoping he could score us some coke, and that was all the incentive we needed to jet.

By 11:45 we were at Ray's place at 14th and 6th snorting fat rails and drinking champagne.

"Where were you before?" Luz asked.

"Oh, a party in Billburg."

"How was it?"

Liv and I exchanged a look. "It was a bust."

At midnight we went up to the roof—eleven stories—and could clearly see the fireworks popping above the skyscrapers of midtown. Turning around, we could even see the fireworks above the Battery. We heard shouts, but traffic continued to roll by and the city was clearly well-illuminated. Nothing happened. No worldwide computer-borne virus. No financial sacking of the free world. Just another moment, winding away into the sea of circumstance to which we all owe our allegiance.

Loudmouth Greg sparked a joint laced with coke and we passed it around.

"I feel like we should throw a glass," I said, "but your glasses are just too nice, Ray."

"No, you're right. We should toss one down. Liv should do it."

We toasted, and Olive slugged down the rest of her champagne and dropped the glass over the edge. We all leaned over and watched it fall silently, tumbling with a kind of grace outside of time, smashing in a muffled implosion on the sidewalk below, a snowflake barely visible against a pale field.

Downstairs, Ray came out of his bedroom brushing the coke from his nostrils and drew me aside. "Listen, Liv and I were just making out in my bedroom. Is that all right?" I wasn't fussed, and a few minutes later, Olive and Luz were locked in a beautiful clinch in the living room. I quickly said our goodbyes as Ray tried to extricate himself from his own party. Cabs were nowhere to be found, but the L train was running.

At our place we fell into bed, all four of us, undressing each other in a mass of twisting bodies and taking turns going nuts on one another. There was so much love in the room, such an ease of understanding among friends—or maybe it was the coke—that we ravaged each other for hours in a sexual tumult. I fucked Olive savagely with Ray's cock in her mouth, so at ease that I wouldn't have minded if Ray had fucked her next, but he, as usual, had done entirely too much blow, and certainly wasn't capable. I picked up the slack, possessed, and when I crawled on top of Luz, Olive was hypnotized, kissing her breasts and commenting on our beauty, as Ray and I did when Olive and Luz held each other, exploring each other with subdued caresses.

Around six in the morning we were all in the kitchen wrapped up in robes, Olive cooking as Ray rolled a joint and racked up lines and Luz sat and beamed quietly. Olive set out eggs but no one wanted to eat. Instead, I got on the floor and put my face between Olive's legs with ravenous desire, and Ray kissed her breasts and put his dick back in her mouth, and Olive came with a shuddering climax that rated on the Richter scale, and then Luz was touching me, and the kitchen filled with the squeak of chairs being shoved out of the way, and my cock was passed between three pairs of lips. I felt like a god.

We were the only rational beings in Williamsburg, that first morning of the year 2000. The apocalypse had not come to Manhattan, because it was unfurling itself deep in the heart of Williamsburg, but for once, and forever in that moment, the four of us were divine and far above the concerns of mere mortals.

Nothing could ever touch us.

PORTRAIT

Hoagy had taken the next step in his self-education as a painter. After working exclusively on self-portraits for the better part of eighteen months, because, by his own declaration, he was "always on hand," he had begun a series of portraits of other people. But when he ran out of extra money to pay models, he turned to his friends to sit for him.

He painted a portrait of Olive sitting at a school desk in a wife-beater, staring intently at the viewer with her elbows resting on the desk. Hoag admitted to having a hard time with the painting. "She's just so intense, that look in her eye. Every time I look up there she is, just staring at me, and it's like—*Aah!* I just want to look away." But he whipped out a stunning portrait—and I was next.

Once or twice a week I went to Hoag's studio and sat on the floor in a hospital gown, looking up at him with the radiant, satiated smile of the insane, pissing on myself in an asylum somewhere and happy as a half-wit, absent-mindedly pulling on one of my toes. It was fun watching Hoag work, his concerned brow shading his eyes, surprising himself, talking to himself and jabbing at the canvas with brushes, scraping it lovingly with knives, wiping off mistakes with a finger and then attacking it again, wiping his fingers on his Jackson Pollock pants, holding a big aluminum oven pan—the kind you use to cook turkeys—as a palette. With two brushes crossed in his hand like confused chopsticks, Hoag moved about the studio fussing with thirty-dollar tubes of paint, with turpentine and linseed oil, mixing up glazes and subtle hues like a mad scientist in an exercise of exaction that would all be destroyed when six different colors mixed on his brush, recreated when the brush touched the canvas, destroyed finally with a wipe on a rag, thrown on the floor like so much trash.

I was eager, walking briskly down to his studio on Grand between Wythe and Kent. It's a great block, with stunning views of the Williamsburg Bridge stretching towards the runaway sky and a quaint park filled with the ambient echoes of children playing. I was excited because Hoagy said he'd been working on the painting, using a Polaroid for guidance, and that it was almost finished, that this should be our last sitting—one last session to look at my face and get it cemented in oils with his delirious brushstroke. After half a dozen two-hour sessions we were approaching completion.

When I got to the studio I called Hoag to buzz me in. I glanced over at the gallery across the street, which had a bizarre effigy crafted in screening, hanging Christlike above its doors, looking out into the royal-blue sky completing its dusk descent to black. I heard Hoag's voice on the answering machine, and saw that the door to the studio was ajar. *Weird*, I thought. *He never leaves it open.*

I walked in and found the door to the stairway and walked down, trying not to trip in the dark, and stumbled through the dim workshop that was once a homespun fly shop, nearly walking right into the shut door of Hoag's studio. The door stuck, so I lifted it from the handle and pushed it open and saw Hoag in the glaring worklight of the white-walled studio.

He hung in the center of the room with a bona fide hangman's noose around his neck, suspended from cheap, hardware-store eyebolts screwed into the ceiling. One of them had pulled out but the others held. One shoe was half off, gently caressing the up-ended leg of a steel folding chair that had been kicked over beneath him.

I moved forward into the room with the harbinger of eternal sleep breathing hot along the back of my neck. I smelled a vague tinge of shit. His cut-off pants, stained with a full spectrum of paint, were sticking out at the fly. I righted the chair and stood on it and touched Hoagy's high forehead with the backside of my wrist. He was still warm but he wasn't breathing, and when I held my forefingers to his carotid, just above the swollen chafing of the rough rope, there was no comforting rhythm to be found. I'd found him with a boner and a butt full of poop.

After calling 911 and giving a full description of the latest tragedy, I slipped out, leaving the door open, sidled down Bedford to the Greenpoint Tavern, ordered one of those four-dollar styrofoam quarts of Budweiser, drank it as quickly as I could, lit a cigarette and ordered another. An old man with a big goiter on the side of his cheek bellied up next to me and tried to interest me in a handful of old silver dollars. He had a couple from the late 1800s, some from the 1920s. He held one up and said, "Here, feel the weight." I took it from him. It was heavy. "That's pure silver. Pure silver that is."

"Wow. Yeah. That sure is. Pure silver." I was trapped. The conversation grew circular, him repeating "pure silver," and me with absolutely nothing. Then he slid into a discourse on the Romans. "You know why Rome was destroyed?" I assured him I had no idea. "I'll tell you why Rome was destroyed. Rome was destroyed because they didn't believe in God. That's why Rome was destroyed. Because they didn't believe in God."

I cocked my eyebrows. "Maybe they just didn't fear him."

"They didn't believe in God," he insisted. "Do you believe in God?"

I washed back the last of my beer, set the styrofoam down and headed for the door.

Olive was on the phone when I came in, flying from room to room and stopping in at the kitchen to suck on a mangy hand-rolled cigarette. "Hiya, bud." She paused to kiss me and went back to her conversation. It was obviously with another actor; she talked in her loud, theatrical voice. It was nails on chalkboard.

I scared up a shot glass and poured myself a bourbon, lit a smoke and sat and waited.

"I know… I know… listen, I think I better go. My boy just came in and he looks a little blue… yes, do that. All righty. Bye now." She hung up. "What's up, babe? You look a little dismal. The painting not going well?"

"The painting is phenomenal." I could still see it, the image seared into my brain. On hold with the 911 operator, I stared at the immense canvas on the wall of Hoag's studio: a perfect likeness of me, leering up at the viewer with the irrational glee of the clinically demented. The mad face foremost, balanced beautifully by the complex configuration at the bottom of the canvas, fingers and toes interlaced in a casual gesture of simplicity… a rough grey background offsetting the white and blue hospital gown, a flowing angelic robe over the blessed hopelessness of the figure, a vision of wonderful innocence tucked away in a quiet little asylum upstate somewhere. Sunlit garden walks in the afternoon, catered meals, great mind-numbing pharmaceuticals….

"So what is it, babe?"

"Hoag's dead."

"What?"

"Hoag's dead."

"What do you mean, he's dead?"

"I mean he's hanging in his fucking studio."

"Don't joke around, Benson. I'm this close—"

"I'm not joking, Liv. I wish I were. Hoag's dead. He hung himself. I'm sorry."

"Did you—did you try CPR? Did you call anyone? What did you—"

"He's fucking dead, Liv, and no, I couldn't get ahold of Jesus."

"Don't—don't—"

"What do you want me to say?"

"I want you to say you're pulling my leg."

"I wish I could."

"You liar!" She exploded, turning it on me. "You fucking heartless, evil liar! Hoag's not dead!"

"He's dead, Liv, he's dead."

She yelled even louder, "He can't be dead! He wouldn't!"

"I'm sorry."

"I don't want to hear anymore," a little more calmly. She shook and the tears were coming.

"Liv, please, don't, don't cry—"

"Don't cry? My friend is dead and you're telling me not to cry?"

"He was my friend too, all right?"

"And I don't see you crying," she said, rich with spite. They came in force, thick rivulets of tears streaming from her crinkled nose and racing down her cheeks.

"I just… can't."

She raised her face then, her bloodshot eyes animal and accusatory. "You're not human."

"I'm glad for that. The humans around here keep winding up dead."

"You bastard you fucking motherfucker you heartless son of a bitch—" and with that she hit me fiercely in the arms, pounding me and yelling. I took a couple more blows, grabbed her by the wrists and pushed her back and forced her to the floor. She finally stopped struggling and crumpled into me, her lithe body shaking uncontrollably, and I put my arms around her and squeezed the tears out of her until she whimpered at me through a snotty nose.

"I can't do this anymore, Benson. I can't."

"Can't do what, baby?"

"I can't live here."

"Don't say that. I'm here, I'm right here. I got you. I'm yours. I'm never leaving you."

"I gotta go home."

"Sssshhhhh."

"I can't live here, Benson."

"Come on, hush now. Don't say that."

"I can't live here."

THE REAR GANG FOLDS

My initial impulse was sheer horniness. With Olive back in California, I felt angry and naked and capable of anything.

I walked down to Jamie's and knocked on the door but there was no answer. I walked back up to Bedford, thinking she might be at the Greenpoint Tavern. At the corner of the bar was one of her friends, whom I've only ever seen sitting on a barstool next to Jamie, so I reintroduced myself and asked if she'd seen her.

"No, she said she was coming over tonight but she hasn't come by. I tried to call her but got the machine."

"Yeah. I just went by there but there was no answer at the door."

"I thought maybe she was with you." She gave me a little wink and a cocked eyebrow.

"No such luck."

I walked back to Jamie's house and tried to find a way in. It's a beat-up old place, a former auto shop or something, with a graffiti-covered metal roller door that's been walled up on the inside, and no real windows to speak of—at least not anything large enough, low enough to the ground, and without burglar bars. I walked around to the side of the apartment, remembering that Jamie shared a kitchen and a bathroom with the tenants in the other half of the house. Their door moved when I knocked, so I pushed on in, thinking the worst.

A cool kid and a hipster chick embraced on the couch.

Closer inspection revealed that they were bent doubled over in the echo of a spasm, folded into each other in a madcap seizure, their bodies contorted in a tableau reminiscent of a lover's embrace. There was a bottle of Drano on the coffee table and bile everywhere.

"Fucking A, people, a bottle of aspirin would have been cheaper."

I found my way to the communal kitchen and tried the door to Jamie's apartment. The door was locked but I forced it, splintering the dead bolt in the dry-rotted wood. There was no sign of Jamie but her kitty was mewing, so I found him some food and left him smacking his lips happily.

All right. So maybe she's all right. Maybe she met a boy or something… you know Jamie, always falling in love with the wrong guy and disappearing for a month and resurfacing when he breaks her heart. Relax. Let it go. You're not her keeper or anything. Okay. I gotta take a piss.

The bathroom was lit up with candles placed on every available surface in the tiny room, some burned out and all burned down low, standing in still pools of melted wax in front of the mirror, sending reflections of flickering candlelight dancing across the room, wonderfully illuminating Jamie's face and knees rising out of the tub. The surface of the water was covered with red rose petals, the alluring aroma filling the space. It was beautiful… a truly romantic scene. She was smiling. She was so lovely, her skin smooth in the rosy water, candles flickering on flesh….

I fished an arm out of the water. She had done a good job, a deep, vertical slit running from the joint of her wrist almost to the elbow. Nice work, babe. Nice work.

My hand dripped with bloody water but I didn't bother to wash it off.

Belle, my upstairs neighbor, overdosed on sleeping pills and wound up stiff in her bed in the fetal position. Scarlet moved out and shacked up with her girlfriend, but when her friends Ronnie and Maciej offed each other with dueling pistols in a homoerotic suicide pact, it was all too much for Scarlet and she skipped town completely. I heard a rumor that her girlfriend strung herself up before they could get out.

Everett, downstairs, cut the hose from the faucet in the courtyard, went over to Ronnie and Maciej's place, broke in, got their car keys, and sat in the car with the engine running and the exhaust siphoning through the hose into the sealed car. No one noticed until the car ran out of gas and lurched forward in a paroxysm of death itself and banged into the car parked in front of it, setting off the car alarm and bringing the owner out of her house to find her car hit by a dead man, his flesh cast-iron black from the smoldering exhaust.

Sam, Everett's roomie, was a complete prince about the situation. He went to great lengths to contact Everett's family in D.C., made arrangements to have the body shipped, held long, teary conversations with Everett's mom in Germany, and packed up most of his effects. As soon as the whole affair was tied up he told me he was going to stay with his parents in Queens, and the next morning I heard a firecracker pop at around seven in the morning. I went downstairs, broke through the window with a rock, climbed into the apartment and found Sam sitting calm as can be in his easy chair, a look of utter tranquility on his face, a Mona Lisa smile playing at the corners of his lips. His brains were mostly stuck to the ceiling.

On the floor by his side was an old World War–II issue .45 that I'll bet had been in his family for years. I didn't guess that his folks would need to see it again, so I took it, along with the box of shells. I put in a call to Queens; his mother wailed like a widow about to commit suttee.

So… Sam and Everett, Scarlet and Belle, Jamie, Ronnie and Maciej, and Hoag, the crew I'd come to know and love here in the neighborhood, all gone. The Poles from the front building have vanished, the sweet old Italian couple next door who used to break my balls about our courtyard parties have left, and even the old Asian man who kept the garden next door and did Thai Chi in the mornings on the rooftop patio are gone, gone, gone.

And Olive is over three thousand miles away.

No choice but to keep walking.

CONEY ISLAND

It was easier, back when all I did was beat myself up about the incessant problem: moolah, juice, jack, scratch, lettuce, bread, dough, clams, coin, bucks, bones, semolians, smackers, greenbacks, dinero, cash, money.

But the summer's almost over, and we can't pass up a delicious invitation. Ronnie and Maciej have a car, a rare commodity in my New York world. Ronnie, an old friend of Scarlet's from Texas, stands six foot something with salt and pepper hair closely cropped, tall and gaunt as a Calvin Klein model, with his boy in tow, sweet Maciej, blond boy with a little belly and a thick Polish accent.

Olive and Scarlet and I pile into Ronnie and Maciej's dingy white urban cruiser. We hit the BQE and ride, watching the afternoon speed by all lit up with the reflections of chrome, promising a Saturday of inane pleasure that even my nihilism and empty wallet can't spoil.

"We're at Coney Island!" Olive screams, bouncing crazily out of the car, jumping up and down, excited as a seven year-old at the zoo.

The day winds out before us like a well-remembered

dream… the enormous Wonder Wheel, a Ferris wheel with sliding cars, over seventy-five years old and "never an accident," Scarlet squealing as our car slides over the turn and swings madly, high above the kiddie park, and Ronnie wishing we had a joint to smoke… the Cyclone, the roller coaster with a steep opening plummet, a heart-wrenching drop curving in on itself, reaching down our throats and coming out with screams and shaking knees and the four-dollar temptation of riding again. The kids are all out, the small kids with parents in tow, the high school kids looking to ogle, the college kids with their sweethearts, the slacker kids like us out for a day in the sun with bad food and the beach. I feel so comfortable, the sights and sounds and smells of the ocean mingled with seedy hotels on the outskirts and beat-up old signs from the fifties, like a massage for my soul, a place I recognize with my mind's inner eye, the soothing mustiness of aging memories and the rundown, ramshackle beauty of it all.

We eat Coney Island red hots and corn dogs, walk down the beach admiring the surf. I feel at home among my fellow poor, my friends and neighbors in this city of big dreams and high rollers, all the Puerto Rican families swimming in the ocean and laughing and screaming and running at each other with fabulous, gleeful abandon, diving in with clothes on and rolling around on the wet sandy mud and jump-skipping barefoot through the fiercely hot sand. No money worries today; this is all free—this beach, this water, this view, a peek at a young girl's ass in a bikini, a glance at a bored lifeguard. These are my people and I love them.

The afternoon wanes, the crowd begins to thin, and we go to the freak show. A midget in clown makeup twists up some balloon animals. A leather-clad, purple-haired punk insults us and pelts us with patter so stale it's crumbling. He's bored as hell and we can all see it, but it doesn't stop him from driving screwdrivers into his sinus cavity, swallowing swords, and otherwise grossing us out. Scarlet loves it, can't take her eyes away, and I don't want to look but I can't take my eyes away either. Olive seems fascinated without evidence of repulsion. Two slacker chicks do a lame straightjacket-escape bit—I think the jacket is supposed to be tight. A hotty comes out in sexy black leather and dances with an enormous yellow-white snake, sticking out her tongue in imitation and letting it kiss her, opening her mouth wide and performing fellatio on his head, eliciting the predictable whoops from the pigs in the audience.

At the end of the show they pass the hat—despite the fact that we paid admission—and announce the blow-off, the eleventh act, that we have to pay more for but that is oh-so worth it. Ronnie falls prey and comes out swearing. "It was just a stupid video," he whines, "a teeny little *tee*vee showing a videotape of, like freaks around the world or some shit." The barker at the front door, a slick-looking carny in a vest and a bowler, shrugs and says, "Why do you think they call it the blow-off?"

The line takes on a deeper meaning to me, somehow emblematic of the towering reputation of Coney Island, a shadow of the infamy of New York City itself, the lure, the attraction. The barker always praising that which does not exist. The party that no one can remember attending, the fabulous bar that no one can find because there's no name on the door. The unbelievable dream job that's just been filled, or the legendary drug dealer who vanished without a trace. The vicious circle of life attending no one's needs but its own.

Welcome to New York, New York, so great they named it twice. You're broke? Busted? Destitute? Why do you think they call it the blow-off?

How's your beautiful, wealthy wife, the high society dame, the perfect mother, your trophy, your salvation? The best fuck you ever had, you've said it a million times. That gracious woman of the world, a lady in public and a whore in the bedroom. The apple of your eye, the anchor of your soul. She left you for a dishwasher? Why do you think they call it the blow-off?

How's your high-salary job, your powerful friends, your influential associates, your company car, your fat pension plan? What, you're unemployed? They downsized you? Forced you into early retirement and swindled you out of your 401(k)? Why do you think they call it the blow-off?

How's your lovely apartment, that impossible-to-get piece of property in the perfect neighborhood on the top floor with roof access and river views that you got for a song with the gravy of rent control? How's your doorman, your in-house washer and dryer? What? You got evicted? You're homeless? Eating out of a garbage can? Why the fuck do you think they call it the blow-off?

I quietly climb into Ronnie's car and rest my head against Olive's tender shoulder all the way back to Billburg. We had a great day and yet I feel empty, brushing an intangible doom, like a turtle on its back, its feet turning in vain, grasping silently for what none of us truly understands.

LISTLESS

The night came cool and blustery and he caught a chill walking around in just a T-shirt. But he walked on anyway, deliberately into the wind, and cut up Bedford to the Greenpoint Tavern. He wanted a beer, he wanted to smoke in a public place, he wanted conversation. And yet even as he thought that he knew it to be a lie; he'd never had a memorable conversation in that bar without taking someone with him. The aging barmaid wasn't much into idle chitchat; there was no pool table; the jukebox was tired; the television was always on and that always had a tendency, in a narrow bar, to draw drinkers' to it and lull them into a trance of languid staring.

He ordered a mug of Bud even though for a couple dollars more he could have had a quart. He tried not to look at the television but he did, peering through his cigarette smoke, and caught a disturbing image of a deformed man and a rather attractive woman. He turned away and caught one poorly formed line of TV dialogue filtering over the Cher song on the jukebox: "No one's interested in your opinion."

He shook his head and gazed at the row of bottles and thought, *You really ought to be careful about what you let into that mind of yours.* He finished the smoke and the beer and hit the door without thanking the barmaid, and walked into the cold feeling like a hounded man, as if at any moment someone would stop him and ask, "What are you doing?" and he would be forced to answer with feeble responses. "I was at the Greenpoint having a beer. I'm heading home now. Well, it's that way but I thought I'd take the long way around. I know it's chilly out but I felt like walking. I just felt like getting out. I didn't speak to anyone and no one spoke to me." He felt like a criminal convicted of a crime he wasn't aware of, like some absurd figure out of Kafka. He felt this way often.

He walked up Bedford to 7th and turned toward the river, walking with a purpose to get a look at Manhattan, and thought he'd walk up to the water but shied away when he saw the cop on the corner, cones in front of the dirt driveway, and cars parked beyond it. He remembered that the chain-link fence had been fixed and he didn't want any altercations trying to get around it. He saw the twin towers of the World Trade Center in relief beneath a thin wisp of high cirrus clouds, gently tinged in the fading orange of the dying light.

Looking the other way he saw figures in the field between him and the water and decided he definitely wouldn't try to make the docks. He wasn't in the mood to look at anyone, let alone talk. He turned and glanced at his favorite building, the Chrysler, and the Empire State, and at other, unnamable buildings winking through grim fluorescent windows in the coming dusk, and saw again the outline of the dim figures in the field between that last street and the East River.

He cut up to 9th towards Bedford, surprised at the ghost town quality of the street before him. It was at Wythe that he saw an American flag, and stepping over a few squares of sidewalk saw the "Engine 212" sign that he had never seen before, and wondered how he had managed to miss it for so long—a fire station, just a few blocks from his house.

At the corner of 8th he stopped to watch a pretty, dark-haired girl jogging by—such a jolt of normalcy—and in a fraction of a moment lived a complicated, detailed fantasy. Coming to watch her jog by every evening, her noticing him eventually and finally, one night, pausing, doing that running-in-place thing that joggers in this town seem obliged to master as they wait at the walk-don't-walk, and saying something to him, something accusatory, something about stalking or minding his business, and his saying something simple and disarming, like, "Am I really taking anything from you that you can't afford to give?" Because it pleased him to look at her, and would it be such a bad thing to look at her for a brief moment every night as she jogged by? But he knew he wouldn't see her again, and he walked back down to 6th and climbed the stoop to his building and was gone from the watchful eye of the street.

III. The Vulture's Beak

LOVE

Everyone wants to fall in love. The search for the wild ride, the unending quest for the unexpected, is a cab ride with an astronomical fare, a driver who doesn't know the city but cruises endlessly through West Village crooked back alleys, up the West Side Highway and down the FDR, cutting off traffic in Tribeca and repeatedly passing your hotel and refusing to let you out. He has to restart the meter because it's reached its maximum fare, and you know if he ever does let you out you'll have to make a run for it: Trump doesn't have that much money.

You want to fall, you want to be taken aback by a moment that catches you unawares, an extra wink from someone pouring coffee, an unsolicited compliment that leads to a date, a seduction, an intrigue, a gravitational force that pulls you in and makes mincemeat out of you. You want to fall in love and be swept off your feet. You want someone to come along who has a plan, an agenda, that will save you from indecisiveness and plot out the rest of your life with no effort on your part. You want a driver who knows where he's going. You want to dance and not have the pressure of leading. You want someone who turns on the radio to your favorite station without having to ask what it is, and who will always turn it on at the exact moment that your favorite DJ is introducing your favorite song. Someone who will slow dance with you to the muzak on the elevator, squeezing your ass playfully and smiling at you in infinity in the parallel mirrors. You want to be teased, you want to be led along by a warm and caring hand. You want to be free and trustful enough to explore all your kinkiest sexual fantasies without fear of retribution, without recurring traumatic memories, without the cops finding you raped and killed and handcuffed to the radiator, naked and covered with bodily fluids which will never even amount to a DNA match. You want to be safe. You want to be respected and adored and placed high on a pedestal by a devotee worthy of worshipping you. You want your parents to be proud of you. You want your friends to be envious of your magical, perfect romantic match. You want to go out for expensive dinners and never worry about having to pay, but be reckless and flippant and order oysters and lobster and caviar and crème brulée and expensive bottles of champagne and overpriced bottles of wine and cocktails that boggle the imagination in their consummate beauty, multilayered in fine crystal, served by impeccably mannered waiters in tuxedos smiling the ingratiating smile of the modest, sincere sycophant.

But you don't want to have to explain yourself. You don't want to be blamed for your mistakes, or mistrusted for your inconsistency of character. You think your contradictions make you interesting, complex, fascinating in a world populated by bland character actors forever typecast. You want to believe that you are the only one left living who is really special, who is truly unique, a gem among polished rocks, an exploding supernova in an endless sea of slow-burning stars. You need someone else to recognize it and validate your belief. You don't want to hear excuses, or talk about money, or feel jealous about the existence of other lovers, or be the object of jealousy. You need reassurance. You don't want to hear that your career is an interference, and you don't want to say it. You want to believe that Cinderella left the ball and entered a better life, that all dogs go to heaven. You know the world is a dirty place but your own little corner is immaculate. Your friends are the coolest, the most fun, the most intelligent conversationalists since the Golden Age. Your mirror tells you that you are the fairest of them all. You deserve better. You deserve fame, fortune, and the undying admiration of this world of blank-faced dreamers from the cabinet of Dr.

Caligari. You want the best. You want to be safe. You want to fall in love, fall and fall and keep on falling, never reaching the bottom, never having to recover, never on the rebound, never on the outs, never in reality but merely sculpting your perceptions to convince you that all the shit in the toilet when you rise to flush was somehow magically deposited by someone else while you were turning on the tap to start your hot, sanctifying shower. No one really believes they are ordinary. No normal person, anyway.

You just want to fall in love.

SPREADING

As cynical as I may be, the Talia incident scared the shit out of me.

I met Talia a couple weeks ago. I was at Swift, on 4th near Bowery, with Phil and some of his NYU cronies, berating the hell out of him for going to see the new Richard Foreman show without me. Apparently, he and Toni went with her friend Pamela and her boyfriend, and they didn't call me because the boyfriend is still pissed about Olive taking Pamela to bed late last summer.

"But, Phil, I didn't even get to fuck her!"

"But did you… do anything?" Phil is a consummate voyeur.

"Well, yeah. I mean, I did kiss her all over and lick her pussy."

"And?"

"But I didn't fuck her, and—you were there that night. It was all Liv. I didn't come on to her, it was all about the girls. They barely noticed I was there. At one point, I was fucking Liv while she was going down on Pamela—I think that's the only time Liv looked at me. Mostly it was the two of them fingering each other."

"I understand, my friend, but Pamela's boyfriend is not exactly what you would call reasonable." Phil checked his shoulder to see that we were still out of earshot. "So all things considered," he asked, "how was it?"

"Super yummy. Her pussy is sweet as a sixteen-year-old's." He laughed. "But still, I want to see that show, and now I have to get a date and deal with all that—"

"Here's your date, right here," Phil said, gesturing to Talia at the bar. He grabbed her and brought her into the convo. "Friday night okay for you kids? I'll call and make a reservation."

Talia was a cute, short brunette weighing maybe a buck, another doctoral candidate at NYU, who had tagged along with Pamela. But Talia seemed different, calling herself a writer, not just a deconstructionist critic like the rest of those kids. I went with it and took her number, more to humor Phil than anything else. But I couldn't get tickets for Friday—it was sold out—so I got tickets for the following week.

Saturday I headed up to the W Hotel on Lexington, with pastel-colored meeting rooms and an elegant simplicity to the overall design, a smart-looking bar and an unpretentious air. We were supposed to load in a small, silly wedding that promised to be cake, and I hopped out of the cab a good twenty minutes late. I didn't see a truck parked outside, so I talked my way past the guard at the service entrance and took the stairs to the ballroom and saw no one. As I headed back downstairs to smoke I ran into Luz.

"Hey...." We exchanged kisses and hugs. "I just talked to Ray. He's running late and said we should go get a cup of coffee or something."

"I could use a sandwich."

"Let's go."

We strolled down Lex and Luz told me about her harried

day. She was directing a show and had arranged with one of the guys in the shop to illegally "borrow" a few lights. She'd conducted the whole transaction by cab, from her place on the Lower East Side all the way up to Harlem, getting the lights, dropping them off at her producer's house in Chelsea and speeding back up to the east side of midtown. "And the cabbie waited for me. He was so great. He even turned the meter off while I went in, and he got out, helped us put the lights in the trunk. It was amazing."

I got a turkey burger at a deli, we both got coffee and were just walking by the W when Ray pulled up in the truck. He got out and we all hugged and kissed, and Luz took one look and said, "God, Ray, you're really stoned." He rolled up the back door and climbed into the truck, looking around at the gear. He did a take, one of those, *Oh, wow, what was I looking for?* moments, reminding himself where he was and who he was and what he was doing.

"Man, Ray," I said. "You really *are* stoned." We all laughed, and Ray held his hand to his head and squinted with a grin.

Greg had bagged him, which wasn't surprising. Loudmouth Greg bags all of us. He's the most replacing-est motherfucker I know, always overbooking himself, or booking a better-paying gig on a day he's already booked, and calling everyone up to say, "Can you replace me on this"—shitty—"gig?"

"He wanted me to take him and a couple bins down to Cipriani," Ray complained. We groaned. "He talked me into it. He said he'd smoke me out. Traffic sucked, it took us forever, we dropped off the bins and the crew started asking me to do shit. I finally get out of there, and I'm driving up and I realize, he walked off with my bowl."

"That sucks."

"So, B, you have your bat on you?"

"Of course."

"Weeeelllll… I think it's time for us to smoke a bowl."

They found seats on milk crates and I squatted on a boom base dolly and ate half my burger, and we passed my pitch hitter between us and looked out the truck at the grey day, strolling pedestrians, and passing traffic. The anonymity of New York.

The gig was a joke, just the three of us, so it barely felt like work, going through the motions with easy laughter.

In the middle of the day, Talia called to see what I was doing that night, even though our official date was a week away. Ray and I weren't dancing during the party, and he didn't need me on the stay-through, so with a break from seven to midnight, I agreed to meet her at Smalls in the West Village to hear some jazz.

The music was all right, if not great, somewhat clouded by the bass player's humming along to his own melodies in a grating, groaning sound pressed through a distorted face. I half expected him to squeeze out a baby right there on the stage. Talia and I ducked around the corner to Kettle of Fish to have a cocktail, and she told me about the guy she was sort of dating, with some bizarre medical condition that makes his nuts swell up the size of grapefruit. He's out of town, they're taking a little break from each other… I was still wondering what was on her mind as far as I was concerned, and finally asked her flat out.

"Well, I don't have that many friends, and I thought you were cool, and I wanted to go out and have a drink, and I thought you would be a cool person to go out and have a drink with."

"You've got to be crazy to think you can hang out with me and not have me come on to you."

"I was afraid you were going to say something like, 'It's a

good thing you just want to be friends, because I'm not interested anyway.'"

We both had a good flirty laugh and I started to like her.

We left the bar and I gave her a ride on her bike, standing on the pedals as she giggled uncontrollably, perched on the seat gripping my ribs, both of us laughing as I weaved through traffic.

Her apartment was gorgeous, right on top of Union Square in the Zeckendorf Towers, the complex of buildings topped with lit-up pyramids. Her family owns the place, so she pays sixteen hundred for the enormous pad and rents out a room for fourteen, giving her a grand bedroom with two bathrooms and a Martha Stewart kitchen overlooking Union Square for two hundred bucks a month. We were there ostensibly to go to the roof and get high, but she had a king-sized bed, and when I saw it I took a running, playful leap, diving into a lush field of feathery comfort. She snuggled right up next to me and we started kissing. She was on top of me, grinding, and jumped off, startled but laughing, when she felt my cell phone vibrating in my pocket.

It was Ray. "What do you want? It was just getting interesting."

"Are you coming back?"

"Yeah, I'm coming back, if you quit bothering me. I might be late."

"Take your time." I could hear him smiling at the other end of the line.

I kissed her some more and she started pulling her clothes off, wriggling out of them as quickly as she could. "Hold up a minute, girl," I said, "we don't need to be in such a hurry. I'll only be at work for an hour or so, and I can come back over and we can do it right."

"I'd like a quick one now, if it's all right with you."

I was mostly naked with a boner, so I figured what the hell.

A week after our spontaneous first "date," we took in *Bad Boy Nietzsche!*, the new Richard Foreman show at the Ontological Hysteric, in St. Mark's Church, as per our original agreement. It was good, but not as good as *Benita Canova*. Talia was dead quiet, and afterwards she said she was just going home. I let her get about half a block up 2nd Avenue before I ran after her.

"I don't mean to be a prick or anything, but I have to say, this is totally rude. Last week was rude enough, but fuck, I thought we were going out tonight. It's only ten o'clock. If I thought you were just going to bail on me I would have taken someone else."

"What have I done that was rude?"

"Begging a quicky off me and refusing to see me when I called you back after I got off work? That wasn't rude?"

"You wanted to do it too, or you wouldn't have."

"And tonight?"

"What about it?"

"We had plans to go out tonight. I asked you if anything was bothering you, you have nothing to say, and now you just walk away? You can't even come out for a drink? No explanation? You don't think that's rude?"

She didn't. It was impossible. After a brief argument on the street, barking at each other as if we were actually dating, she suddenly flipped her attitude 180 degrees, smiled and walked me around the corner to what Luz calls the Tile Bar, a dark dive at the corner of 7th and 1st with a rockin' jukebox. Talia opened up a little, and even kissed me at the bar. And then we ran, racing each other, up to her place. She was pissed because I dogged her. "I run every day," she whined. "I can't believe you beat me."

We went to the roof and smoked a quick bowl; the view

was stunning. Standing underneath a glowing pyramid seen so often from the ground, peering down onto Union Square and uptown to the Empire State and that towering genius of chrome, the Chrysler Building, I wanted to maul her right there on the roof.

I was beginning to feel like a tool, but I stood her up in front of the full-length mirror and stripped her to the waist, kissing and caressing her thin, childlike body, dwelling lovingly on her tiny breasts and tantalizing erect nipples, her adorable belly button that was merely a dimple. We moved to the bed, and the more we got into it the more ridiculous I felt, as if it were all part of a scene she was writing, a fantasy that she controlled, and yet it was as if I were the only willing participant. She was controlling all the moves but didn't even want to be there. When I got inside her I said, "What do you want?"

"I want you to come." What is the rush with these early-twenties broads? I'm just getting started here, I want to ride until four in the morning, I want to make you come a dozen times before I even consider it, I want us to satisfy each other completely. I had already made a concession since she refused to either give or—this was too much—receive oral sex—and now I was supposed to come quickly and get it over with? The more she lay still and silent and unmoving, the more bored I got, no matter how delicious her body. The more I tried to get her into it—biting her to get her blood up, trying unsuccessfully to roll her over and mount her like a raggedy horse—the more she resisted me, lying still, in the missionary position, compliant but resistant in her refusal to participate, merely spreading her legs and allowing me to violate her. I felt distant and removed, like a puppet tangling the puppeteer in the strings. I finally said, "If you want to control the entire experience you should just get a vibrator."

"You're right," she said. "We should stop." *Like hell. I made it this far, I may as well bust a nut. That's what you want, isn't it?* I refused to relent and attacked her with a voracious, animal urge, letting her lie as still as she wanted, putting my hands under her grapelike ass and holding her up and into me, turning up the volume, the heat, the strokes per minute, the pounds per square inch. And when I broke through, it was a deep, double orgasm, one and then another following it, right on top of the first, digging deeper, plunging closer to the core, pulling my soul from my body and throwing it all into her, whether she deserved it or not.

When she went to the bathroom I lay still on the bed sideways, my head dangling over, feeling spent and dizzy and ready to pass out. All I wanted was to see her lovely little frame waltz out of the bathroom, pull her back down onto her comfortable bed, cuddle up, and nap and talk about absolutely nothing, nuzzling each other like gushy teenagers. But I thought, *When she gets back in here she's going to ask me to leave, so I should just ditch right now and be done with it.*

I was almost dressed when she came in with a towel wrapped around her, looking more desirable than I could have imagined. She sat on the bed with her tan, shapely little legs folded underneath her.

"I guess I'm a bit of a masochist, and a bit of a sadist," she offered by way of explanation. "I just want you to know that I sometimes find pleasure in things that other people wouldn't necessarily consider fun. And I had a good time tonight. Even with everything… I had a really good time."

"But you never asked if I had a good time. And I didn't."

The next three seconds lasted a lifetime. It was my exit line. I was out of there, I was gone, I never wanted to see her again. She was a lousy lay, and completely unaware that there were other people on the planet besides her. I couldn't deal with her. I said the words "and I didn't" and turned towards the door. I saw it all out of the corner of my eye. She slipped a hand underneath her and pulled out a large kitchen knife, a nine-inch blade shaped like an upright sail. In one quick, deft, repulsively committed motion, the knife flipped itself in her hand to face her, and plunged itself into her throat with a sickly wet thunk. The force of it pushed her back and off balance, her legs coming unfolded, the towel coming loose from around her, her head striking the backboard of the bed and the tip of the knife, protruding from the back of her neck, making a slight nails-on-chalkboard sound as it scraped the wooden veneer as she slid. The blood flowed in thick rivulets, soaking the coke-white sheets and pillowcases behind her, trickling delicately down the front of her elegant neck, collecting in tidepools in the hollows of her exquisite collarbone, painting her smooth brown body crimson on a white field... as it choked and sputtered slowly, slower, slower....

I looked at her legs and the soft bit of mystery that had so recently held me. I felt like a necrophiliac already. There was so much blood. It was already beginning to coagulate. Her head was askew at a surreal angle, her eyes wide open and accusatory.

I dialed the all-too-familiar number and cleared out her weed drawer—stash, pipes—before taking the walk.

To get to the street I had to take the elevator to the seventh floor, then walk to the other side of the building to catch another elevator to the ground. I walked the stale industrial carpet and saw the EMS guys in white, with a gurney and a body bag.

"What's up?" I would never admit to being in that room.

"Oh, that's a good one," said the man closest to me, with dry, icy cynicism. He looked as if he hadn't slept. Ever. The guy pushing the gurney attempted a smile but couldn't bring one all the way to the surface. "Another suicide, man, what else?" He said it with the sadness of routine. The gurney rattled on behind me and I made the elevator before the door closed and pushed the button for the lobby. When the polished stainless steel-door closed in front of me, I saw my own haggard reflection, and it dawned on me, slowly, like a hangover: I was in Manhattan.

It was spreading.

DENIAL

Ray and I pulled a gig at the Metropolitan Club, sneaking off to shoot pool in the immaculate billiards room. We got the party set up, dismissed the rest of the crew and put on our dancing clothes. As we tore everything down after the last glass of champagne ran dry, Ray started to work on me. "I know you want to come back up to the shop with me and tip and turn a truck."

"Oh, man…."

"Come on. It'll be another couple hours on the clock. We'll do a few lines while we're waiting."

We rolled out in a pounding, freezing rain, rode to Harlem, did lines, and waited for the truck to come, spilled it, pulled the gear for the next day, and loaded it back up again. It was six by the time I passed out on Ray's couch. He stayed up, took a shower, roused me, and at seven we were at the Whitney Museum, unloading the truck we had just packed. We put in a fourteen-hour day, got drunk in the East Village, and were back at the Whitney at eight the next morning.

When we opened for guests, the party looked so inviting that instead of napping, I busted down to Macy's to pick up some decent duds and went back to the gig, posing as a guest and slamming Wild Turkey. Ray and I snuck into a stairwell to do lines off his cigarette case and cruised the party for possibilities—we wanted to cash in on the company's four-hour bonus plan. I didn't score, but did some dirty dancing with a trashy blonde named Ariella who had come with Robert Mapplethorpe's brother. She gave me her card.

After a couple days of sleeping it off on Ray's couch, I met Ariella for drinks at the Spring Lounge before taking her to a company party at Wetlands—it was the secretary's birthday. When Ariella confessed to having some coke and shared with us, Ray whispered, "If you don't fuck her, I will."

"I'm breaking all my rules with you tonight," she said to me.

"What rules?"

"Don't kiss a guy on the first date. Definitely don't kiss him in the bar. Don't take a guy home on the first date…."

"You haven't taken me home yet."

"Let's go to my place… but I don't want to have sex tonight."

We fucked until nine o'clock in the morning. She was shy and elusive at first, but when she opened up, she was a blooming rose anxious to fall to pieces, spilling petals to the wind. She came completely unglued, shaking, moaning, screaming, "You bastard… you bastard."

"If you come on my tits and in my mouth, can you come again soon?" I fulfilled the first clause but was busted on the second, and since it was taking me forever she howled, "What are you doing to me?" finally begging, "Put it in my ass." We napped until noon and went at it again, and it was two in the afternoon by the time I got out of there. Despite it all, she seemed afraid of kissing me on the lips.

"If I really kiss you, and you really kiss me, then it's something else. Then we're not playing."

I tried to stay far away from Williamsburg, geographically and metaphorically, hoping to outrun the nightmare like a man trying to outrun his own shadow. I set a personal record for not setting foot in my own apartment. I jumped from gig to gig, sleeping and showering wherever I happened to be, borrowing clothes, eating on the run, looking over my shoulder and avoiding the eyes of strangers.

Ray and I became partners in crime, weaving drunkenly over the line between blue-collar stiffs and elegant dandies, executing costume changes in hotel kitchens and lying to everyone, spreading the wealth that was bulging from our obese wallets to keep all the players happy. We were dancing boys for hire, we were electricians, we were cocaine middlemen, we were continually under threat of being fired from one employer or another and passing out the payola to cover ourselves. For those few flamboyant weeks we were everyone's best friends and devil's advocates, begging favors from electricians to cover our dancing exploits, paying in cash and cocaine, begging favors from other dancers to cover our electric gravy train, paying in cocaine and cash.

What a perfect drug for New York. Amps you up, makes you fearless and egotistical and fast fast fast, a perfect motif for evading a life and subsisting on a lifestyle. Ray was becoming prone to nosebleeds; I couldn't remember what it was like to wake up without my head splitting like I had slept on the subway tracks.

But the money kept rolling in. The big boss threatened to rescind his four-hour pay policy for getting laid on the job because Ray and I were putting in so many "extra hours" he was afraid his accountant would find out. The dancing-boy gig was a gold mine. It was our job to flirt with the guests, and almost nightly we ducked into quiet hallways, disappeared into a janitor's closet, or bribed a chambermaid to let us into an unoccupied room. The bar mitzvahs were the worst; the mothers were lascivious and anxious to cuckold their husbands, slumming with "the help," and the daughters were young and desperate to be shown around the block. We tried to stay away from anything under eighteen, but it was impossible to guess the age of rich debutantes who could easily pass for twenty, with perfectly developed bodies and unnaturally developed appetites.

Ray complained of being bloody after popping a cherry standing up in a hotel stairwell. He was an endless amusement to kitchen staff, who laughed and chattered at him in a dozen languages when he asked for vanilla extract so that his other lovers wouldn't notice the metallic smell of rich pussy on his hands.

But before Ray could face the string of other lovers that were waiting for him after a gig was struck, we indubitably hit a bar—any bar, whatever was closest. The Subway Inn at 60th and Lex, the Lava Lounge at 55th and 8th, Siberia inside the 1/9 station at 50th, the Bull Moose on 44th—wherever we happened to be—and swilled our prerequisite string of cocktails, sucking down our dinner and parting ways with our minds reeling from the inundation of abusive influence.

Overall, I was doing a great job of ignoring reality. I was riding a train, but I hadn't purchased a ticket and I couldn't get off. The gigs bled together, the days overlapped. I put Williamsburg out of my mind; I put Olive in a corner of my brain that I never visited. I shut down, and Ariella's apartment was the perfect garage for the hull of a jalopy that I was driving around town.

My thirty-five-year-old Jewish nymphomaniac was the perfect lover. Her Jewish sensibility left room for none of the guilt and sexual hang-ups that I'd become so accustomed to with Catholic-background women like Liv. She had no compunction about sex whatsoever, and if she saw me as nothing but a shegetz then so be it. She struck me as a perfect pornographic princess, a ravenous beast I could never satisfy but was determined to try. She never broke character, always true to her invented image, taunting and teasing me coyly, talking trash, moaning in anguished ecstasy, sniffing a line of coke off my cock or surprising me with amyl nitrates, all with the demeanor of a hired slut in a porno—better than that, like a porn queen who has won the admiration of her peers through her genuine acting ability, exquisite sexual performance, and endurance. I spent sleepless nights at her cloistered apartment locked in a tangled, frenetic duel, and no matter how hard I threw myself into her, no matter how many throws per night, she was always standing naked next to me at the door on my way out, smiling mischievously and pushing herself into me, turning around and pressing the greatest ass in Manhattan at the fly of my black jeans, begging me not to go.

Everything changed with a gig at the St. Regis. I'd always hated that hotel—the gigs are a bad scene no matter how you slice it. Inevitably, we do one setup on the second floor and another on the twentieth. The split is a backbreaker, and on the twentieth floor, booms won't get you a decent shot at anything, so we have to hang the lights off pipes suspended from Airwall hangers in the ceiling—which is far from safe. The slots were designed to hold Airwalls, nothing else, and I'd heard of pipes falling in the middle of parties.

The roof of the St. Regis is divine, and Ray and I took ample breaks to do lines and smoke bowls, looking out at the Plaza Hotel, Essex House, and the grandiose vision of Central Park, and peering out over 5th Ave. with its endless line of buses.

But the gig was sucking and I wanted out. In a Genie Lift, I hefted eight-foot pipes loaded with lighting instruments, trying to hang them from the Airwall hangers without taking out any of the chandeliers. Our boss and both our supervisors stood on the ground watching, which only made my cocaine hands twitch all the more. I brushed a few crystals on a chandelier and everyone flipped. I lost control and barked, "I'm the only one in the room besides Ray that is even physically capable of doing this, so step off already." The big boss decided that I needed a break and pulled me off. There was no dancing—St. Regis events are always conservative geriatric affairs—so I ditched with no intention of returning for the strike.

I went to Ariella's. She had stocked up on cold cuts and dolmas and other delicacies, and she fed me and petted me and made quiet love to me without my having to do any of the work, and she talked to me softly until I passed out.

When I woke she stood naked in the kitchen, toying with a spatula, looking off into the distance at nothing, and strangely silent.

"What's up, baby?"

I gave her a kiss that evolved into a long, deep soul kiss that sent shivers along the inside of my veins. It was lovely and sensual, and yet I had the disturbing sensation I was kissing a corpse.

"I was just waiting for you to wake up." The look in her eyes was distant and somehow familiar.

She touched my shoulder and kissed it gently, and then stepped past me and broke into a run, dashing through the railroad apartment, through the spare room she used as a closet, past the bedroom, running at full tilt through the living room and throwing her body into a dive, crashing through the window and disappearing from view.

I got dressed as quickly as I could, in a panic, like a murderer escaping the scene of the crime. I ran down the four flights of stairs without a glimmer of hope, no chance that she had survived. I hit the street and looked over my shoulder at the halted traffic, her nude, crumpled body covered with glass scratches and inhumanly askew on the pavement, a contorted mass of crumpled flesh, a Rorshach test of spattered blood providing a misplaced patch of color on the dirty street.

I walked, trying to lose myself.

To ever have sex again, even if random and casual to a fault, was futile in such a city—a death factory working overtime. That live, warm body writhing beneath you will be a cold corpse tomorrow. I tried to shake the guilty feeling that it was all punishment for refusing to live monastically in Olive's absence, for my lustful desire to continue getting laid on a regular basis. Was this my punishment for trying to move on? To watch my lover die by her own hand? Had I caused her demise? Somehow led her to it? Was Talia my fault too?

The inanimate artifacts of the city hummed along as if nothing out of the ordinary had occurred. The street seemed to sing to me as I walked, bathing me in the brash intensity of Broadway, grinning along with David Letterman's face on the billboard in front of the Ed Sullivan Theater. Times Square winked away in the night, the neon stretching towards heaven.

I found myself waiting for traffic at the corner of 5th Avenue and 55th, where roadwork required the placement of eight-by-six-foot sheets of heavy steel over torn-up asphalt. There were maybe ten or fifteen of these in the street, half in one lane and half in another. As the Taxicabs rolled by, each hit the steel and drove over the sheets, missing some, hitting others, followed by the next car, hitting some, missing others. The steel rattled against the pavement under the weight of the cabs with a shuddering boom, resonating and ricocheting off the sides of the buildings, an uneven rhythm of booming steel, loud and unforgiving, a manmade thunder echoing to the sky in resounding torment. I stood and listened for a long while, letting the thunder wrack my body and deafen my ears, before I began to scream over it.

It was late when I rang Ray's buzzer.

"Hey, you. Come on up—meet me on the roof."

I took the elevator to the tenth floor and walked up the stairs and found Ray watching the city.

"Man, I'm so glad you're here. I'm having the most fucked-up day."

"Glad you stopped by," he replied, and handed me a wineglass and poured me a slug of Merlot. "Missed you on the strike."

"Sorry, man, I—"

"Don't worry about it." He picked up his own glass and we toasted. The glasses gave out a melodic ring.

We drank. After a few moments of silence Ray turned to the edge. "Hey, do you remember this?" and he dropped his glass, leaning over to watch it tumble, and I looked in his eyes and listened to the distant crinkle as the glass shattered on the sidewalk, an echo of New Year's Eve and the false nostalgia for less complicated days. His eyes… there was something in them. Something I recognized.

"Ray—don't!"

But I was too late. He stood up on the ledge and faced me, his back to the street, his arms outspread, like a high diver preparing for a difficult trick. I reached for his chest and my hands grabbed empty air as he slowly fell away, leaning backwards, and I tried to grab his feet as his body became horizontal, perfectly relaxed, and my fingers slipped from his ankles as the soles of his boots abandoned contact with the ledge of the roof.

I remained there, watching, long after gravity had stopped his movement forever.

COLD

Even though you had money for a cab you walked home and didn't mind the cold. You would have been grateful for brief spatters of rain to attack you with glancing blows, glistening on the asphalt with oily rainbow streaks. You let yourself in the front door quietly, even though no one else was there to hear you, and climbed the steps as softly as possible in heavy boots. You keyed the lock and opened the door, sat on the edge of the miniature davenport, slowly manipulated your fattened fingers, working dumbly at the laces, and pulled the boots off your swollen feet. You padded over to the fridge and took out a withered piece of yellow bell pepper, the hardened end of a purple onion, a sausage about to turn and a half cube of butter. You reached above the stove and opened a slender cabinet, finding a can of black beans and a package of saffron rice. You eyeballed the water into the pot and started it boiling, fumbled for a can opener, up-ended the beans into another pot and got them going, turned on another spurt of blue flame under the cast-iron skillet to fry the lonely sausage. When the water was boiling you dumped in the rice with a fork-shaving of butter, turned down the heat and put on the lid. You sliced the onion, threw the bits into the beans, added garlic powder, black pepper, and hot sauce, and stirred, taking the odd moment to turn the sausage. You cut the sausage into slices, seeking out the pink parts and pressing them into the skillet. You diced the pepper and added it to the rice. You stirred the beans until they began to collapse in on themselves, becoming a chunky mush. You added more hot sauce. You opened another cabinet and almost dropped a bowl, nestled inside another. You turned off all three burners, found a clean fork, served yourself some rice, scooped some beans on top, and almost burned your hand on the raging-hot skillet. You found a pot holder and tried again, fork in hand, flipping the sausage slices into the bowl on top of everything else. You set the bowl down on the table and took a seat. And you put your face in your hands and wept, as the grease congealed on the sausage in the forgotten bowl, and the beans grew cold and hard.

YELLING

I didn't leave the house for so long I lost track of time. It was a long while before I could admit that it was me who cried, uncontrollably, inconsolably, with the desperate sobs of an infant. It was even longer before I was able to admit to myself that it wasn't just the coke blues—the irrational depression that sets in after a cocaine bender. I cried for Ray. I cried for Ariella. I cried for Hoagy, for Jamie, for Sam and Everett. I cried for Liv.

There was a hole in my heart and my whole world had seeped out while I was dreaming of a rock star lifestyle. My friends were gone. My neighborhood was a death camp. My body was a wreck and I didn't care. But Liv... the only woman who had ever aroused in me a spirit of optimism, the only lover who had ever comforted me in sadness, insulted me in pride, fucked me in passion... was gone. I had chased her away. Liv always said that she would never leave me unless I made her miserable; I conveniently forgot that. I thought it was only Hoag's death that drove her away, but in my grief at her absence, I realized it was my fault.

I exhausted what little food I had in the house and subsisted on a diet of cigarettes, tea, and dry tortillas. I watched bad daytime television and avoided the news—not that there was any mention of us. My cell phone rang steadily at first, but since it was always about work I ignored it. Curiosity got the better of me, and I listened to the messages. They were almost all from the girl at the office who booked us on gigs, and they became increasingly frantic as the days went on, filled with horror stories of death in every way I had ever imagined on the job: jumps from Genie Lifts, jumps from truss rigged to high ceilings, electrocutions. Loudmouth Greg was killed doing a live tie-in, grabbing the neutral with one hand and a hot with the other. Luz had disappeared. All my electrician buddies were dead; the calls stopped coming.

I didn't bathe and I stopped brushing my teeth. I never played the stereo. I didn't want to think this was really happening to me. I had wandered into the wrong movie theater by mistake.

So when the front-door buzzer went off one afternoon, instead of just buzzing the person in, I pulled on a pair of pants and walked downstairs and down the hall of the front building and saw a large, long-haired man standing in the vestibule. He called me by name, and I realized it was Ty, the bartender from Black Betty.

"I didn't know you lived here."

I shivered. "Yeah, I guess I do."

"Listen, we're just ringing bells at random today. Trying to round up some new recruits."

"For what?"

"Collection."

The word hung in the musty, mildewed air like an allusion to a book that had never been published.

"You're picking up dead bodies."

"Yeah. There's a lot. The city is doing what it can, but we need more people. When the weather gets warmer it'll be worse."

"What do I do?"

"We start every morning around seven. Meet in McCarren Park. A guy named Joe is heading it all up. I'm in Group C, if you want to try to get in with us."

"Yeah… all right."

"So… see you tomorrow?"

"Yeah. Why not."

"Thanks, man. Go get warm."

I went upstairs and took a shower. I took Ty's visit as a sign, a shove from an unseen and unknowable force. Perhaps my callousness could still prove to be an asset.

The next morning I stepped over the stiff, naked bodies of those who had offed themselves through the cheapest imaginable method—sleeping outside on a cold night naked, dying of exposure and hypothermia. I hadn't been out in the neighborhood for so long I was aghast at the emptiness. Even the bus stop was deserted.

I met a ragtag band of miscreants at McCarren Park. I waved to Ty and introduced myself to Joe, who assured me that he would forget my name immediately. That was fine with me. He assigned me to Group D, which would spend most of the day combing the area around the Lorimer station, down by Kellogg's, at Union and Metropolitan.

The Group D leader was a tall, gangly fool named Mick who took his job extremely seriously and wielded his power with a death grip. It was obvious he had never done anything meaningful in his life, and this morbid occupation was his chance to redeem himself in a noble if macabre manner. He was about thirty-five and seemingly uneducated, but he did know the neighborhood well and he was a hard worker, and he led more by example than by inspiration.

Garbage trucks and converted dump trucks and the occasional pickup came through every other day. Our task was to round up bodies, pile them up at the drop site for our area, and be on hand to load them into the trucks when they came by. The routes were constantly shifting and the trucks were

145

always late, so inevitably one member of the crew would wait at the drop site half the day, running around and rounding up the crew when the truck finally came, making the truck run even later.

That first day I started at the drop site, as ours was one of the first stops on the route. The collected bodies of the last two days were stacked up in a pile, and as the weather had been consistently cold and wet most of the week, the bodies were largely frozen together. We huffed for almost an hour, prying them apart and throwing them into the back of the truck. Most of the other Group D crew members were skinny office-types and former coffee-shop employees; they were weak and they tired quickly. It didn't help matters that they kept averting their eyes from the task at hand, not wanting to look the dead in the face. Whether they were afraid of seeing someone they knew or just squeamish about death didn't matter.

Crawling out of my chrysalis, I was awed by the change that had taken place in Williamsburg in my absence. My neighborhood had undergone a crippling metamorphosis that seemed at once permanent: it was devastated. Most of the businesses were shut down and the streets were entirely unoccupied, discounting the cleanup crews that stalked the sidewalks like mangy jackals, discounting the inert and life-less bodies heaped at the curbs like lawn clippings awaiting collection on a suburban street, discounting the rats seething across the street in broad daylight. What few people showed their faces glared at us in still shock and quickly skittered away. I recognized no one. Even the few kids I thought I'd seen before were impossibly changed, a look of abject terror worn on their faces like Halloween masks—hair matted into fright wigs, red rings under the eyes and perverted frowns betraying a conflict of emotions. Fugitives; refugees. Survivors of the neutron bomb. We walked through a ghost town, and even the ghosts were gone.

The remainder of the day was spent walking around, finding dead bodies and carrying them—or more commonly, dragging them—back to the drop site, starting a new pile for the day after tomorrow. Jumpers, car runners, gunshotters, plastic baggers, exposures... the method of kevork barely mattered. In the homogenizing monochrome of the snowy day, all bodies looked alike, and even the gore surrounding them was muffled if not washed away. I had no curiosity about who they were or how they died. They're dead now.

There were about eight of us in Group D, and collectively, we did the work of maybe four good workers. The two women in the group were good at spotting bodies but would do little else. Mick did the work of two or three men.

At midday we took a break and walked back to McCarren Park for our coffee and sandwiches. A gang of tired women passed out the homemade victuals, and the crews stood around not talking and sipping lukewarm coffee out of styrofoam cups. Then we walked all the way back to our area. The break sapped two hours out of our day.

I told my brain to shut up and stuck to the task at hand. I didn't even know what happened to the bodies after the trucks took them away.

We spoke seldom, but we called out to one another repeatedly. "A yelling body is a live body," Mick said, "and a live body is good." We yelled when we found a body, we yelled when we needed help, we yelled for no reason but to encourage one another to keep our heads up, our feet moving steadily from one step to the next. I began to yell louder than anyone else, finding the blast from my lungs a welcome and focusing disturbance, like the strike from a master in the practice of zazen.

One of the girls in Group D I recognized—I had seen her

147

once at the L Café in happier days, a cute redheaded girl with a gorgeous face and a broad, winning smile, smoking long, black cigarettes and sipping a glass of wine. She looked a little worse for wear now, bundled up and hiding her face in a hooded sweatshirt, but when she pointed out a body to me and waited for me to drag it out, I remembered her smile and I thought it wouldn't be bad if—

I told my brain to shut up.

THE BRIDGE REVISITED

After a few weeks of working steadily, I've found my rhythm.

I wake as early as I'm able and hit the streets of Williamsburg, sniffing out stiffs and coordinating their disposal to the nearest drop site with the ever-dwindling team of misfits the local cleanup effort has managed to recruit. I've become a floater, so I wrap everything up as quickly as possible with Group D, get Mick to release me, and check in with Joe who coordinates with the other crews to see if anyone needs a strong back or an extra grunt for a few hours. When I get clearance to leave, I walk the Williamsburg Bridge to help out in Manhattan, where the epidemic is blooming.

The Williamsburg Bridge is 135 feet above the surface of the East River, and the towers are 310 feet. I've seen a couple people try to climb the towers to jump, but most just scale the pedestrian fence. Some just jump from the beginning of the walkway and fall to the ground; they always die. The ones who jump into the water sometimes make it and have to swim to the side and climb all the way back up again, or they close their cloudy eyes and sink to the bottom of the East River without so much as an attempt at a doggie paddle. At 135 feet, even including wind resistance, it's possible to exceed fifty miles an hour before you smack the water.

Mr. Buck's masterpiece opened in 1902, the second bridge

across the East River and the object of severe ridicule for its ugly design. What the critics didn't realize was that it was a perfect bridge for the neighborhoods it was intended to serve: it was cheap. It was the first suspension bridge with completely steel towers, needing none of the masons that Roebling's masterpiece required, and it was built in half the time it took to build the Brooklyn Bridge, and with considerably less funding. At the time it was the longest and heaviest suspension bridge in the world, and it went up in only seven years. Thousands of Jewish immigrants walked the bridge from the slums of the Lower East Side to begin again in Williamsburg, and the Hasidic communities near the base of the bridge are a reminder that it was once called the "Jew's bridge."

I can't help but be reminded of the Orange Widow, the most popular suicide destination in the world, more heavily trafficked than the Eiffel Tower, the Space Needle, the Empire State Building, Mount Mihara, or Pasadena's Arroyo Seco Bridge.

The Golden Gate Bridge is 220 feet above the surface of the San Francisco Bay, and jumpers are said to reach speeds of seventy-five miles per hour, their splash sending a plume of water forty feet in the air. The Coast Guard unofficially estimates the average at around three hundred jumpers a year. They suffer massive internal injuries, sheared aortas, ripped off ears. One jumper hit the seawall with his head, which smeared along the wall while his body fell intact into the water. Romantic legend has it that every jumper has vaulted from the East side of the bridge so that the lovely city of San Francisco, framed in panorama with the Marin Headlands, would be their very last sight on Earth.

It's a better view than my compatriots are seeing, the dingy grey water of the East River and the oppressive midtown skyline, the east side projects scowling to the west and the Domino sugar factory frowning from the east. I always wave at jumpers. Not out of any spite or irony, but just to be nice. Why not wave? The bridge has seen worse and it will still be standing long after we're all dead and buried. I wish it could do for me what it did for the Jews escaping the tenements of the Lower East Side, but there's nowhere to escape to anymore, on one side of the bridge or the other.

How high is the Williamsburg bridge, anyway? I mean, not in feet or anything, but when you jump, how long does it feel like you're falling? Can you see the water coming up at you? Does any of it, any of it at all, race through your mind as you hurtle towards the water? Or is it just too much. Is that what it really is—that it's all just too much, and the nauseating specifics and traumatic memories, impressions and reactions bleed together into a homogenous hue of brown dishwater, until there is only the rush of air as the East River hurries to your face and the bridge recedes above your head.

Might as well live.

If you see something beautiful, don't cling to it. If you see something horrible, don't cringe from it. It's what I remember, some translation from a Buddhist tome; I'm sure I'm misquoting but that's the gist. The nihilism thing works pretty well, most of the time, but when you're looking at this huge pile of dead bodies, and all your mind can see or feel or recognize is the *stink* of it all, it's kind of hard to believe that there's nothing, because you know more than you know you're alive that there is this awful stink of human existence. This is something. I don't know what it is, but it's definitely not nothing.

Life always sucked on this planet, no one's disputing that, but the twinge of nostalgia in my black heart keeps winking at me, telling me that, surely, things must have been better back in the day when the suicide rate was only thirty thousand people a year in the whole U.S. It may as well have been a million years back.

There's a small clan that meets at Union Square every day. The men are mostly old-school blue-collar boys who attack their work with vigor and valor, acting as if it were just another union job, without the constant interference of coffee breaks and arguments over meal penalties and double overtime. Some of them are completely unhinged, like the guy with the squint who mumbles a continuous monologue: "And the fatter they are, the more they stink. And the littler they are, the more they stink," and so on, all afternoon without rest. No one judges. Every day the men are different, and no one bothers to introduce himself anymore. The man picking up bodies next to you today—tomorrow you'll be picking up his. The vicious cycle of disease. What the ever-shifting labor pool lacks in organization we try to make up in concentrated effort and endurance.

We stay out as long as we can still stand, running reconnaissance and hauling corpses, and negotiating the undignified depravity of the situation with those unfortunate enough to outlive their loved ones. The weeping never stops, and sadly, we all recognize the horror of human bodies piled into garbage trucks for unceremonious transport with hundreds of other corpses. At the end of a night our eyes are glassed over with the protective sheen of resistance to sorrow; there just isn't time. Too many bodies, not enough graves. We still retrieve IDs and take names, but we've stopped asking about the daily toll.

The dregs of the day are dedicated to reviewing the latest government mandates and instructions in confused huddles, a steady dispersal of misinformation and paranoia. The best facts are all speculation, relayed dutifully through the grapevine, communicated in quiet, serious tones, told like ghost stories. We are students of the trade of death.

In normal times, the fate of a suicide is simple. The body is collected from the site of death by a mortuary wagon belonging to the morgue of the county in question—Bellevue in Manhattan, Queens General, Kings County Brooklyn. The wagon takes the body to the office of the chief medical examiner, who performs an autopsy. At that point, if arrangements with a funeral home have already been made, the story ends like any other. But if the body goes unclaimed—or worse, is unidentified—then the body goes to the county morgue where it will be held for as long as thirty days. If it is still not claimed, it goes to Potter's Field, a secret so deep most New York residents don't even know it exists.

The name comes from Matthew, Chapter 27. After Judas hangs himself, "the chief priests, taking the pieces of silver, said, 'It is not lawful to put them into the treasury, since they are blood money.' So they took counsel, and bought with them the potter's field, to bury strangers in. Therefore that field has been called the Field of Blood to this day."

Hart Island, in Long Island Sound in the Bronx, was purchased by the Hunter family in 1868 and established as the city's public cemetery for indigents and unclaimed bodies. In the first year, almost two thousand bodies were buried. Since then, Hart Island has been the site of a yellow-fever quarantine, a charity hospital for women, an insane asylum, a tuberculosis home, a reformatory for young delinquents, a World War II stockade, a Nike missile base, a narcotics rehabilitation center—and of course, more than once, a prison. Hart Island has always been the home of the unwanted, the pariahs, and Potter's Field is a ghost town on the island of the dead.

Three-quarters of a million is a safe estimate, but it's more likely that there are at least a million dead on Hart Island. The burials are performed by inmates of Riker's Island, who are overseen by corrections officers, which is to say that the only way to get onto the island is to be a cop, a convict, or a corpse.

In addition to amputated limbs, three thousand bodies a year are buried in Potter's Field; at least half are infants and the stillborn. The plain pine boxes are stacked three high, two across, 150 per plot, and are buried without last rites save an annual memorial service.

It's all anyone in the Union Square task force can talk about, the age-old tradition of caring for the indigent dead and the reluctance to abandon such a noble undertaking. There is a stubborn, common thread of thought, a recreation of the myth of civilization: order must be imposed on a disorderly situation. Grown men make false promises to one another, swearing that they won't allow each other to end up in Potter's Field, like adolescents playing at blood brothers. But most of these hacks are conspiracy theorists and spout all the stock inanity: the epidemic was designed by the CIA, the FBI, the KGB, the survivors of Heaven's Gate. Some refuse to drink tap water because of fluoridation. And the rumors that abound are worse than the lonely prospect of the forgotten fields of Hart Island.

The medical examiner's office has shut down completely due to suicide of the entire staff. The bodies now collected are merely stored in walk-in refrigerators in restaurants all over town; the Williamsburg dead are waiting in meat packing plants on North 6th. There is a death train, a Long Island Railroad car stacked top to bottom with inert bodies, an image so fecund and flickering in the mind we almost can't wait to catch a ride. The bodies are taken far out across Long Island and thrown into the Atlantic, sent to mass graves packed with lye, stored underground in unused subway tunnels, ground into protein powder and shipped to Japan. The carcasses are hauled to landfills in Staten Island and New Jersey, buried with common garbage like any other city refuse.

No one knows if any of this is true. No one has a decent answer as to why the government is doing so little. No one understands why the press won't report it and why our friends in other cities don't believe us. No one wants to believe this is really happening at all, and the characters from day to day are so interchangeable it's easier to believe it is all a bad dream, an unfathomable bridge from one world to the next, from the living to the dead, or from a dream state to the phenomenological world—it makes no difference.

We're doing everything we can. But rumors or no rumors, it isn't working.

JONESTOWN

It isn't just the Bug anymore—that's what we call it. That irresistible urge to suddenly off yourself by whatever means available. We don't know what it is any more than we ever did: lack of desire to live, hopelessness, despair—only the fad caught on and never went out of style, just spread like an airborne plague.

But it's not just the Bug anymore; people are leaving. All the fat cats with pads in the Hamptons have moved out there indefinitely. Everyone with an aunt or uncle in Hoboken is permanently couch-surfing. Anyone with a home to return to—college kids, slackers from Wisconsin, recent immigrants—has gone home. I never thought I'd see it happen; I always thought New Yorkers were stoic, indestructible, able to endure anything and never slacken the pace. But more and more are buying one-way tickets out of town, leaving their apartments and running like hell.

I can't blame people for leaving, any more than I blamed Olive. This is hell, like living through the book of Revelations.

The woes are overwhelming, and the true nightmare is that the saved, the saints, live through it all, while the damned get to die early. The fear is more contagious than the Bug. And we've all seen just how easy it is to kill yourself in a jungle of concrete like New York City.

There is still a struggling population trying to live with as much normalcy as possible. In a city with eight and a half million people, even with so many dead there are still an awful lot left living, however they can, trying to get by without falling to pieces and welcoming the Bug. But it's sinking all around us, like an ancient Otis elevator crankily starting its descent.

Cats, "now and forever" at the Winter Garden Theatre, has closed.

The *New York Times* grows thinner every week, the quality slipping. It would seem that journalists are quick to go, a fact that isn't without irony. I remember a cartoon in the *New Yorker*... a cliff with lemmings rushing over it, falling with arms outspread and disappearing into the distance like tiny paratroopers. At the top of the cliff one lemming holds back. The caption: "'Nobody told me about this.'"

The *New Yorker* has "temporarily" halted production.

The press and the government still refuse to deal with the issue head-on. In the brief local news broadcasts, with ever-shifting commentators and declining production values, only the barest, most vague and indirect reference to the catastrophe is ever referred to, and then only tangentially. "The unusual phenomenon," "the undisclosed rumors of an epidemic," "the apparent trend of relocation." We're fed unnerving statistics on the incredible availability of jobs and the exceptionally low rate of unemployment, quickly overridden by news from other states and other countries—canned stock footage of distant tragedies.

Giuliani, to his credit, is wearing a stern face and making his moves surreptitiously, underhandedly trying to manage without recognizing that there is anything to be concerned about: classic politics. He has dedicated what's left of the city government to addressing the body count, since putting a stop to the actual epidemic is beyond anyone's grasp. But organized aid isn't forthcoming, and most city officials have already fled.

The police force is drastically reduced. There are more cops lying in their cruisers wearing bullet holes and muzzle burns than there are walking a beat. There are no cops in my neighborhood, and even in Manhattan the donut shops are lonely. It would seem that having an exit portal strapped to your hip is all too alluring a temptation.

Cab drivers, too, are flocking to the exit sign and clogging the doorway. The yellow cabs that used to congest the streets of Manhattan are now as rare as trustworthy attorneys. Actually, any kind of lawyer is pretty rare in New York these days—they went quick, also not without a certain black humor.

The subway is completely shut down. At first it was just the Williamsburg stations that were boarded up. The L still ran to Canarsie, and the other Brooklyn lines ran from downtown Brooklyn to Manhattan, and the G was as reliable as it ever was. But a conductor aboard the L train ran it into the wall at full tilt at the end of the line at 8th Avenue. He was killed instantly, and he took a lot of people with him, not just passengers, but people standing on the platform. After that little incident, the MTA and the DOT pulled out completely— no train service in New York. Stay where you are. The previously madcap Lexington Avenue line is dead, the A/C/E is an express memory, the N and R tracks are collecting dust and providing fertile breeding ground for rats now that the distraction of thundering trains has been silenced.

It can't hurt. The last time I surfed a train was at Union Square, trying to catch a 5 uptown. The computer voice warned us about the moving platforms as a 6 was about to roll into the station. A suit stepped by me, and I knew what even he hadn't yet realized. He leaned back, and I took a step as he lurched forward to jump, spun my body with an out-stretched arm and clotheslined him. His feet left the ground, and he fell flat on his back and looked up at me with hatred.

"What the fuck is wrong with you?" he snarled.

"I just saved your fucking life."

"The hell you did."

People stared. "Forget it," I said.

He rubbed the back of his head and muttered, "Asshole."

Seconds later I felt a rush of air, and caught in my periph-eral vision the blue blur of a Brooks Brothers suit shooting through the air. The 5 came in, and the suit intercepted the nose of the train, was thrown to the tracks and disappeared from view. The echo of his scream rang in the station as the wheels squealed to a halt and my feet beat a quick tattoo up the cement stairs to the street.

I never again tried to stop a suicide in progress. Once it happened behind the eyes, it was destined to happen, no mat-ter what.

Walking in Manhattan has its own risks and inconven-iences. Jumpers are common. New York hasn't seen so many bodies fall from the fifteenth floor since 1929. No one uses the sidewalks anymore; it's too dangerous. We've heard too many horror stories of people taken out by falling bodies. A woman jumped from the sixty-eighth floor of the Chrysler Building and took five other people with her when she met Lexington Avenue. Now, people walk at the edge of the street, in the gut-ter or on the outside of parked cars. Most jumpers step right out the window and fall on the sidewalk next to the building. Very few make it to the street—it's harder than it looks.

It was an exceptionally warm day with the seductive allure of spring, balmy and with a quiet intensity, like an orgasm on the rise. I was on autopilot, but I doubt I could have done anything to stop it. I didn't see it coming, but none of us still walking ever saw any of this coming, so a few more tragedies can't tip the balance. No one is guilty here; the dead and the survivors are all victims.

The day started out pleasantly enough. The bells from the church down the street rang vigilantly, the melodies floating in my window, blending perfectly with the songs of the birds, riding on sunlight. I hit the pavement with a bit of a spring in my step and was grateful for it, reliving crisp mismatched memories: Olive bouncing off to Little Poland to ravage ninety-nine-cent stores, dancing in the street to live salsa music on the Fourth of July, sliding on beer-soaked asphalt. I slipped on my fingerless gloves—nosepickers—but left my leather jacket behind.

The sudden onset of spring seemed like a break in the action. We saw fewer new suicides every day and I was beginning to believe that in Williamsburg, at least, the disease had largely run its course, having eaten its way through almost all available fodder and emaciated the neighborhood population. We were beginning to make headway on the overwhelming number of corpses and I thought I'd soon be dedicating all my time to Manhattan.

Group D had gotten a late start, but by midafternoon we were ready to call it quits. The cute girl I had been avoiding since the first day was nicer than ever, and I came out of my shell a little and said a few words. I was about to cross the line into flirtation when Mick found us and told us to go over to

McCarren for coffee and a conference with the other groups.

The sight of McCarren Park that day... I still can't get it out of my head, and I still don't have the slightest idea how it came to pass. The best I can figure is that a chemist or pharmacist had been overcome by the Bug and had taken, for him, what was the closest available exit. But somehow—and this is what keeps me up at night—somehow, he staved off the urge long enough to leave his exit door open for others. Or perhaps it was just some cruel bastard who didn't want to die but knew that half of the urge is proximity of method. I read somewhere that when a handgun is available, a suicide will choose that method almost every time.

Don't trust anything you can't see. What you don't see will kill you. After McCarren Park, I trust myself. I trust the men and women in arm's reach. I trust the pieces I put in motion. I trust what I put my hand into willingly, and I will do everything in my power to keep my hand in as deep as it will go. Death is on the line, and I won't take orders from sergeants who blindly take orders from colonels who blindly take orders from unseen and manipulative generals, far outside the fatal reach of the virus that has turned my thriving neighborhood into a scene from Dante.

Someone spiked the cleanup crew's coffee with cyanide.

It's possible that someone drank first without knowing what it was. The rest of these desperate souls clustered together and hoping for a caffeine fix crawled over each other like rats when they realized what it would do, desperate to get their hands on the life-sapping elixir—a feeding frenzy over a poisoned watering hole. When there was nothing left, they attacked the other pots, and finding them filled with only coffee, they went at each other.

Group D was late. We got to see the aftermath. The scene presented itself to us as an unholy triptych:

In the center panel, a tableau of bodies piled up on top of each other like sacks of sand stacked by flood victims, with the odd styrofoam cup fallen just out of the hand, lying neatly on the grass. In the left panel, a tangled mass of bruised bodies, brutally beaten to death by each other with various implements—sticks, lengths of rebar found in the park, a coffee pot. In the right panel, the twisted remnants of a craft services table, overturned with coffee urns still steaming in the grass. I picked up an empty cup; it still had that strange almond smell. The bodies were relaxed, every heart still, the visible skin untouched.

"We should check their pockets for rolls of quarters." It was Ty's voice, and I turned and saw him smiling helplessly. "Steal their Nikes."

I swallowed hard and forced a grin. He was riffing on the Heaven's Gate suicides. "No phenobarbitol for me, thank you, but I could go for some vodka."

Another voice wafted across the park, singing the chorus of an old song by the punk band the Judy's, "Guyana Punch," emulating that Buddy Holly "oh oh" whine. It was Jack, a skinny, pale, pimply Puerto Rican kid from one of the other groups. He was a loudmouth with an evil laugh, and never seemed even slightly fazed by any of the proceedings.

I looked around and saw a few hangers-on, including a few of my own Group D who hadn't gone running for cover or a method of death. Some people wept, some just walked aimlessly.

Jack approached Ty and me and screamed, "Wazzup!" Ty gave him a dap and I just looked them both over.

"Benson, you know Jack?" Ty asked. Jack shot a hand out and I shook it.

"Benson."

"Hey, I'm Jack."

"So…" Ty let the word go past his lips in a pucker. "Guess this is it for today."

I snorted. "Don't trust anything you can't see, man."

"What?" Jack kicked at a styrofoam cup in the grass.

"You can't trust anything you can't see. You know, this whole government cleanup project."

Ty had lit a smoke and offered me one. "This isn't a government thing," he said. "Joe started all this."

"Really? On whose orders?"

"Come on," Jack yelped. "Let's go break into that liquor store up on Nassau and get polluted." He looked at Ty, but Ty was looking at me.

"What's on your mind, Benson?"

"Fuck this," I said. "I'm starting my own goddamn crew." They both looked at me and said nothing. "You guys wanna work for me?"

"Sure," Jack said, noncommittally. "Long as you send us to the liquor store."

"Yeah, I'll work for you," Ty said, taking a long drag off his cigarette. "Now let's go have a drink."

BENSON'S CREW

For my first coup, I teamed up with Neil at the Luncheonette, who still continued to open up every morning to serve coffee and bacon, egg, and cheese on a roll to anyone who came by. He talked to everybody and had the best handle on available information, and he agreed to let us use his joint as a meeting place.

The Monday after Guyana Sunday, I hit the street and waited at a drop site for several hours until a guy in a truck rolled up, looking for bodies that were mysteriously not stacked up waiting for him. He jumped from the cab, lit a cigarette, looked up and down the street, and finally allowed his gaze to rest on me. I barely came to his chest and was maybe half his weight, and he looked me over like a man accustomed to talking to smaller men.

"What, taking the day off?"

"Nope." I lit a smoke of my own and waited for him to ask.

"So what the fuck? They ain't gonna bury themselves."

"Everybody's dead, yo. Everybody's dead."

"Everybody?"

"Most of the cleanup crews bought the farm yesterday."

"Shit."

"Yeah."

"Guess I'll cruise the neighborhood and see if anyone's out. Back to Manhattan if not."

He turned to go and I stopped him. "How 'bout you work for me."

He looked at me like I'd asked him to kiss my ass, but I had his attention. "Why the hell should I work for you?" he asked, almost laughing. "You're young and you don't know shit."

"I know I don't know shit," I said, "but I'm strong, I'm smart, and I know how to run a crew. And I'm never gonna kill myself."

"No?"

"Nope."

"Well, all right. Fine. I'll work for you. Get in."

He started up the truck and pulled away from the curb. I had to ask.

"So, why do you want to work for me if you know I don't know shit?"

"Well… you asked. I figure if you're stupid enough to ask, then you might just be smart enough to do something right."

That was good enough for me and I showed him the way

to Neil's, and we sat down over an endless cup of coffee and he filled me in.

His name was Bernie, and he was a truck driver for Local 1, the electrician's union, and when I told him I had done some electrics work, albeit as a scab, he gave me a little respect. Bernie had a kid sister in Williamsburg who disappeared, and he found her in her apartment with a dozen empty strips of roofies. He saw what was going on in the neighborhood and stole a truck from Local 1. Trolling the streets he was stopped by Mick, my group leader, who, incidentally, did the lemming off a twenty-story building in downtown Brooklyn late Guyana Sunday.

Bernie was one of those blue-collar guys who seemed to know damn near everything.

The Mayor's Office of Emergency Management was New York's answer to FEMA. It was established as an independent agency that could "plan for and help mitigate any emergency that threatens the safety of New York City's people or property." It was supposed to guarantee accountability as well as manage coordination and communication between various city agencies, headed up by a director who reported directly to the mayor. The forty-three-person agency included personnel from several different jurisdictions, including New York City's Fire and Police Departments, Emergency Medical Service, Department of Environmental Protection, Department of Parks, and the American Red Cross. The OEM's goals were to assist in minimizing the human impact of an emergency and to restore normalcy as quickly as possible.

In short, the OEM should be all over the suicide phenomenon. The legendary "bunker," the emergency management station in World Trade Center 7, rumored to rival NORAD with its pantheon of big screens, should have picked up evidence of the epidemic and unleashed its own wrath, bringing in city, state, and federal aid to deal with the over-whelming problems of medical care, corpse disposal, rat infestation—everything.

"So where are they?"

Bernie shrugged. "I don't know everything, kid. Maybe they know, maybe they don't know. The World Trade Center is blocked off. No one's heard shit from them since they passed the buck in the first place."

The suicide phenomenon was an embarrassment. In an attempt to keep a low profile, the OEM, under the direction of Giuliani, passed down certain mandates and delegated their instrumentation to low-level officials, who, in turn, passed them along to even lower-level officials, until the dirty work was eventually taken up by civilians. This is what I had seen happening in Union Square; half of those paranoids were on the government payroll.

"Oh, yeah," Bernie said. "Those wackos are half the reason everything's so fucked up. They get the go-ahead to install some kinda order, then they sit around all day bullshit-ting about how it's all one big fucking conspiracy."

When he said it "wasn't a government thing," Ty was only half right. But I was only half wrong. Joe, the leader of the Billburg effort, was only a little more than a neighborhood local with a mind for organization. He had been given his power officially by the OEM, but beyond that, the system was his brainchild, the driver routes and drop sites his design. The bulk of the cleanup effort as we knew it was largely the work of generous souls striking out on their own. The right hand knew that there probably wasn't a left hand, but kept on out of a sense of duty and a stubborn resistance to giving up.

The hands-off method of dealing with the situation had undermined the central power the OEM had to begin with. At this point, it was anyone's guess how many members of the

OEM were still alive, or still in the city.

"Just tell me what you've seen," I begged.

Bernie couldn't get onto Hart Island, but he had it on good authority—from a Union brother incarcerated on Riker's who volunteered for burial duty to get some fresh air—that they were overworked. The crews were doubled, as were the work hours. They filled in trenches double time and there was no end in sight. The civilian truck drivers were closing the gap left by the limited number of mortuary wagons, but the real source of the bottleneck was the medical examiner's office itself: it couldn't even begin to handle the overwhelming magnitude of cadavers. They had all but ceased performing autopsies, and even then, it was impossible to get the bodies processed and back to the morgue and eventually transferred to funeral homes. And since so many family members were following death's trail, bodies weren't being claimed. The mortuaries in all five boroughs were stocked to capacity.

The death train was a myth, as were most of the other horror stories the wackos in Union Square liked to tell, but Bernie knew garbage collectors who, for lack of any better idea, had indeed taken corpses to landfills and dumped them. And it was true that the meat packing plants in Williamsburg were loaded with corpses.

"Shit," Bernie shrugged. "At least they're off the streets."

The cemeteries had, for the most part, barred their doors.

"We gotta burn 'em," I said. "Billburg might be almost done, but Manhattan is heating up."

"You know, buddy, I thought of that," Bernie said, a worried look knitting his brow, "but there has to be some kind of… emergency legislation to allow that. You know, this whole damn thing is chock full of bureaucracy."

"But a renegade garbage man can dump bodies in some Staten Island landfill?"

"Hey, I didn't say that was kosher."

"All right. I, Benson Lee, hereby pass a motion before this, the Emergency Suicide Committee, stating that from this day forward, we institute the immediate and urgent cremation of all bodies belonging to those persons who have died by their own hands, for reasons of public health, and by the power vested in me by the living citizens of the city of New York. Do I have a second?" Bernie shifted uneasily in his seat. "Come on, Neil, help me out," I said.

"Sure, kid," he said, wiping the counter. "I second the motion."

"So I put it to a vote. All in favor?"

"Aye," Neil said.

Bernie shot me a toothy grin and said, "Aye."

"Aye. All opposed? Okay, we burn 'em. We need mass cremation. Find an incinerator or something."

"Yeah," Bernie mused. "I remember when my pops died he wanted to be cremated. The funeral home did it for us."

Bernie's memory led us in the right direction. The next day we drove out to Middle Village, Queens, just north of Maspeth, and found the Fresh Pond Crematory. The kid at the counter, no older than me, was eating a bologna sandwich. Bernie and I played good cop–bad cop.

"Can I help you?"

"We're taking over your operation here," Bernie said. "We got a lot of dead people to burn."

I pretended to calm Bernie down while stifling my laughter and trying to explain the epidemic to the kid. He had heard rumors, and in a little less than half an hour we had his commitment to the cause and his boss—cringing under Bernie's gaze—committing as well. We promised to send along extra help when we could.

Fresh Pond has four cremation ovens that hold one body

each. They burn at temperatures of between sixteen hundred and two thousand degrees, and in two to three hours will reduce a human cadaver to a mass of ashes. The ashes are mechanically pulverized—looking like crushed seashells—and are put into a six-by-six-by-six-inch box that weighs, on average, nine pounds. We figured that with a team working 'round the clock we could incinerate thirty bodies a day. I thought we had taken a big step, but Bernie, a type A overachiever, already had his sights set on the Evergreen Cemetery and Crematory in Hillside, New Jersey, and the Rosehill, in Linden.

In the coming weeks I became a walking, talking PR campaign for the survival of humanity. I harassed everyone I saw on the street and posted signs in the neighborhood, tearing down reams of forgotten sublet-available signs and announcements for bar gigs for bands that doubtlessly no longer existed. I listed my home phone number and left a message on my machine encouraging people to stay alive, to stay in touch, and to meet me at Neil's if they wanted to help.

I rounded up the survivors of the original groups, who now resembled hardened criminals out on parole. I kept a notebook at Neil's, and made everyone who came by sign their name, address, and phone number, so if they stopped coming without giving word we could track them down. At the very least, we'd know if they'd decided to catch the bus.

Bernie was a godsend. He made the rounds of Union Square and scared up the least paranoid of the OEM-delegated wackos and put them to work driving trucks alongside what union buddies he was able to track down. The more shell-shocked were sent out to Middle Village for the cakewalk of burning bodies and boxing up ashes for eventual delivery to Hart Island. For the time being, the boxes would sit in dry storage in a warehouse in Bensonhurst that belonged to

Bernie's brother-in-law, long since a suicide himself.

People came and went. For the most part, they would arrive, pitch in for a day or two, and vanish. Sometimes we found them dead in their apartment, sometimes we didn't see them again. But some stayed and stuck it out, and slowly but surely, I was forming a crew. Ty and Jack were there to stay, as was the cute girl from Group D. A wild-eyed lumberjack of a man arrived from Maryland looking for Mick, my old crew chief, admitted to being his brother, and stuck around to help out. A waitress from the L Café came on board, as did a number of enormous Poles who spoke no English but had the strength and stamina of ditchdiggers. Two big Brooklyn boys joined up, and having big guys around was always a plus. But for the most part, the crew represented the neighborhood: Puerto Ricans and Dominicans that straggled up from the Southside, and young, hip white kids who were largely from suburbia and had migrated to New York in search of success.

All of us shaved our heads, all the guys on my crew. Hair absorbs odor... we all know the feeling of going out to a bar and reeking of smoke the next morning, our hair polluted with the stench of a thousand cigarettes. But the smell of death doesn't wash out.

We continued scouring the neighborhood. At first, we decided it was easier to keep it together if we went out in threes and fours, and we did away with the concept of "drop site" because the piled bodies were breeding grounds for maggots and rats, an eyesore for the living, and a suggestion to those on the edge of deciding to die. We met and split up and re-rendezvoused several times a day, calling in to leave messages on our whereabouts with Neil, who became like a taxi dispatcher. Bernie handled all transportation issues, managing a motley crew of gypsies like a labor pool, getting us around so we wouldn't exhaust ourselves walking, and having corpses picked up as quickly as he could and shuttled to the crematory.

I still went to Manhattan in the late afternoons. Having a car helped. I'd revived Ronnie and Maciej's car, the one Everett used to off himself. I drove cautiously across the Williamsburg Bridge, meandering to avoid the wrecks that remained—steel carcasses of crashed-up cars, the detritus of attempts to break the guardrails and drive off the edge.

I picked my way uptown, always driving too slow to be a moving death method. I parked at Union Square and sat on the hood, as conspicuous as I could be, talking to everyone I saw and recruiting whomever I could. I was usually disappointed.

I sent everybody out in search of information, scattering my people to all corners of the city. Northside Williamsburg, we knew, was decimated. I could only ascribe the relative sanity of the Southside to the demographics; above Grand was mostly white, and I already knew that more whites killed themselves than any other ethnic group. I wondered if being bashed around regularly made one more immune to the suicide reflex, as it doesn't take a bleeding-heart liberal to recognize that the first-generation immigrants south of Grand had a tougher time than the suburban transplants up north. The Southside was suffering from suicide, yes, but was more wounded by the exit of live inhabitants and by the utter lack of goods; trucks bearing food and other necessities just weren't rolling anymore.

On the same page, the Bronx speaks for itself. I sent Jack to check it out, and he came back howling, "Yo, that place is a wreck." But if the Bronx was a mess, it was reeling from the steady onslaught of immigrants fleeing north from Manhattan, a boiling kettle of racial tensions worse than usual, and frequent lootings and random acts of willful violence. If the suicide rate was up it was impossible to tell. No wonder it didn't make the news; no one's ever given a shit about the Bronx.

Staten Island was relatively stable. Empty, but stable. Suicide was up, in "alarming numbers," but the self-contained nature of the island and its proximity to New Jersey kept it afloat and under the radar.

Queens was spotty as ever. Supposedly the most culturally diverse area in the world, Queens bore the epidemic like a small planet digesting a new disease. The effects varied from neighborhood to neighborhood, and it was difficult to take a pulse on the borough as a whole. The only thing we knew for sure was that the areas closest to Williamsburg—Maspeth, Ridgewood—and to Manhattan—Astoria, Long Island City— were the worst off.

And Manhattan was fucked.

We had our work cut out for us, but the focus was Billburg and the haunted island of Manhattan. And always, without fail, all the members of my fledgling crew, except for those who were sent out on special duties, or those helping Bernie steal a truck, or those out on crematory detail, or those too exhausted or unsteady to work that morning, or those who were AWOL in search of the missing, or those who had vanished in the ether that lay outside the city limits, or those who had succumbed overnight to the bizarre epidemic that had us all on the run in the first place—all these good soldiers were to be found drinking coffee and chewing on bacon, egg, and cheese on a roll at Neil's Luncheonette at nine a.m.

BREAKING & ENTERING

It was Chico who had the idea to start making house calls. I call him Chico because, to be honest, I've forgotten his real name. These days it's hard enough to remember important information, like where the nearest safe house is if you can't make it home, or what delis and bodegas still have unspoiled food for the looting.

Chico is the Mexican kid who used to work at Anna Maria's Pizzeria at Bedford and North 7th, dealing out slices to the young hipsters of Williamsburg. He's young, a kid, really, with Mayan features and a sparse, ambitious mustache, and when I ran into him in front of the laundromat, looking beat-up and emotionally destitute, I recruited him immediately.

The owner had put his head in the pizza oven and cranked up the gas. No one knows if he was dead or alive when the sealed pizzeria finally blew. All we know for sure is that Chico went by well after closing, maybe four-thirty or five in the morning, with a strange premonition. He peered in the window and saw the hunched-up body kneeling on a stool in front of the high oven, head out of sight. The door was locked, so Chico picked up a garbage can and hurled it through the window. There must have been a pilot light somewhere, because air rushed in and the place blew, the concussion blast throwing Chico into the street. Fortunately the place didn't burn, tiled top to bottom like an airport bathroom, but merely smoked half the night like a kiln.

Although he'd suffered only a few scrapes from flying debris, Chico was one fucked-up pup when I found him on the street. Now he's my right-hand man in my crew, which we laughingly refer to as Los Hombres Hermosos sin Misericordia, or Los Hombres for short.

We were sitting in the fishing chairs bolted to the front of the pier at the end of 7th, dangling our feet and drinking warm Fosters oil cans. Chico said to me, "Main, all we do is pick up dead bodies on the street."

"What the hell else are we supposed to do?"

"What about the *pinche* apartments?"

He was right. All we've done is pick up the remains of *public* suicides. By now, it's only obvious to assume there are empty apartments all over this city hiding remains.

Chico and I did our first B&E job, at night, just the two of us. Some of the guys we run with are even more sketched-out than we are, and we didn't want to give them any delirious ideas. We started on the Lower East Side, tooling for dead-looking apartment buildings and watching for unbarred windows.

"What do you think?"

"Shit, I don't know," Chico said, shrugging. "I bet they're all full of remains."

We only say people to refer to the living. Suicides are called suicides, or corpses, or remains. After the Bug, they lose their right to be people.

We picked a place on Suffolk, just above Delancey: an old immigrant-era tenement, typical of those on the block, with an unbarred window to the left of the front door. We tried the buzzer and rapped on the window. Nothing. I shattered the glass with my wrench.

I had instituted the standardized equipment of my electrician days—crescent wrench, knife, mini-Maglite—the tools of the trade. As an electrician, it was common to have your C-wrench attached to you by a length of trick line, or better yet, a fusilli phone cord, so that if you dropped it while you were up on a ladder, you wouldn't kill anyone. In the bar mitzvah world, even dropping a C-wrench onto a decorated table from twenty feet up in a Genie Lift would be devastating. The wrench-and-phone-cord combo was also an excellent instrument for gaining access to bodegas and domiciles: throw the wrench through the window and jerk the phone cord back with a deft flick of the wrist. Small windows are best; perishable food goods should be kept from the elements at all costs. Nothing comes into this city anymore.

"Give me a boost, yo." Chico pushed on my Doc Martens and I pulled myself up to the window ledge and stepped in, banging my head on top of the window. It was black as my lungs inside and I took out my Maglite, stumbling around until I found a light switch.

The lights came on, of course. All the amenities here still work; you could run up a thousand-dollar phone bill and your line would never get disconnected. The lights are on, just nobody's home.

I wound my way through the apartment, and out the front door into the hall to let Chico in, and we combed the place. It was empty. The beds hadn't been slept in recently and the fridge was a science experiment. But we didn't find any bodies.

"Chico."

"What."

"Smell."

His nostrils flared and he looked back at me.

"I don't smell nothin'."

"Exactly. *It's* not here." I meant death. Not the smell of decay, not the burning stench of rotting flesh, not the foul fecund odor of breeding maggots, not the gamey, rancid scent of rats on the make—but death itself. That sharp, dry scent of maudlin regret. The perfume of the grim reaper. It simply wasn't there. We had found our first safe house.

"Check the closets."

Clothes were missing, drawers were empty, hangers hanging lonely and naked, skeleton wires with no skin on. We couldn't find any suitcases—not even a duffel bag.

"*Se fueron.*"

I agreed. "They got out."

"Hey… look at this." Chico had found a bottle of tequila and we dug out some glasses and knocked back a few. I passed out. In the morning, half asleep, I dreamed the idle dreams of the nine-year-old girl whose room it had been… flowers and snapshots and teddy bears, Spice Girls and 'N Sync, visions of cute boys and sweet little sundresses, a fascination with the young, cool drunks who inundated my neighborhood on weekends, school field trips to the zoo, heated arguments with my mom, late-night slumber parties with girlfriends giggling, an innocent vision shattered by flailing bodies hurling themselves off the roof.

Chico later confessed that it was nice to sleep in the midst of someone else's loneliness, a loneliness incomplete in that the residents didn't stick around long enough to see how bad it had gotten. At your house, you know what you're missing, how wrong the quiet is. In a safe house… it's just someone else's memories, snapshots of better times, couches still creased with the imprint of happy asses.

The more I thought about people leaving town, the more I wondered: What happened to Phil? I had emailed him, called him, left messages on his home machine and on his cell phone… nothing. But I couldn't imagine he'd succumbed to the Bug. I hoped he'd gone back to Kentucky to ride this thing out. NYU had closed its doors for the remainder of the semester, so I knew he was out of a job.

I drove across the bridge to Delancey and cut up Essex and tried to get in. The front door was locked, so I waited around for a few minutes to see if anyone would come in or out. It was broad daylight, and I was nervous in spite of myself, so before breaking in I walked down to McDonald's on Delancey, where the double cheeseburgers are still ninety-nine cents.

It was bizarre, the oasis of corporate evil, a welcome sight for sore eyes. McDonald's was still taking money, its freezer apparently not yet depleted, still the same young black kids working the counter, and a handful of stragglers silently munching cheap burgers.

I got a double and some fries and sat down and ate. I was just about to walk out when I saw, in the corner, by the front door, hunched over by the window, Phil. An empty burger wrapper in front of him, he was pale as a Klan hood and looked thinner than usual.

"Phil!" I strode over. He looked up at me with a total lack of recognition, and looked down again and sideways out the window.

"Phil, it's me, man. It's Benson. I shaved my head, bro. It's me."

Phil looked up again, and I saw the glint of understanding flash in his eyes. He tried to grin but gave up halfway.

"How you been, man? Shit, I'm so glad you're alive. You look thin. Are you all right?"

He shook his head.

"Well what's up? Pretty nuts around here, huh?"

He nodded.

"Phil. Speak to me, my friend. Say something."

He shook his head.

"Ya gotta say something. You're giving me the heebies."

He shook his head emphatically.

I looked around. "Have you been surviving on these god-damn burgers?"

He nodded sheepishly.

"Come on. I'm getting you out of here. You have to eat something."

I stood him up and walked him to his apartment, passing a man slumped on the sidewalk with his legs splayed out before him, a carving knife buried in his belly up to the hilt, moaning quietly in excruciating pain, a puddle of blood next to him. He was already remains, but hanging on by a thread. I had Sam's .45 on me—it's dangerous work, and many of us had taken to carrying guns when we could find them—but considering Phil's shaky condition I was disinclined to pop the guy with Phil watching. "Phil, stand over there a second, okay? No, no, just look up there." When Phil was safely a few feet away and facing uptown, I took out my wrench and hit the man across the temple, breaking the skin and splattering my shirt slightly with juice. The man collapsed further and I checked his carotid… fucker still had a pulse, but hopefully he'd sleep through the worst of the pain and wake up dead. Horribly painful, they say, belly wounds.

"All right, come on." Phil stood at his stoop, fumbling with the keys, and I took them from him and got him up the four flights of stairs. It was tough going since he's so much taller than I am, and his gangly legs kept buckling under him. But he weighed nothing, and moved in a daze. I got him in the door and into his room and sat him down on his couch. His iMac lay sideways on the floor, still running a screen saver. Clothes were strewn everywhere and all his books had been pulled from the shelves and lay in piles on the floor.

"I'm gonna put some food in you, all right?"

He looked up at me and held two fingers to his mouth.

"I can't imagine that's the best thing for you right now."

He repeated the gesture, so I broke down and lit a cigarette and handed it to him. He drew on it with a pasty, withered hand that shook like Los Angeles during a 4.5.

The kitchen was hopeless. Nothing in the cupboards, nothing in the fridge, not even ketchup. But when I stepped out of the kitchen I smelled it.

"Shit, he's living with remains," I muttered, and opened

the door to one of the other bedrooms. It was immaculate, and I checked the closet: empty hangers. This roommate got out. It was the German's room, the six-foot-six longhair who had lived with Phil... he must have gone back to Krautland. Must be the other one, the computer programmer with the harelip. What was that guy's name again?

In a moment I realized it didn't matter in the least. The smell was overwhelming. It was remains, all right. Hadn't been a person for a long while. Gotta give the guy credit for creativity, though... lived by the sword and died by it. He had wrapped the cord from his computer keyboard around a clothes-peg on the wall and caught his head in it; the cord was wrapped around his neck three times, and he leaned slumped against the wall, still suspended by the cord, the keyboard dangling near his right arm. Gravity and the softness of decaying flesh had allowed the cord to cut halfway through... another couple weeks and he'd have that cord wrapped around nothing but vertebrae.

I went into the German's room, picked up the phone and called Chico.

"Chico."

"Yeah."

"Yo. Get a couple of guys and get over here. I'm on the Lower East Side."

"Find something sweet?"

"No. It's remains."

"Come on, *jefe*. You said we'd take the day off."

"Don't fuck with me on this, all right? It's a friend of mine."

"Sorry, yo. I didn't know."

"I got a guy coming apart at the seams and I gotta get this stinking corpse out of here."

I gave him the address and went to check on Phil. He looked like Bob Geldof in that scene from *The Wall*, not moving, an entire cigarette of ash in his fingers, defying gravity.

"Don't move, Phil. I'll be right back."

I ducked out and found a bodega, and was just about to put my C-wrench through the front window when I saw a person inside. I pushed the door open, and a Paki said hello.

"Still in business?"

"I'm not leaving."

"Glad to hear it. Look, I just need some soup, all right?"

"Take what you need, my friend. Until it's all gone, it's here for you."

"You're a champ."

I grabbed a couple cans of soup and some saltines and slipped him a ten-spot despite his protest and headed out. On my way back I passed by the corpse with the knife in his gut, just to check. The bastard was conscious again, gripping the knife by the handle and digging it into himself like he was whipping cream in slow motion. Nothing else to do, really, so I took my .45 and shot him in the head and kept walking.

Back at Phil's I heated up the soup and sat him back up on the couch—he had collapsed into a fetal position on the floor—and made him eat half a bowl and a handful of saltines. He wiped his mouth and tried to grin again and held two fingers to his mouth. I gave him a cigarette and he managed to light it with a trembling match.

"Are you gonna talk to me now?"

He shook his head.

"All right. Can I ask you a couple things?"

He looked unsure but nodded.

"Okay then. The German guy… did he go back to Deutschland?"

He nodded.

"And… do you know your other roommate is dead?"

He winced and nodded.

"So how long have you been holed up here? Since NYU closed?"

He nodded at first, then shook his head adamantly.

"So it's not that."

He shook his head.

"Phil, I just want to know what's wrong. Why aren't you talking? I know people are dropping dead left and right, but… you knew about this. You knew what was happening in my neighborhood. We joked about it." I thought for a second and looked at him. Hangdog. Defeated.

"Phil." I took a deep breath. "Is Toni dead?"

His chin wrinkled and pushed his lower lip out; his mouth stretched into a whimpering frown and then his whole face broke open. Tears crept into view as he moaned softly and buried his face in his hands, nodding frenetically like an epileptic. I grabbed his head and held it to me, joining him on the couch, caressing his head and stroking his hair. "It's all right, man. I know. But it's gonna be okay. You're not gonna get the Bug. And I'm not gonna leave you. You'll get through this. I'm sorry. I know how much you loved her." I wondered how she went but it didn't matter. He was out of control and inconsolable, a broken thing that had been taken apart and would never go back together again, a unit whose pieces had undergone a fundamental change, rendering it effectively useless, like frozen lettuce.

Phil was passed out when Chico yelled up from the street. I untangled myself from Phil, who didn't so much as blink, and leaned my head out the window. Chico stood before a beautiful mid-sixties Chevy Impala with the two huge Poles from our crew.

"Nice ride, amigo."

He looked up, smiling proudly at his latest acquisition. "*Gracias*."

"Here's the key." I threw it down. "And Chico."

"*Que pasa*?"

"There's one more, too. A guy over there with a knife in his belly."

"I saw him. Hey—you all right?"

"*Sí. Soy ya muerto.*"

He laughed.

We cleared out the remains and installed Phil in the safe house on Suffolk, just around the corner from his place—I had to get him out of that tainted space. We took his computer over and some of his favorite books, like *120 Days of Sodom*. I set him up in the little girl's bedroom and kept an eye on him for a few days. He slept and ate and slept some more. When he started to get his color back I told him about my crew, and he enlisted right away.

But he still won't speak.

Again, it was Chico who found the place in Greenpoint. We had broken in with our boys Jack and Phil, and the second we set foot in the apartment we pulled out our bandanas and put them over our faces—another electrician tool, for handling hot bulbs, now used to mask, however scantily, the pervasive reek of Thanatos.

The corpse lay on its side in front of the couch, bloated like a beached whale and buzzing continuously with so many flies we may as well have been in some tropical malarial hell. Drugs, I was thinking, as it didn't have any marks on it. It had clearly been heavy while alive, but the body was now grotesquely swollen.

"Methane," Jack said.

"That's bullshit. Ain't no methane in a corpse," Chico countered.

"Whattaya call farts?"

"It might be gasses," I intervened. "But I doubt it. That bag's got fifty fucking pounds of maggots squirming around in it."

Jack leaned forward for a closer look, and he must have seen the flesh undulate because he pulled his head back and squinted his eyes in disgust.

"Fuck, let's get out of here."

"I'm right with you," I said. "We'll call it in to Bernie. Phil, take down the address." The dreaded black book came out and the black pen scribbled. Phil had taken over bookkeeping responsibilities and was a lot better at it than I was. He took copious notes, a description of every body we interred, with all viable data: ID or driver's license, when available, place of residence, if known, place and estimated time of death. Description of appearance and of method, time of discovery. He also noted empty apartments, and anything we heard on the street about people missing or people known to have evacuated.

"Jack, let's look for some ID—check the mail." I looked around. "Where the hell's Chico?"

From the back of the apartment came a joyous whoop that sent the flies reeling. It was completely out of place—I couldn't remember the last time I'd heard such elation. We scrambled to the bedroom and found Chico kneeling on the floor with his knife in his hand and a three-by-two-foot piece of sheetrock lying across his knees. "It's a closet." The doors had been removed and the molding taken out and the whole thing walled up. "Look," Chico said, and held up the sheet-rock in his hands. It had a poster of the band Cypress Hill. "A bedroom with no closet? A poster low to the floor like this?" He grinned a wild, leering grin. "Look!"

I knelt next to him and peered into the closet and busted a grin of my own. I stuck my head right into the hole and breathed deeply. The sweet, sticky scent filled my nostrils and burned out the stank of death....

Chico beamed. "I hit the fucking jackpot."

"I'd say this shit is about ready for harvest, wouldn't you?"

We harvested a few pounds of killer hydroponic marijuana and took the rest of the day off, smoking fat joints in my courtyard and drinking skunked beer and laughing ourselves stupid. The black market was one of the first things to go, not having the permanence of the standard trappings of capitalism—like offices and steady employees. I also think the type to make a career out of drugs would be quick to succumb to the Bug. It had been some time since any of us had smoked any reefer, and we reveled in our score, divvied it up and left a pile in the middle of my kitchen table to be imbibed before sundown. Even Phil smiled.

I was glad to see him cut loose, but in my stoned state I thought him braver than any of us. His girl was dead. At least mine had gotten out, and I could harbor a clandestine desire to seek her out someday, when this was all over, and possibly rekindle whatever had been trampled by the epidemic. But Phil... his girl was gone, dead, a casualty. She had entered his heart and broken it and left nothing behind but the shell of a man who, by all rights, should have followed suit. But here he was, riding with us, keeping records for the entire crew—sitting up at Neil's and compiling other people's notes late into the night.

More than that, his silence was a strength, a fierce resistance to the banal coping mechanisms the rest of us indulged: denial, ignoring the obvious, and subsisting on a steady diet of callous reactions and caustic humor, laughing in the pestilent face of death and creating distracting preoccupations— Chico with his cars, me with my drug of authority, Jack with his adolescent ride for kicks. Phil's silence was an utter refusal to play, a refusal to come outside at all.

"Phil, laugh with us," Jack said. "Damn, you are one hard bitch."

BOMB-OUT

There was hope. I met other folks struggling to form crews, and we banded into a loose conglomerate. Information was key. The more you know, the more you can see, and the more you can see, the more you can trust that you might live to see another day. Word of resistance to the contagion spread as quickly as denial had spread initially, and the underground gossip line was rife with chatter of the cleanup effort. Crews had started to pop up in Manhattan, and just as in Williamsburg, a gang-style grassroots mentality bred more survivors than any "organized," centrally located effort. You can only trust the people you run with, who will save your ass because you saved theirs yesterday, whether that means fighting off a maniac in the throes of a suicide attempt, swatting away rats, or just offering an encouraging comment to someone about to slip into despair.

Los Hombres had undergone a mitosis-like division, and Ty had started his own Billburg-based crew, the Cripplebush Criers. We all worked in close association and under the umbrella of Bernie's task force, which had grown in both size and numbers—more men, more trucks, more crematories.

I had what I considered to be a crack team of crackpots and looked after them with fierce loyalty. I had Chico, and I had Phil. And I had Luz, my former electrician buddy, whom I had spotted on one of my tours through Union Square, a young girl with a butch haircut, sitting on a bench. I called out and she came running and threw her arms around me.

"Baby, it's so good to see you," she said.

"You too, baby, I'm so glad you're not dead."

She laughed. "I wish I could say that's a weird thing to say. What are you doing here?"

"Seeing if I can round up anyone for my crew. You wanna come work for me? I mean, I know you were always pissed about the crew chiefs always being men and all, but—"

"Shut up. Of course I'll come work for you. How's the money?"

I grinned. "Bad as ever."

And I had Jack, who was a freak and a goof-off, and often a pain in the ass, but his antics never stopped, no matter how grim the work, and he helped everyone blow off steam.

The five of us were always together, usually with the two huge Poles and the Cute Girl from Group D, who quickly became Luz's trusted accomplice and confidante.

"All right, I'm going in," Jack said. He gave me a nod and I threw the door open. We were investigating a squatty building off of Bushwick that was rumored to be a mess. Other crews had backed away from it. We were on the top floor— you always work your way down—and this was the first apartment we'd tried.

The door blew back open and Jack jumped back into the hallway. I slammed the door behind him.

"Rats! Holy shit, I've never seen so many rats," he said, his bloodshot eyes rolling. Phil rapidly took notes.

"All right, let's fucking bomb it." I made the gesture for *bombs* to one of the huge Poles, who was carrying most of our auxiliary effects, shaking my hand like I was holding a spray can and making a *psssst* sound. The Pole handed me a four-pack of bug bombs, the kind you use to clear a house of fleas or cockroaches. They don't kill the rats, but the rats hate them and will generally leave the room when they smell the foul gas. But when the gas clears, the rats come back, so we have to evacuate bodies double time.

Luz tied her handkerchief around her face, and her voice came out soft and muffled. "How many years are we taking off our lives with this stuff?"

"I don't know, babe," I answered. "How many have you got?" I smiled and put my handkerchief on like an Old West cowboy in a dust storm.

Chico, Luz and I shook bombs and Jack pulled the door open and we hit the buttons on the bombs and threw them in. Jack slammed the door and counted to twenty to give the rats a chance to get out. We all started yelling as Jack opened the door again and the eight of us darted into the apartment with our eyes stinging. Rats swarmed about our feet, dizzy and disoriented and confused, scrambling for cover. I stepped on one and almost fell. I caught myself and heard the Cute Girl from Group D squealing and Chico muttering.

"Don't even look! Fucking fan out, people! Let's get out of here!"

The two Poles disappeared into a bedroom, reappeared through the haze carrying a corpse between them, and started for the door.

"Window! Window!" I shouted, and picked up a TV remote from a side table and threw it at the window to get their attention. You don't have time in a bomb-out to mess with stairs. The Poles broke the window out with a boot and a gloved fist and tossed the body. They headed back into the same room and I knew there were more.

"Phil, follow!"

Phil and the Cute Girl from Group D followed them in. There was another doorway, and Luz and Chico came out pulling a bloated corpse. There was another on the front couch, and Jack and I hoisted it up and out the window. As we were about to dump it over, a rat fell from the curtains and Jack jumped a foot.

"*Chingale!*"

Luz buzzed past me, stepping over rats. "That room's clean."

"The back," I said, pointing in the direction of the Poles. We saw the Poles coming out with another, and behind them Phil and the Cute Girl from Group D, each cradling a small, crumpled shape. They had found the remains of two dead children, no older than eight or nine. Tears streamed down the Cute Girl's face, and I didn't think it was just because of the gas.

I jumped forward and took the body from her hands and barked at Chico, "Get her out of here!" and tossed the body unceremoniously out the window, watching it fall four floors to the grassy front yard. Phil followed suit and gave me the sign for clean, like a salute that missed.

"Go! Go! Go!" I screamed, and we all piled out of the apartment stumbling on the running rats, and Jack slammed the door. A rat squirmed under and Chico took aim and shot it dead.

We ran downstairs and fell outside, collapsing on the front stoop and panting for breath and tearing at our masks and scratching at our eyes, tearing involuntarily. Phil passed out water and we tried to recover. As soon as I could breathe I reached for my cell phone.

"Neil? It's me. Listen, we gotta get some more guys over here. Yeah. I'm at Bushwick and Devoe. It's fucking bad. If anyone calls in, get them over here. And tell Bernie to send someone over with more bombs. Yeah, it's that bad. Right on."

I hung up and shut my eyes, tight, watching the blood flow through my lids and trying to make the headache go away. I opened them when I heard someone screaming.

The Cute Girl from Group D had her knife in her hand and was plunging it into her breast. Luz was wrapped around her, a tangled mess of extremities, trying to wrest the knife out of her hand.

"Get away from her!" I barked. "It's too late!"

The Cute Girl managed a swipe at Luz and cut her a good one across the forearm. Jack and I were hopping but Chico was closer, and he grabbed Luz and pulled her away, yelling obscenities and thrashing her head from side to side, as the Cute Girl from Group D shoved the knife in and out of her chest until her torso was a bloody confetti of shredded sternum and tissue. She lay flat on her back in the matted grass with the knife protruding, her hands out to either side, hands open and begging for forgiveness.

"Damn it, damn it, damn it, goddamn it!" Luz spat, as Chico tried getting her to sit down on the stoop so he could look at her bleeding wound. One of the Poles took a blanket out of a rucksack and laid it across the girl's cute, dead face so we wouldn't have to look at it. Phil scribbled in his notepad. Jack walked away and picked up a rock and threw it at the building across the street, murmuring, "God damn I wanted to fuck her." I prayed Luz hadn't heard him or I'd have two corpses on my hands. I reached for the cell phone and called Bernie.

"It's me. Yeah, Bernie, I'm sure you're busy. You need to get someone over here, right now. Bushwick and Devoe. I don't care. Leave them there. *I don't fucking care, Bernie, I got a man down and I want her remains removed.*" I hung up, sat down on the curb and ran my hands across my stubbly head.

I've seen better days. I have to have seen better days, somewhere in the back of this tangled mind I have to believe that, or how can I ever begin to wish for better days again? Is there no limit to the level of tragedy that I can be called upon to endure? It's as if tragedy begets tragedy, multiplying in a steady onslaught of one ridiculous, needless waste after another, heaped one atop another until the resulting Tower of Babel threatens to blot out the sun itself... and the blight on the heart grows, eating its way from the outside in, turning the entire fruit to a useless, mushy paste that festers and molds and shrinks down to nothing, folding in upon itself like a fanatical physics project proving the infallibility of gravity and the irresistible nature of entropy. We've finally passed the point of no return, the marker in the road that spells our misfortune in every language known to man. Before this point, every tragedy hardens you for the next; after this point, every tragedy makes you that much more susceptible. Your callous demeanor is not a lie that you are beginning to believe; it is a truth that you are beginning to doubt. The cancer fermenting in your soul is the painful opposite of the numb remedy you witness on a daily basis. As it eats you, it will not do you the courtesy of bringing you closer to death. It is performing the radical disservice of bringing you closer and closer to life—unending pain, unrelenting sorrow, limitless frustration, infinite sadness, capacious fear, and rabid, animal hatred for everything that threatens this pain itself—life. If living in New York, before the epidemic, was an exercise in being kicked in the ribs on a daily basis, then life after the Bug is an examination of the endurance of having your heart and soul trampled by a leviathan beast every unending day after the next. Sisyphus pushing the stone only to have it roll back down. Prometheus having his liver torn out and devoured only to have it grow back again. All these terrors, and more, will be practiced and perfected before the sun sets, and when it rises again, in its fruitless fury, you will gaze at the azure sky and welcome their return like an unkindness of ravens descending upon a glimmering field of fresh eyeballs grateful to be plucked from their sockets.

I must have seen better days.

MARLIN

Chris Marlin sat with Luz at one of Neil's tables, filled a hypodermic needle with local anaesthetic and injected it into her arm as she winced. Moments later she smoked a cigarette as he bent over her arm, moving his gaze only to readjust the goose-neck reading lamp Neil had set up on the table, or to take a hit from a joint burning in an ashtray by his elbow, and in a few minutes he was dressing the laceration, now sealed up and decorated with a tidy little row of spidery sutures.

We had managed to stop the bleeding, but the cut was jagged and nasty and a wide-open candidate for infection. I was faced with the truly dodgy issue of medical care, which wasn't easy to come by anymore, even if one had money or insurance. But I knew she needed stitches and she was part of my crew, and therefore my responsibility.

Neil, Jack, and I got on the horn with a vengeance. Ty went out looking for better painkillers. Luz lay down on the cot in back, seeming much more concerned with the passing of the Cute Girl from Group D than with her own wound. Chico presided over her like a doting Mexican grandma, and Neil worried over her, crinkling dark Italian half-moons under black eyes wet with concern.

Jack dialed a safe-house phone that was answered by one of his compadres in the Carrion Crew—a crew on the Lower East Side—who just happened to be lounging on the couch smoking a joint with an acquaintance named Chris Marlin.

Chris Marlin was a man with a dilapidated, cloudy past. He had graduated from Harvard Medical School at the top of his class and interned at the Mayo Clinic, but then joined the Peace Corps and went to Somalia. He came to New York three years later with his ambition shattered, and took a job as an EMT for a mediocre private ambulance company. He was grossly overqualified. This was a man who had abandoned his original dream of becoming an overpaid plastic surgeon doing nose jobs for Jewish-American princesses to pursue a more righteous dream, but he no longer understood the point of trying to help people who would wind up dead for one ridiculous, wasteful reason or another. His humanitarian change of heart had become a shattered, stained-glass pipe dream, and he remained bitterly content, if not exactly happy or fulfilled, to stick with a dead-end job.

The onslaught of pandemic suicides broke what resolve he had left. He abandoned his post, as many EMTs and ambulance drivers had done, all too many becoming morphine addicts. But Marlin was merely a hophead, usually sitting out smoking at Roosevelt Park, where Rivington disappears for the block east of Chrystie. It used to be a great area, bubbling with energy, a perfect place to whittle away the hours of a sunny afternoon to the echoes of spry old men selling *paletas.* Marlin persevered at this idleness as the neighborhood drowned.

Jack doesn't smoke a lot of weed, so after the Greenpoint haul he sold most of his share to a Southside huckster who's determined to make a buck off this disaster come hell or apocalypse. The kid discovered Chris Marlin, who became his best customer, sitting out in the park hour after hour, smoking joints and gazing up into the bleak tangled sky.

Chico took Luz down the block to my place so she could pass out in peace after Marlin gave her a handful of Tylenol 3s.

"So," Marlin said. "Give me a ride back?"

I had picked him up, since Bernie was having a hell of a day and the afternoon had devoured our inclination to do anything more than tend to our wounded. I recognized him as the same bleary-eyed hack I had seen at the Zeckendorf Towers the night my inadequate lover decided to bury a knife in her throat. It reminded me of my early days in New York, when running into a cat on the street that I had known seven years before in another city was a common occurrence. It's a small town.

"Where you going?"

"To the park."

"Can I get a hit off that?"

"Sure."

I took a long drag off the joint and handed it back. "Why did you bail out?" I asked.

"Whattaya think?" he said, squinting through the sweet, acrid smoke enveloping his face. "I got tired of handling dead people."

"Isn't that part of the gig?"

"Look, if I wanted to be a mortician I wouldn't have gone to school for ten fucking years. Know how much debt I incurred?"

"No," I said. "I don't."

"Yeah, well..." he looked outside.

"Can I get you a cup of coffee or something?" Neil offered.

"No, never touch the stuff."

"You hungry?"

"No thanks, Pops. Just waiting on a ride." He looked at me.

"So why'd you come out here, anyway?" I asked.

He shrugged. "The kid promised me some free dope."

"Oh yeah," I said, "that. I can hook you up now, if you want to come by—oh, you know, Luz is laid up at my place."

"I'll get it later."

"Maybe I can just pop in for a minute. She's probably not out yet."

"Look," Marlin snapped, "is there some particular reason why you're trying to keep me here? I did you a favor, now please, take me back. And if you're not going to, just say so and I'll start walking."

"Work with me here. We could use you. You know a thing or two and none of us know shit. You're tired of handling dead people… all right. I'm not asking you to go out in the field with us and heft bodies. But I've got a great crew of live, walking, talking people. Work on them. You'll come in real handy."

"No. I'm sorry."

"You could help us out a lot, Marlin, and it's gotta be better than smoking by yourself in the park, wasting away to nothing."

He put the joint out and shot me a chilling look. "No." He picked up his bag. "It's not."

"Why the hell not?"

"Because I just don't feel like it."

"Fair enough."

There was a long pause and Neil shifted his weight uneasily behind the counter. Marlin moved his bag from one hand to another and looked outside again and back at me. "So will you take me back now?"

I shook my head.

"Why? Because I won't work with you?"

"No. I just don't feel like it."

He huffed and pounded outside and disappeared around the corner. I sat at the counter and Neil fixed me a cup of coffee.

"You tried."

"Yeah… but I shouldn't have let him off so easy."

"You can't make anybody."

I took a sip of the lifeblood and leaned my elbows on the

counter. "Neil… what are we doing, anyway? I mean, is it even worth it?"

"Listen, kid," he said. "You're doing great. Don't get discouraged just 'coz this guy's breakin' your balls. You're all right, kid. You're all right."

"Yeah…" I focused on my coffee and thought about Luz, and remembered that look of sincere and total tragedy on the face of the Cute Girl from Group D when she came out of that room with a child's remains in her arms and a rat crawling over one of her boots.

I heard a thump and turned around. Marlin stood in the doorway and had thrown his bag onto a chair.

"Can you get me a place around here? Something respectable, with some decent light?"

"Yeah," I said, masking my surprise as best I could. "I can arrange something."

"All right." He didn't know what to do with his hands. "I'm in."

Ty came bursting in, breathing hard, already talking rapid-fire: "—man I couldn't find shit and I ran all the way down to—" he saw Marlin and broke off, looking around the room and not seeing Luz.

"Ty, I'd like you to meet Chris Marlin." I couldn't resist smiling. "Our company medic."

WALL STREET

It was sick, really, but we did it anyway. Somewhere in the bottom of our cold, lifeless hearts was a lingering stain—our hatred of suits. As a result, the spectacle still had something to offer us in the way of entertainment.

You could almost set your watch by it. Ty, Luz, and I sat against a building on Broadway just south of Wall, in a kind of urban alcove. We were safely tucked under a portico, hunkered against the glass smoking cigarettes. Every fifteen minutes or so, we would feel, unconsciously, a sudden rush of wind, or hear in the back of our minds the echo of a scream filtered through the Doppler effect, ringing and rising in a crescendo of lust, cutting out sharply with the dull, wet impact of a body striking the concrete sidewalk or the blacktop. When we heard it we looked up anxiously, like ballplayers tracking a fly ball. Our eyes, drawn by a flurry of movement, would find a suit flapping in the breeze, and the remains sped toward the ground in a rapid accumulation of acceleration, gravity taking its grave toll, the body flailing and gesticulating wildly, helpless as an astronaut at the event horizon. Every time, when the body struck the pavement, we winced in unison and looked away, looking back quickly at the broken remains haphazardly arranged on the surface of our planet like a discarded de Kooning sketch.

For a long time there was no sound out of any of us save the finger flick of a cigarette butt and the butt striking the pavement.

Luz broke it. "Can you believe this?"

"Ironic, yeah?" I offered.

"How so?" she asked. "I mean, I can think of a million ways that it's ironic, but what were you thinking?"

I took a last draw and flicked my smoke and waited for the sound of its landing, and then I waited again because we could hear wailing up the street. Ty craned his neck to peer around the building, and we followed his gaze. A black pinstripe was hanging out to dry. "I was thinking that seventy years ago the stock market crashed and all the brokers jumped out the windows. And now… the brokers are jumping out the windows and the market's gonna crash."

"Pretty funny, huh?" said Luz, and didn't laugh. I didn't laugh either. Nobody laughed.

Again, the unmistakable sound of imploding glass, and that weird vacuous sound of the atmosphere reestablishing a balance of pressure after a windowpane of an air-conditioned building is busted out. A suit propelled through the spiking shards of a mirrored building, jetting out like a pop-up book, suspended for a brief Wile E. Coyote moment before the mighty demon Gravity clutched him in invisible jaws and sucked him to the ground. The glass tinkled after him.

The thing about the Financial District is that, even before the Bug, few people lived there. You can't trust a neighborhood without residents; it's like trusting a drug dealer with a listed phone number. Wall Street at night is the shadow of a hundred-dollar bill—thin, almost invisible, and marked by razor-sharp loneliness. People come for one reason and one reason only, and then they go to their nice homes and rest up for the bloodbath the next day. No one is here to clean up the mess made by the failure of the suits to return home.

Phil had taken on the habit of long, self-obsessive walks that lasted until four in the morning. He had become the poster child for sleep deprivation, mastering insomnia like a fine art. His eyes were persistently bloodshot and hung with a fine drapery of baggy grey. On one of his long walks he ventured south toward Battery Park, stumbling on bodies, and met me the next day with a crumpled note scrawled in his inscrutable handwriting: "Wall Street remains." It wasn't a fervent prayer for the immortality of the American Dream.

I had worked in that neck of the woods, before all this started, dodging the vast hordes of army ants moving with dedicated fervor in their exoskeletons of blue blazers and spotted yellow ties. No more… the tourists that used to flock the streets and wait in line for hours for the rare glimpse of the frenetic floor—they were gone. The dry-cleaned permanent-press secretaries were few and far between. Gone were the coffee carts, the grills on wheels serving strange-smelling meats in pita bread, the book tables, the fruit stands, the energetic men hawking three-dollar ties and leather belts and the lost, lackluster people that weaved around the obstacles, fighting their way through the jam of the sidewalk to duck into revolving doors that spun and spat out replacements.

The air itself seemed unnaturally cool, devoid of the pressing humidity of hustling bodies brushing each other with the sting of static electricity. No more. The few people on the street moved hurriedly, not with a sense of purpose, as before, but with the rhythm of fugitives—breaking from one building to the next like agents in a trashy spy movie, like so many woebegone cockroaches scrambling for a refrigerator to skitter under when the overhead light snaps on with a flick and a flash.

We were joined by a heavyset, ruddy-faced man with six chins and a beer belly in a coffee-stained pink-striped dress shirt open at the throat. "One of you got a cigarette?" There was a wet sound to his S's, like he had a gob of spit in his mouth. I reached for a smoke but Ty beat me to it. I offered him a light and he drew and recoiled as if he were going to cough, but he didn't. "I quit twenty years ago."

"Welcome back," I said. No one had anything to add. Three months earlier the man would have thought us punks if he saw us sitting outside of 55 Wall in work clothes, taking a break from some broker party we were lighting, and he would have been right. But today, sitting with us and smoking one of our cigarettes, he was the one out of place.

"What are you guys doing down here?" he asked, again with a sibilant S.

"Waiting on a truck." I said.

Luz laughed. "Some things never change, Benson. Here we are, still waiting on a truck." It was reminiscent of better days. But the truck we were waiting on would be empty when it arrived.

"A truck?" The man sucked so hard on his cigarette it seemed to crumple in his pinched fingers.

I looked him over and he caught me looking and held my eye. Late fifties, early sixties… wedding band, with kids, to be sure. Maybe grandkids.

"We're here to pick up your dead."

We were silent as a body tumbled from the sky executing a perfect half gainer.

"Fucking change the channel already, Ty, I've seen this one."

We continued to pollute our lungs and gazed out toward the reflected sunlight like Old West drovers staring down the horizon. The man sat with us and Ty fed him cigarettes without his having to ask.

Two box trucks rolled the wrong way up Broadway and stopped in front of us, spilling Jack, Chico, Phil, most of Ty's Cripplebush kids, about half the Carrion Crew and a few others I didn't recognize, including an unbelievably thin woman with jet-black hair and a sexy sway to her hipless hips. They walked toward us with eyes raised to the building above us, like soldiers spying for snipers. Chico had a deli bag and passed out bottles of water and Gatorade. There were handshakes and hugs all around, and the newcomers lit up smokes of their own. The woman I didn't know approached me boldly and extended a hand.

"I'm Alexis," she said. "I chief the Midtown Martyrs. Bernie brought us in on this one," jerking a thumb toward the skyscrapers and the crumpled jumpers.

"Check it out," I said to Luz, "a chick crew chief. See? We're not chauvinists—anyone can pick up dead bodies."

"Yeah," Alexis said, bearing a sideways smirk, "I heard

you were kind of an asshole."

Luz laughed and introduced herself, and Alexis shook Ty's hand and then turned to the broker, not realizing he wasn't one of us.

"I'm Tim," he said, "Nice to meet you, Alexis," his snake-like *S* already becoming endearing.

I stamped out a smoke. "All right. Let's do this thing."

We watched our heads for the rest of the afternoon. There were no casualties, just one close call when Luz and one of the Martyrs went for a corpse and a jumper came from above them. Alexis shrieked from half a block away, and Luz and her partner moved the wrong way, positioning themselves even closer to danger. Luz dodged at the last minute, and the other kid jumped a full three feet in the air when the body hit and an arm bounced up from the pavement, the hand seeming to grab the kid's ankle in a last grasp of desperation.

Tim was out of shape but didn't complain. He worked alongside us with a grim determination and I wondered if he had been to war, but didn't ask.

LONGING

I miss the yuppies. I miss them with a categorical, styptic awe.

I miss the Williamsburg bohemian yuppies with their designer dogs and their square-shouldered swagger, the women's hotblack slitted skirts and minimalist make up, the men's casual slouch jeans and no-starch shirts. I miss the Upper East Side mavens with their haughty Oscar de la Renta noses, made to be looked down with the incisive air of an undertaker, their Lexus smiles and gleaming BMW teeth. I miss the West Village old-schoolers with their pretentious and patient endurance of the come-hither gay boys, the "what has the neighborhood come to" and the "I have to leave town on Gay Pride and Halloween," and I miss the homosexual yuppie ecstasy culture, wannabe Republican and insisting on "We're here, we're queer, get used to it." I miss the Technicolor yuppies clogging the former drug jungles of Alphabet City, slinking down lettered avenues all dressed in black and anointed with delicate scents of microbrew beers and Nat Sherman cigarettes, gathering in hibiscus clusters to preen and guffaw over the latest office gossip and last week's episode of *Sex and the City*. I miss the Union Square late-afternoon sunset watch on the southside steps, the huddled backpack-bearing masses yearning to spend free, to worship at the altar of the Virgin Megastore and pray for more meaningful one-night stands and more Helmut Lang minimalism in their lives. I miss the afternoon Soho runway of crowded, narrow streets speckled with oversize sunglasses and begging-to-be-recognized wish-I-were-a-model nymphettes, tiny and anorexic in Calista Flockhart glee, seemingly on the edge of slipping down a storm drain and disappearing in a dreamlike flush of glamour, laced with the delicate aroma of Obsession by Calvin Klein. I miss the Central Park matching jogging outfits and the Rollerbladers decked out in fashion-forward crash gear, the hushed conversations held between panting breaths, betwixt the rhythm of two-hundred-dollar running shoes with patented features—a peacock mating ritual in pitch-black shades and Lycra action wear only barely containing the whimsical yearnings of the flesh. I miss the Tribeca calvacade of overpriced restaurants owned by celebrities, the reservation-required dominance of overbearing, prettier-than-you hostesses and swishy waiters who specialize in drinks or order-taking only, leaving subservient duties of food running and bussing to the hordes of minority minimum-wagers and welcoming with open arms anyone with the scratch to order delicacies unerringly, drink from the correct glass, shovel with the proper fork, tip exorbitantly, and never break the façade of a stiff smile and cheery, shallow conversation—the agreed-upon convention that dining in public is a private affair. I miss the Coffee Shop on Union Square, Layla on West Broadway, Spa on 13th—all the magnetic meeting points for yuppies and their money-grubbing ilk, these single-minded capitalists with their vacuous simplicity, drawn to the simple pleasures of fine clothes; high-paying, low-impact desk labor; tasty, sweet cocktails that bring lithe intoxication and weak-kneed recovery, and for-a-limited-time-only sexual pleasure exercised in reckless abandon in a stranger's apartment, hushing cries and weeps of orgasm under bedclothes and fancy feather pillows, buried below the radar of a roommate's ear.

I miss the YUPS, the SYPS, the GYPS; the slackers, the hipsters, the whiners; the come-latelies, the girl Fridays, the go-to guys; the suits, the stiffs, the execs; the moguls, the magnates, the self-appointed magistrates; the CEOs, the CPOs, the COOs; the indifferent and ungainly and impressive. I miss them in their terrifying and alienating hauteur, snobbery, selfishness, hedonism, aggression, ambition, delusion, subordination, didacticism, autonomy, and superiority. I miss their takeovers; their sitcoms; their gather-round-the-water-cooler gossip; their rampant capitalism; their greed; their blind subservience to a status quo of their own participation and design; their unerring fallibility in any social situation requiring tact; their pushy manner on the sidewalks and subways; their malicious, derisive glares at street people, the homeless, and blue-collar losers alike; their *Wall Street Journal*s tucked in the armpit of a thousand-dollar suit; their Gucci handbags slung viciously alongside their graceless full-figured or slender-hipped bodies; their phony laughs and guffaws; their practiced smiles wielded mercilessly on the "service industry"; their "keep the change"; and their "Ciao."

I miss their differences from and their similarities to me. I miss their bad example and my bitter reactions and contorted oaths. I miss the color they added to the sidewalks, the density and elbowing they added to a barroom. I miss the hated wheels of progress and consumerism they continue turning, tirelessly. I miss their humanity, epitomizing weakness and strength in every crushed white cigarette, every raised taxi-hailing hand, every signed deal and every Starbuck's double mocha latte Frappuccino and every secluded online call to Cosmo.com to deliver the latest Gwynyth Paltrow movie, a bag of Pepperidge Farm Milanos, a tub of Häagen-Dazs, and a bottle of Pellegrino.

I miss them, more than anything, not for the hole of hatred I once harbored in my heart for them, but for their livid, animate existence purely, no matter how paltry or pale or simpering they ever appeared to me. I miss them because they were alive. They walked, they talked, they ordered a slice. They took cabs and they rode the subway, they made money and spent it, they were upright and mobile. They breathed, they ate, they shit; their hearts beat and their eyes wept. They sweated. They came. They wiped the crust from their eyes in the morning and the jam from their toes at night. They showered and brushed their teeth. They worried. They loved. They hated with abandon. They felt small and inadequate; powerful and fulfilled; empty and frustrated; abandoned and blamed; championed and adored.

They lived.

ORGANIZATION

"Headache, fever…"

"I got those."

"Insomnia and agitation, anxiety and confusion, hallucinations, hypersalivation, difficulty swallowing, and of course, hydrophobia."

"What's that?" Jack looked nervous.

"Fear of water."

"So what happens after that?"

Marlin shrugged and took a long drag off a joint. "You die."

"What?" Jack reached the hysterical boiling point. "What-taya mean I fuckin' *die!* You can do something, right?"

"Nah," Marlin shrugged again. "Once you start getting symptoms it's too late to do anything. Only way to treat rabies is post-exposure prophylaxis, five doses of the vaccine over a four-week period after known or suspected contact with a rabid animal. But once you get the symptoms you're toast."

"What the fuck? You're tellin' me I'm fuckin' dead already?"

"Nah," Marlin said, tapping an ash, "I don't think you got rabies. It hasn't been long enough."

"Man," Jack leaned back and punched the air. "I knew you was fuckin' wit' me."

"I think you have rat-bite fever."

Jack was on the edge of his seat again. "What the fuck is that?"

Ty had just come in the door. "Marlin, you're getting the kid all worked up. Does he have rabies or not?"

"No!" Jack almost screamed, "Now I have rat-bite fever!"

"Isn't that a Ted Nugent song?"

"Shut up, man. This shit ain't funny."

"All right, all right," Ty nodded at Neil who fixed him a cup of coffee. "Tell it to us straight, Doc."

Marlin sighed and sat down heavily, his voice growing tired and bored. "The gestation period for rabies is several weeks—a month at the least, sometimes three. It's not likely that our spasmodic friend here had any impure contact with a rabies-bearing animal that long ago. Besides, rabies is only rarely found in small rodents in New York State, and then usually in squirrels and rabbits. No rat has ever been found with rabies in New York City. What I think is more likely," and with this he cocked an eyebrow and reached for his crutch, the joint still burning in the ashtray, and Neil let out an almost inaudible sigh of forbearance, "is that sometime in the last month, in one of your intimate associations with febrile disease-carrying vermin, Jack here picked up a case of rat-bite fever."

"You're making this shit up, right?" Ty asked, lighting a cigarette and rubbing at his head. His hair had been quite long before he finally broke down and shaved it, and he still mourned the loss. He gave Jack an encouraging wink.

"Rat-bite fever," Marlin asserted. "Fever, shaking chills, progressive myalgia, nausea, vomiting. Sometimes accompanied with a rash on the extremities. You did say you were nauseous, didn't you?"

"I been puking," Jack confessed.

"If it were rabies you'd be raving, not puking. And rat-bite fever sets in after about a week, maybe three, which would line up pretty well with the rat-infested incident that got Luz cut up."

"So… how bad is it really?" Ty asked.

"It's not. It'll probably go away on its own, but a good antibiotic will knock it right out, which would be a good idea, because I wouldn't be surprised if more of you kids come down with it. All that rat business."

I went in the back to take a piss, and when I came in they were talking about invading a hospital with guns blazing to steal antibiotics.

"No," I countered. "You're not going into a hospital with fucking guns. What do you need, anyway?"

"Penicillin would be great," Marlin said. "But really, anything. Amoxicillin, streptomycin—even tetracycline would do it."

Then Miles walked in and asked Neil for a cup of coffee as if nothing out of the ordinary had ever occurred in Williamsburg. Miles used to work at Joe's Busy, and was my favorite there, since he was young and went against the old school grain of the place with his earrings and the fact that he played in a band, but he was Italian and could make a mean hero. I clapped him on the back.

"Miles, I'm so glad you're not dead."

"Well, Ben, I'm glad you're not dead, too."

"Yo, wassup," Jack said, and gave Miles a dap. Marlin nodded to him, and Miles cocked his head and said, "Hey, Chris."

"Does everyone know Miles?" I asked.

"This is the cat I sold my stash to," Jack said. "He gets Marlin all his weed."

"If you need something from the hospital," Miles offered, "just walk in and get it. St. Vincent's is the best. It's almost empty and no one will trouble you. But forget about narcotics, especially morphine. The ambulance drivers have tapped it."

"I could have told you that," Marlin said.

Jack piped up. "You know where to get toilet paper?"

"Of course. There's a big warehouse down off Graham, kind of a back storage building for a ninety-nine-cent store. Loads of Charmin. I've been supplying the Southside and making a decent profit."

"Bug bombs?" I asked.

"Oh yeah. There's a string of shitty home-product stores in Astoria. Some of them are still open, but the ones that aren't I loot and trade for vegetables."

"What about Cointreau?" Ty wanted to know. Vodka was still fairly easy to come by, but you can't make a decent cosmopolitan without Cointreau.

"I can get it."

"Where?"

Miles spread his fingers. "I can't disclose that information at this time. But I can get it for you, and it won't cost too much."

"What about ammo?" Jack asked.

"Oh sure." Miles pursed his lips and nodded solemnly, adjusting his engineer's cap. "I can get you ammunition, maybe a gun or two. But don't ask me where."

"This guy's fucking Milo Minderbender," I said under my breath, and Phil, who had been skulking against the wall in silence, let out a chuckle.

"Who?" Jack asked, but the joke was wasted on him, an undereducated former car-wash attendant. Miles lived on the Southside and managed to keep the neighborhood afloat, since the living residents were suffering from sheer lack of essentials. The Puerto Ricans called him El Gringo and secretly loved him, though they cursed his name and showed abject hatred every time he made a deal to procure vegetables for a grocer or toilet paper for an *abuela* with screaming grandkids.

Tim came in with a large roll of paper under his arm and unrolled it onto the table and started talking logistics with Bernie, who had just rolled in with a box of Krispy Kremes and offered no explanation as to how he got them. The cloying, sickly-sweet smell of heaven-sent, hell-bent fried dough brought even Marlin into the fold. He was on his second joint of the morning and beginning to act a trifle less surly. With a mouth full of doughnut I said, "Boys, meet Miles, our new quartermaster." Miles joined in on the conversation as if he'd known the men all his life.

Tim pointed a glazed half-moon at his paperwork, dropping crumbs. "I've started to compile a list of resources and needs, and I drew up a map last night of the city and the other crews that we know about so's we can expand—"

"Oh no," Miles interrupted, "this is nothing. You got a pencil?" He leaned over the map and marked it up, filling in the blanks of our accumulated knowledge.

"Los Hombres and the Cripplebush Criers on the Northside, okay. But you also got Southside crews… Los Chingados, Puerto Ricans, and Cinco Seis, Dominicans. There's also Met Emet, a Hasidic crew. I think it means 'Death Truth,' some Hebrew wordplay from a Czechoslovakian myth or something. And another, Malach Shomer, 'Angel Guard.' They're tough, though they look kinda ridiculous, you know…" Miles mimed a heavy black coat, *payes*, did a funny impression of a Hasid lumbering over corpses. "Over in Greenpoint you got Zwoloki Wlozyc, a kind of truncated slang for 'Corpse Baggers,' and Pozny Patrol, 'Late Patrol.'"

"Right," Bernie said. "That was started by two guys that used to run with Benson."

"Great guys," Miles said. "Both crews—those Poles are tough. In downtown Brooklyn, you got this all-black crew, the Bombers, the Bailers, Da Boyz—they change their name every week. Good, but scary. They do a ton of blow."

"Where are they getting blow?" Ty asked.

"I have no idea. In Astoria there's a crew called Chloroform, and in Long Island City, the Kamikazes. Okay, you know the Carrion Crew, and the Martyrs in midtown. There's also the Plug Uglies—they kind of work Flatiron and Stuy Town, maybe up to Murray Hill. There's the Fashionably Dead on the Upper East Side… Hell's Cooks, Hell's Kitchen… and there's some crew—I don't know the name—working west of Central Park. In Chelsea, working down through the Meatpacking District, is the crew called—of course—the Meatpackers. The Model Citizens in Soho, and the Converts and the Pink Stallions in the West Village. That's an all-gay crew, and they're growing so fast they'll probably expand south. Oh, and in Chinatown... see if I can remember... Joi Gin— 'So Long'—Kiu Chau Tin—'Autumn Bridge'—and Sei Dei Ha Tit—'Number 4 Underground,' or 'Subway 4,' depending on whether you take the metaphorical or literal translation."

"Fuck, yeah," said Bernie. "Now we're talking."

"That's good," Tim said. "It gives us a place to start."

"We've got to start dealing with the rat problem," Marlin said. "I got crews going out with fucking bug bombs."

"Tell me what you want," Miles said. "I'll see what I can do. Give me a hit off that."

"What about gas?" Bernie asked, a cup of coffee in one hand and a Krispy Kreme in the other. "It's starting to get scary—half the gas stations I used to hit have run dry, there's nothing coming in, and if I have to send my guys the fuck out to Long Island to get gas it sort of defeats the purpose."

"I can get us gas," said Miles, holding the pot smoke in his lungs and passing the joint back to Marlin, "but it'll take money. I mean, I can get a tanker in from Philly or something, I'm sure, but it's gonna take bucks. You can't barter with people outside the epidemic."

"Don't worry about money," Tim offered enigmatically. "I know plenty of guys who won't mind if we borrow a little."

"Not in a position to spend it, huh?" Bernie said, and Tim laughed, his face becoming flushed.

"Anyone need coffee?" Neil asked.

"I'll take a cup," Tim said.

"All we really need is a credit card," said Miles. "One with like, no limit? Give me the go-ahead and I'll start making calls."

"And what about body bags?"

"Marlin, that's gonna be tough."

Ty gave me a slap on the shoulder on his way out to meet his crew. I followed him out, grabbing Phil, and saw Luz and Chico peering in at the brain power through the service window, squinting in the bright sun.

"Leave them to it," I said. "We'll check back later."

"You don't need to stick around?" asked Luz.

"No, I think they're good."

She wasn't buying it. "What happened to 'Don't trust anything you can't see?'"

"But can't you see it?" I asked. "This is what I was talking about all along. I didn't want to work for a faceless government agency that might be pulling strings, or some assholes who can't cop to the disgrace of our suicidal population—but I'm all for organization. I just want to know who I'm working for, and that they want what I want."

"So you trust this broker, Tim?" Luz asked.

"Luz. The guy's crashing in a shitty Billburg apartment, and he's got a house in Westchester. He was up all night last night working. He could go home, but he's here. What else is there?"

"Yeah," Chico said. "He coulda jumped like the rest of 'em."

"And look at that brain power. Tim and Bernie could turn this whole thing around—and now they got Miles, too. I don't have a head for that kind of systemization. It's all I can do to keep my own shit straight."

Luz smiled at me. "You're better than you think."

Tim had a mind for organization and was a master of negotiation. He could see the big picture and pursued it with a vengeance, taking over planning of all operations. He scheduled Bernie's remains pickups, allowing Bernie to focus on maintaining a reliable fleet of drivers. Miles fielded requisitions from crew members and coordinated product procurement and distribution. Bernie got Miles a truck, and Miles brought in a crew of his own and shuttled goods from one part of town to another, moving supply to demand, bringing in Bernie's team when necessary.

Ty, in addition to running his own crew, took charge of recruitment and periodically took easy routes with new recruits, running exercises on basic methods of remains disposal, B&E technique, and small-arms training. Marlin was in charge of all medical emergencies, and stepped up his game, teaching crew members basic first aid and stockpiling supplies in the back of Neil's place.

Tim syndicated almost everything. He had sit-downs with the leaders of other crews, and formally paired resources and abilities. Maps were broken out and lines were drawn, and questions of turf were clarified, with primary responsibility for all crucial areas of Manhattan and Brooklyn assigned to a crew based on tradition and proximity.

Tim gained control of every major crematory in the tristate region. Between that coup, greater efficiency of transportation, and vastly greater efficiency of infantry, the removal, cremation and interment of remains began to operate like a well-oiled machine.

The superstructure helped; we had the information we needed, and if we got in trouble we knew whom to call. Miles got us all Nextels, so if we needed help in a hurry we were instantly in touch with any of Los Hombres. And by flipping to another channel, we were in touch with other crews.

Phil, at Tim's urging, recruited a typing pool of stay-at-home survivors, and rapidly established a network—conducting his communications via e-mail—of data-entry specialists who compiled the vast accumulation of field notes from Phil and other crew bookkeepers. They constructed an interactive database that catalogued everything we knew of the Bug and its havoc. All our information on victims was put into cyberspace and stored on servers in other cities.

The weather was balmier than ever, and Marlin held open-air classes in the garden at Season's, the restaurant across the street from Neil's where Jamie used to work. Marlin strutted in front of a dry-erase board, wearing a lab coat with pockets stuffed with ready-rolled joints, one of them always burning in his hand, gesturing to the board with chaotic swirls of sweet smoke.

"The first thing after you die is your body temperature starts to drop. After a couple days, the temperature goes back up, due to metabolic activity of bacteria—but I'll get to that. First, rigor mortis. Once the body is dead, the muscle cells can only work anaerobically, and the breakdown in glycogen leads to irreversibly high levels of lactic acid. Actin and myosin fuse to form a gel—you get rigor mortis. As the weather continues to warm we may see rigor mortis setting in a little quicker, but as a general rule of thumb, a warm body that is not stiff has not been dead for more than three hours. A warm, stiff body is probably under eight hours dead, and a cold, stiff body is between eight and thirty-six hours dead. After about thirty-six hours rigor mortis will pass, and my advice is, if you find a stiff body, come back the next day, 'coz those fuckers are hard to move.

"After death, the internal organisms in the intestine start getting busy, especially our friend *Escherischia coli*. Gas formation will eventually bring about the rupture of the intestines and the decomposition will spread rapidly. Initially, as bacteria, protozoa, and nematodes in the body go to work, the cadaver will still appear fresh. In the putrefaction stage, the cadaver is swollen by internal gasses, which will almost certainly be accompanied by the odor of decaying flesh.

Then, the flesh takes on a creamy consistency, with exposed parts turning black—this is called black putrefaction. The gas escapes, the body collapses, and the odor gets really strong. At the butyric fermentation stage, the cadaver starts to dry out, and you get a ripe, cheesy odor, with the ventral surface becoming moldy from fermentation. This is some nasty shit. Then you get dry decay, which I doubt many of you will be lucky enough to witness since most of our problems are relatively fresh kills. Dry decay may be hard to look at, emotionally, but the cadaver is now almost dry and easy to carry, 'coz the hardest thing about moving a body is that it holds ten gallons of water.

"Enough about cellular death. I want to talk about somatic death, and this is upsetting. Somatic death is when an individual is no longer considered a unit of society, because he is irreversibly unconscious, unaware of himself and impenetrable to the world at large. For our purposes, you must consider any person who has so much as attempted suicide to be somatically dead. They are no longer units of society. You are hereby given license to speed them on their way to cellular death, and advised to do so lest they show you the way.

"The *only* reliable method of stopping a walking corpse is to decrease the functioning capability of the central nervous system, and by that I mean the brain and spinal column. There are two ways to do this: direct trauma to the central nervous system, resulting in immediate tissue destruction, or lack of oxygen to the brain. For an average male, say, a hundred-fifty pounds, the cardiac output is around a gallon and a half a minute. You got to figure on serious stress, making his heart beat faster, so when you shoot him his aortic flow could almost double. Now, adequate blood pressure can be maintained with minimal symptoms until the body has lost twenty percent of its blood, so, even if you totally sever his thoracic aorta, which isn't likely, it'll take a minimum of four-point-six seconds before this guy suffers any ill effects. And if you don't think four-point-six seconds is very long, just ask Ty how long it took to lose one of his crew members when that maniac on Meserole started shooting off his Saturday night special. The moral of this story, kids, is aim for the fucking head."

I wasn't there, but the way Jack told it, he, Miles, and Marlin walked into St. Vincent's like they owned it, went straight to the pharmacy and stocked up. No one bothered them, and Jack, who was packing despite my admonitions, never had to take his gun out of his pants. When they came back to Neil's they were toting tackle boxes—the crappy plastic kind you get at ninety-nine-cent stores—full of pills. Marlin dosed Jack up on amoxicillin, his RBF symptoms went away in just a few days, and we all stopped worrying about rabies.

Miles came to the meeting one morning with a Hefty bag full of different boxes all depicting rats on the front. "These are just samples," he said, handing them to Marlin. "I can get tons."

"We'll need tons," Marlin said. "I want every crew in the city with a pocketful of pellets, dropping them everywhere they go. Let's see here…" reading off the active ingredients, "Warfarin, pindone, chlorophacinone… these are all crap. First-generation anticoagulants. Our rats will be resistant."

"Anti- what?" Jack asked.

"Most rat poisons kill by causing internal bleeding. The bad news is that even after they take a fatal dose it takes a few days for them to die. Hang on. Brodifacoum. This is the shit, right here. Miles, get a ton of this, in pellets and wax blocks."

"You got it."

"And some of this, too," he said, squinting through his smoke at another box. "Bromadiolone, a couple other agents… yeah, get some. Not as potent, but it says you can prepare a liquid solution." He opened the box and dipped his fingers into the fine red powder. "Yeah. I want to spike their water source."

The Cripplebush crew dosed the rat house, which seemed to make Luz feel a little better, and we all started carrying rat poison around with us everywhere we went. We killed a lot of rats, but we still couldn't catch up. There were too many dead bodies and not nearly enough live ones.

THE TURN

It happened quickly, when it happened, the way most things do—the turning point that puts you over the edge. When asked to tell the story later, you tell it too quickly, condensing it to an anecdote, anxious to get to the good part.

I can't remember when it was, exactly, buried under a constant barrage of rigor mortis, maggots, and the omnipresence of aching feet. I was with my core crew, Phil and Jack and Chico and Luz, working one of those blocks over by Hoag's old place—Devoe, maybe, or Ainslie, maybe near Leonard. I remember walking by that crazy Italian house with the Virgin Mary standing guard behind glass. It was a hot day. Luz wore a sports bra, and I gave her a hard time about flaunting her tits and Chico told me to shut up. Maybe they were already together and I hadn't noticed. I was in a good mood, and kept grinning at Phil, and he wouldn't speak but smiled back. I could almost forget that we were piling dead bodies into the back of a pickup truck.

Phil went through the pockets of the corpses, plucking IDs and scribbling in his black book. Jack took a survey of the buildings, double-checking, and every few minutes he stuck his head out of a different building and yelled "Clear." A civilian had called in some old kills on the block, street remains, but other than those we hadn't found any new bodies all day.

The air crackled with a stutter, the sputtering retort of a car trying to start. Phil and I dropped a corpse and looked around. Chico stood in the bed of the truck and had the elevation. "*Sss!*" he hissed, pointing down the street. Luz followed his gaze, moved behind the line of parked cars, and crept down the street, knife in hand.

There it was again—the unmistakable chug of an engine trying, and failing, to turn over. "*La roja, la izquierda,*" Chico said, barely raising his voice but perfectly audible on the empty street. My boots tapped briskly down the asphalt and Phil took the sidewalk.

As I got closer, I saw him, a twenty-something with a mop of brown hair, bent over the steering wheel of a red Honda. In any other town, at any other time, this would be nothing to notice, but I assumed he was trying to choke himself out. I was almost there when Jack popped his head out, and because Jack never talked when he could yell, his voice cut the block like a jackhammer.

"Yo—it's *cleeeean!*" he hollered, and we all pounced.

The kid heard the shout and looked up. The first thing he saw was Phil walking up the hood of his car, gun leveled at him through the windshield. I threw the driver's-side door open and pulled him out as Luz came around from the back of the car, and as I pushed him against it, Luz put her knife to his throat. Phil stepped off the hood, barrel still focused.

"Whoa—what the—" he sputtered, but I cut him off.

"You offing yourself?"

"What?"

"You offing yourself?" My voice could be heard in Ridgewood.

The kid's eyes were wide, flicking from my angry eyes, to Luz, with a knife, to Phil, terrifyingly silent and holding a gun. He had the easiest out imaginable; one flinch, he was done. But he didn't move, just gaped, panting. He looked like he was going to piss himself.

Luz took the knife from his throat and I eased off him. Phil kept his weapon on him but stepped back, and waved to Chico—coming up behind us, pistol drawn—to stand down.

"Relax, man," I said. "Try to catch your breath."

"Holy shit." The kid sat down into his driver's seat, shaking. "You scared the fuck out of me."

Luz moved in and touched his knee, speaking softly with her husky voice. "You weren't trying to kill yourself?"

"No," he said. "I'm just trying to start my car."

"Sorry," she said. "We didn't mean to scare you, but we always fear the worst."

"'S okay. I guess you would."

Phil put the gun down, took out his black book and snapped his fingers at me.

"Can we see your ID?" I asked.

The kid took out his wallet and I handed it to Phil to take it all down.

"Have you guys been here this whole time?" he asked.

Luz gave me a look. "We have. How long have you been gone?"

He scratched his head. "Five months."

"I think you flooded it," Chico said, reaching into the car and popping the hood. "And your gas is turning to varnish." He opened the hood, leaned in and took a deep sniff. "Old gas. You should let it rest, get some fresh gas and try again."

"I'm surprised the battery's still good," I said.

"It wasn't," the kid said. "I walked all the way to Sunnyside looking for someone to sell me a new one."

That cracked Chico up.

Jack, Phil, and I finished the block. Luz sat with the kid,

calming his nerves and hearing his story—he'd gone home to his parents' house in the Midwest when it started getting bad.

Chico got a gas can and a siphon out of our truck, siphoned off a gallon or so and poured it into the Honda. It started with some difficulty, and Chico kept it running while he took off the air filter and beat the dust out of it. I called Bernie, and he said he'd send someone over with a second driver to pick up our loaded truck, and we walked off to the next gig. The kid waved to us, smiling, climbing the stoop to his apartment. His address was written in bold black ink in Phil's book, next to the first entry of its kind, in block letters: "RETURNED."

We were all lost in our own thoughts as we rounded the corner. "Chico," I asked, "What did you do with the keys to the truck?"

"I left them in the ignition for the driver. Where else?"

Luz got my drift. "Guess we're going to have to stop doing that."

"People are coming home," I said.

"No doubt," Jack said. "Our bad old city is coming back!"

"It's like after a hurricane evacuation," Luz said. "People go back, see what the damage is. Start over."

"Maybe it's over," Chico offered carefully.

"Our city's coming back!" Jack shouted. "We're back, baby!"

Luz laughed and cheered, Chico laughed, and Phil and I exchanged a guarded look. It was great news; it was our first return. It felt like a quiet revolution. But I wasn't convinced we'd seen the last of the Bug.

JACKED

"When I was a kid," I said, "we used to argue about whether or not Batman could beat up Superman."

Los Hombres had finished for the day, and after our newbies had scattered and Chico and Luz had wandered off, Jack and I, with nothing better to do, caught up with the Cripplebush Criers and helped them out for a couple hours just to have an excuse to end the day with Ty and get invited over for happy hour. Ty had taken over the apartment across the hall from his and set up quite a bar, stocked with every conceivable liquor, thanks to Miles. Ty still made the best cocktails in town.

"Easy," Jack said. "The Dark Knight could kick the shit outa Superman."

"But that's just it, right?" Ty asked, grinning mischievously and raising his eyebrows. We were walking up Lorimer, deep down by Scholes, and the streets were so quiet Ty's husky voice seemed to fill them with an authoritative awe. "You want to believe that Batman can beat up Superman, because Batman's this badass everyman, just like you or me, only tougher, and Superman is this fucking alien pansy who's only a big deal 'coz our gravity doesn't affect him."

"Yeah," I said. "Superman's always fighting interstellar villains and creeps from other dimensions."

"Who cares about them?" Jack asked.

"Exactly." Ty said. "Batman's always taking out common thugs and corporate villains—the kind of guys normal people really worry about and would love to smack around. He's like this avenging angel of darkness that swoops in and saves your butt."

"And he, like, knows every kind of martial arts and has, like, traveled all over the world and shit learning how to be the baddest badass ever," Jack said, getting worked up.

"Right," Ty agreed. "That's just it. We all believe that if we had Bruce Wayne's money, we could be as badass as Batman."

"—have a Batmobile and all them cool toys, yo."

"That's why Batman's cool and Superman is fucking lame."

"I'm with you, Ty," I said. "I mean, if Superman were worth a shit, don't you think he'd've bagged Lois by now?"

Jack started laughing but Ty cut him off.

"But I'm afraid, my friend, that Batman could not beat up Superman."

"Why not?"

"Because Superman lives in Metropolis, man, Batman's right here in Gotham."

"Man, fuck you…"

I laughed, but I stopped short when a scream pealed through the stillness. A woman struggled in the third-story window of a building across the street. Trying to get out onto the fire escape, she managed to get her head out the window before being violently jerked back inside, and as her head bobbed frantically, we saw a man brandishing a large kitchen knife, flashing a Jack Nicholson sneer. He threw her away from the window and disappeared from view, and that's when we noticed the hungry orange flames licking the inside of the building through the windows of the first floor.

Jack was off at a run before I had a chance to think. He grabbed a garbage can on the street and overturned it, sending two overweight rats scurrying for cover, and shoved it underneath the fire escape, using it to hop up and grab the bottom rung of the ladder.

"Stay put," I said to Ty, "cover us," and I followed Jack's lead up the fire escape to the second floor and stopped, seeing Jack's legs disappear into the window above me. I wanted to meet him on the other side, and kicked in the window facing me and climbed headfirst into a musty apartment that reeked of death. I picked myself up off the floor and bumped my head on the leg of a corpse hanging by its neck from the curtain rod. I ran through the apartment, already beginning to fill with smoke, and found the door. It opened onto a stairwell raging with flames.

I heard the woman screaming "*Fuego!*" as I ran up to the third floor, rattling in rapid-fire Puerto Rican Spanish something about "He's trying to kill me" and "He's crazy." The door was locked; I tried to force it but the hallway was too narrow to get a running start. Then I heard the deadbolt snap to, and the door blew open, and I was face to face with the hysterical woman for a silent instant before her head jerked back, the man with the Bug tugging at her hair. Jack was picking himself off the floor with his lip busted open, and he grabbed the man from behind as I pulled the woman out of his grasp. The man had lost his knife already, and Jack held him fast by the chin and began to deliver one rabbit punch after another.

The woman tried to get past me and out the open door, but I held her back and slammed the door shut with my foot, saying, "*No posible, fuego,*" and moved her toward the front window. She resisted and clawed at me, jabbering and terrified, and I dealt her a light, quick slap to the face and grabbed her wrist and pointed. "*Ventana,*" I spat, and with a little shove was able to get her safely out onto the fire escape. I jumped up into the window after her and squatted on the sill, my left arm stretched out to the side for support. Jack had gotten the man down and sat atop him, pasting him in earnest. "Jack, come on, fuck him," I said, just as Jack's eyes widened in horror. Jack's hands reached for his belt, and the man stood up from under him and pointed Jack's Glock at me and squeezed off a round.

My arm left the window casing by no will of my own, and I lost my balance and fell backwards off the sill and onto the fire escape. If the steel slats hurt my back on impact I didn't notice; my arm was on fire and I could barely breathe from the shock. From that moment on, time seemed to crawl, painstakingly pacing itself out in moments that were agonizingly long, as if the pain racing through my body were echoing through the space-time continuum itself, and every moment became as excruciating to endure as the last.

The woman screamed beneath me. Ty yelled "Benson!" at the top of his lungs, and in my mind, I said, *Yeah?* but no words came out of my mouth. I looked up at an electric-blue sky. I heard another shot from Jack's gun, and then a whizzing and a muffled squish, followed by the thump of a body hitting the hardwood floor. I felt the fire escape wheeze, pulled to one side by the weight of a large body climbing up. I heard a scraping of fingernails on the windowsill, and the leering face appeared above me, framed perfectly, wearing a look of absolute abandon. I saw the gun in his hand and tried to turn my head, and then I felt the fire escape sway, and was deafened by a shot, my face suddenly scalded by a sprinkling of white-hot pins as a hole appeared just above the man's right eyebrow. I knew then that it was Ty's fault that a corpse was falling on top of me and drenching me in blood.

I felt the deep groan of the building itself as the hardwood floor of the second level gave way with a splintering crack, and I knew that I had to get up.

I couldn't tell how much blood was mine. I crawled back inside and found Jack lying on the floor, laboring with raspy breath in a room filling with smoke. I told him if he didn't get up he was going to burn to death, and he said that he was already dead, the motto of Los Hombres. "I'll kill you again if you don't get up," I said, and I helped him to his feet and got him as far as the window. Ty pulled Jack out onto the fire escape and carried him down.

From my vantage point on the sidewalk I saw a crotchety old fireman struggling with a big hose with the help of Ty and a couple other living bodies I thought I recognized. Time seemed to be back to normal. I had a bandage on my arm and powder burns on my face and was in a hell of a lot of pain, but I was more worried about Jack. I got up and found him a few feet away, spread out on a blanket with Marlin hunched over him. Jack's face was contorted in a mask of pain but he seemed unable to groan. His eyes were wide when he looked up at me.

"You're fine," I said. "You got shot in the belly, and it takes a long time to die of a belly wound. Didn't you see *Reservoir Dogs*?"

Jack cracked a grin and seemed to relax for a moment before his face bent itself with another wave of pain. Marlin gave me the deadeye gaze and took a hit off a joint and handed it to me. I took a deep drag and said, "What's up, Doc?"

"He's shot through the left lung," Marlin said. "He'd make it if he were in a hospital, but this is more than I can handle in the middle of a goddamn street with a burning building behind me."

"So what are we doing here?"

"Bernie's on his way."

After a hard stare Marlin took the joint out of my hand. "I don't understand, Benson. What happened here?"

"Jack's a fucking hero," I said. "That's what happened."

All our weapons were scavenged, so who knows where Jack got his gun. It always shot a little to the right and Jack just got used to it. That idiosyncrasy had probably saved my ass. I was lucky; the bullet had gone right through my bicep without hitting any bone, passing cleanly out the other side. Jack was lucky, too. The bullet had missed his heart and he still had a chance.

Bernie drove the pickup with cool reserve, his unwavering hand on the wheel never betraying that he was close to breaking the land speed record. I was in close attendance over Jack in the camper shell; Marlin talked on the phone to an acquaintance at Woodhull, trying to secure us a table and a surgeon when we arrived. I'd never felt so lucid.

"I've got a Hispanic male, twenty-five. Bullet wound. Single entrance wound, left fifth intercostal, five inches lateral to the sternal border."

Jack seemed to be leveling out. "The girl?" he asked.

"She's with Neil," I told him. "She's fine. You saved her life, man. She'd be a flame-broiled burger right now if it weren't for you."

"Blood pressure 120 over 80, pulse 105, temperature 101.9."

"Cool," Jack said. "She was hot, right?"

I had no idea what the woman looked like. All I could remember were those frightened eyes. "Yeah." I told him. "White hot. And she's gonna wanna nail you for sure when you get out of the hospital."

"Slightly diaphoretic skin. Acute subcutaneous emphysema."

Jack's eyes sparkled with a rare light. "*Yo soy ya muerto.*"

"That's right," I said. "We're all dead already."

"No exit wound apparent, concern about possible pulmonary contusion."

"Cool to be a hero," Jack said. "Always wanted to."

"You're fuckin' Bruce Willis, yo. Twice as tough."

We made it to Woodhull, but by then Jack had slipped out of consciousness and deteriorated into what Marlin called "fine ventricular fibrillation." Marlin tried CPR, but the hospital was a mess and we couldn't get a fucking table. I'd never seen Marlin cry before and I had to take the joint out of his hand.

Ty didn't want to see anyone, and I couldn't blame him. He was such a gent, cordial to a fault, that he apologized to me for not wanting to have a drink, his face red with tears. I kept thinking that if it weren't for the Bug, he and Jack would never have met. Maybe if Jack had gotten a dishwashing job at a bar Ty was tending, sure, they might have shared a snide comment after hours. But in a pre-Bug Brooklyn, it would be hard to imagine two such different guys becoming so tight, sitting up together night after night arguing about cocktail recipes and what superhero was the baddest ass.

I had my arm in a sling when I pounded on Luz's door.

"Benson? That you?"

"Yeah."

"I'm sleeping. Can it wait?"

"Let me in, Luz. I know you're naked and I know Chico's there and I gotta talk to you both.

Luz cracked the door and peeked out.

"Jack's fuckin' dead."

The door flew open, and Luz was indeed naked and so was Chico, who had opened the door. "The fuck you mean, *amigo*?"

Luz made tea in her robe and Chico sat across from me in his boxers and we all chain-smoked. Chico took it the worst. The more the news settled into him the more he seemed to turn to putty.

"Main," he said, weeping uncontrollably, "maybe we should all fuckin' follow him."

I jumped out of my chair and grabbed him by the throat and jacked him up against the wall, screaming, "Jack's not dead because he offed himself, motherfucker! He's not part of the problem. He fucking died trying to save an innocent, damn it, and if you want to die—" I took my gat out and shoved it up under his chin with my free hand "—if you want

223

to die, my man, just say the fucking word and I'll do it for you. 'Coz I'd hate to lose you, but I'll be goddamned if I'm gonna lose you to the Bug."

Luz had to take the gun away from me.

Jack had been with us from the beginning and his exit hit everyone hard. We made an exception.

On Broadway, where Wall Street begins, stands Trinity Church, the Gothic Revival building that was finished in 1846. It's actually the third Trinity Church on that site; the first was destroyed by fire in 1776 when the British decimated lower Manhattan, the second was structurally compromised by heavy snows and torn down before it was finished. South of the church is a cemetery with a statue of John Watts and the grave of Alexander Hamilton. To the north, at the intersection of Broadway and Pine, is a big stone gazebo-like monument with an inscription reading, "Sacred to the memory of those brave and good men who died whilst imprisoned in this city for their devotion to the cause of American Independence."

In the narrow strip of grass between this monument and the sidewalk of Broadway, we buried Jack's remains under a marble gravestone reading, "Juan Javier Marquez, 1975–2000, Valiant Hero of the Second Civil War. Peace."

GLOBAL

I never wanted to be on TV. We had just finished a big push with the Carrion Crew, a five-day marathon of humping remains that almost ruined us and ultimately resulted in the deaths of two Carrion members.

Miles had been doing a few B&E's on his own. I'm sure he had less-than-honorable motives, but regardless of the circumstances, he discovered a midtown apartment building top to bottom with remains. He tried to hand the job off to the

Martyrs, but the Martyrs countered with a building of their own—an equally messy situation in a yuppie complex on Orchard, one of those old tenement buildings that had been renoed into expensive studios, and was now eight floors of remains with so many hangings that negotiating it was like spelunking through stalactites. Los Hombres and the Carrion Crew spent most of the week cleaning that place out, and then we moved up to midtown to help the Martyrs, who still weren't finished with their vertical graveyard. It was bad news from the get-go: no elevators in either building, a clusterfuck of humping down narrow winding stairways, wrestling with remains in Hefty bags since coroner-issue body bags were still so scarce. Halfway down a stairwell a corpse would slip, or someone's fingers would dig through the soft, mushy flesh, and the bag would rip apart and cover us with gore. We'd spend extra time getting the pieces together and then take a break to brush off maggots and lean out the window to puke.

On the last day, we were in a stairwell, about six of us, struggling with a 250-pounder, and a tall skinny white boy from the Carrion Crew snapped in half, screaming, "Fuck it! Fuck it!" Of course the guy had a gun, and instead of just catching the bus and leaving us out of it, he tried to take the rest of us out first. He popped a cap into one of his own crew—a wiry Latino who clapped his hands to his chest and fell to the floor without so much as a death rattle—and was drawing a bead on Alexis when Chico shot him in the neck. The guy stood his ground for a moment with a fountain of blood shooting out from under his chin. Chico put another round in his torso and Alexis kicked him in the chest, and he flipped backwards out the window and fell six stories. Alexis spat on the floor and walked downstairs to retrieve the gun that had gone out the window with him. No one spoke. We had an extra corpse to carry.

Then Chico looked at me warily and said, "*Tranquilo, jefe, por favor,*" and it broke the tension and we all laughed. Right after Jack's death, we were ambushed by a Bug victim with a shotgun who was holed up in a room full of corpses. A green-horn on our crew almost caught a bellyful of buckshot, but got out of the way when I hollered after hearing the pump from behind the door. Sheetrock went flying with the blast and I stepped into the room, saw the man with his wild eyes, shot him in the head and said, "No one else dies on my crew," shot him in the head and said, "No one else dies on my crew," shot him in the head and said… until I felt Luz's warm hand on the back of my neck and her soothing voice say, "It's all right, Benson. He's not getting up." Since then, Chico'd been busting my balls.

When the midtown building was clean, we decided to take the next day off and do a little partying. We'd salvaged enough alcohol from the two buildings to start our own speakeasy, so we gathered at a Martyrs safe house up above Union Square—slightly out of their jurisdiction, but Union Square was still a bit of a free-for-all. As the crews drifted in they were all buzzing about the president and the National Guard and the news vans outside. We clicked on the TV.

President Clinton was at a press conference, all flashing bulbs and the bobbing heads of the press.

"…concerning the recent state of emergency in New York City, I vow to do everything in my power to bring a stop to this crisis. The National Guard has been dispatched to put a stop to this alarming trend, and the Red Cross is in the process of establishing a presence to console survivors and to evacuate where necessary."

"Gee, thanks a lot," said Alexis. "Right on time."

The big black kid who headed up the Carrion Crew sang,

"Go Billy, go Billy, getcha groove on…."

"I want to assure the American public, and the citizens of the world, that the New York Stock Exchange will not, repeat, will not close its doors. We have a crisis on our hands but we will not allow it to affect the global economy. There is no immediate cause for alarm. We are working on the problem and doing everything in our power to resolve it."

On Wall Street, when I joked about the brokers jumping and crashing the markets, I was more right than I knew. Tim and Marlin were both installed in the building in front of mine, and we often sat out in the courtyard at night telling stories and getting drunk. Tim painstakingly explained to us the inner workings of Wall Street, and he called the epidemic a "global catastrophe."

Forget the NASDAQ and forget the recent explosion of e-trading. The New York Stock Exchange was founded on the concept of human interaction and negotiation, and the old school boys' club nature of the operation isn't the only reason the Exchange persists, two hundred years after that first meeting under the buttonwood tree.

The brokers hustle from the clerks at the booths to the trading posts and back, getting put up and picking up the yellow phones to call in to desk traders taking orders from clients. The vast majority of the trading on the floor is moved in large quantities by clients who are themselves large industrial corporations, and all these transactions ultimately take place at a trading station between the broker and the specialist. The brokers and the specialists make money off of each transaction, and the clients make money or lose money depending on whether they sell higher than they buy. It's simple economics: supply and demand. But the brokers and the specialists can never be replaced by computers. A broker with an order to buy a large number of shares can buy half now and the rest later, always shopping for the best price, and the specialist oversees the auction process, insuring fair trading and making markets.

Everyone's objective is to keep the market moving. Because whether the trade is a DOT or a GTC, a round lot or an odd lot, whether the bid is three teenies or the offer is seven, whether the specialist acts as an agent or the principle, whether the order is market or limit, whether the client ever gets the look or even understands the lingo, the only hard-and-fast rule is to make money—and in order to make money, money must change hands.

The New York Stock Exchange trading floor sees in excess of two hundred million shares traded a day, with ten thousand institutions investing in three thousand listed stocks—literally billions of dollars changing hands five days a week, thanks to the 1,366 seats of brokers and specialists, and an army of clerks and desk traders pushing money around, which may not make the world go around, but it is the sheer movement of money from one human hand to another that is the backbone of capitalism, which is the backbone of America, which, like it or not, is the backbone of our planet, especially in economic terms, which can have dire political consequences.

When Tim called the epidemic a global catastrophe, he meant that the world as we know it sets its watch by the activities that take place behind the blue line of the Exchange. The sudden lack of living brokers, living clerks—living anyone—had finally brought the problem that began as an ignored, isolated outbreak to the vanguard of the world's concern.

On TV, the president took questions from the press.

"What is the current death toll?"

"I can't answer that at this time. Those statistics are not in yet."

"Is this going to affect international flights routed through JFK?"

"That remains to be seen."

"Mr. President, are you aware that this phenomenon has been going on for months?"

Everyone in the room leaned forward.

"That is a vicious and fallacious rumor. I'm certain that all pertinent information has been brought to my attention in a timely manner."

We all started yelling.

"Mr. President, my sources—"

Clinton stepped aside and an aide took the microphone. "I'm afraid we're out of time. No further questions." The reporters erupted in shouts, and in our safe house, the shouts were louder and accompanied by peanuts and beer cans thrown at the screen.

"Asshole!"

"Fucking liar!"

"What are we, just Jews and niggers?"

"Eight months!" I screamed. "The first suicide in Billburg was *eight months* ago, you dumb fuck philistine!"

We had all finally calmed down with the resolve of getting shitfaced when a boot kicked in the front door, introducing us to the business end of an M-16. It was a National Guard yahoo. "All right, everybody out." Just as we had, the Guard was starting in Union Square.

"What the hell for?" I was half drunk and really pissed. One of those hilarious claymation iced-tea ads was on and this meathead was spoiling my buzz.

"We're evacuating this building."

"There's no one here to evacuate."

"We have reason to believe there are dead bodies here, and we're evacuating everybody so we can clear the building."

Alexis stepped up before I could speak, pulling out her black book and flipping pages. Alexis keeps her own books. "No… no… the Martinez family on the fifth floor… and John and Jeff are still on the third. Other than that we're the only people in the building. We cleared remains out of the ninth floor, the sixth, this floor, and the ground floor. All the other apartments are EPD."

"EPD?"

"Empty, Presumed Deserted."

The Army man blinked.

"Listen, pal," I said. "We're the ones who have been swimming in dead bodies while you were out protecting the president from his sex scandal. You're higher than I am if you think we're evacuating."

Alexis countered. "And the Martinezes have seen enough heartache already—if you kick their door in you'll hear about it from me."

He thought about it for a moment, I'll give him that much. His orangutan brain was doing loop-the-loops: orders, free will, orders, free will. Orders won out and he leveled his M-16 at me.

"I'm afraid I have to ask you to leave."

I stared him down, listening to the irritating hum of a car commercial. Phil had been at the table just inside the door, cleaning my gun for me, so innocuous and invisible it was no wonder the soldier walked by without noticing him. Phil stood up behind the armed man and leveled my .45 at the back of his head, only inches away, and calmly slid the clip into place with a click.

"I'm afraid we can't do that," I said. "It's our day off."

The soldier stood his ground and stammered, "Listen, I don't want any trouble—"

Phil slammed the bolt back. "You've fucking got trouble,"

I said. "What, is this not Hollywood enough for you? You want me to give you some Sly Stallone ultimatum? You're already dead. Welcome to New York. We're all dead, just waitin' to get buried. Now drop your prop and go back out the way you came in, or we'll put your remains in a Hefty bag and carry you down the stairs. Which would really piss me off because that's what we've been doing for the last five fucking days."

Alexis pulled her new piece out of her pants and rested it casually on her hip, and Chico fidgeted with his nine and grinned. The Carrion Crew chief, who was just a big sweetheart but looked intimidating as hell, put his foot on the couch and drew an eight-inch blade from a boot sheath and languidly picked at his nails, which I thought was a real nice touch. The guard lowered his weapon and backed out of the room.

"Damn," Chico said when he was gone, "I wanted that *gun*. Why didn't you get it?"

"Can't carry remains with that giant thing in your hands." I turned to Alexis. "We're not getting the day off, are we?"

"I don't think so."

We cruised Union Square en masse and consulted with other crews and civilian spectators alike. The mayor was to give a speech and the press shot background footage, but for the most part they didn't want to see anything messy so they were going to keep it short.

"Thousands die in Sarajevo and we can't get enough footage," Alexis said. "It happens in America and the public doesn't want to see it."

We sat back on the stoop and Chico rolled a joint, and we watched the media run around like ants under a magnifying glass. Every time they got the reporter and the camera set up, a rat would sneak into the shot and the reporter would lose her nerve. Then it was announced that Giuliani had bailed, and would make only a televised statement from indoors.

"We certainly wouldn't want anybody to rob his prostate of the privilege of killing him," Luz said.

"He's been a pain in everybody else's ass for so long...."

"Like he's really got cancer. We all know why he pulled out of the Senate race. If Hillary ever set foot in this town she'd pull out too."

A pimply-faced kid with a press badge walked up to us with clear trepidation. "Are you guys part of the cleanup crew?" I was about to say something cruel when Alexis, always the polite one, spoke up.

"What is it?"

"We'd like someone from the local cleanup effort to make a statement."

"A statement?"

"Yessir. About what's going on here."

The Carrion Crew chief whistled and drew the edge of his hand across his throat, making a sound like a seam ripping. The gang cracked up.

"That's a pretty good summation of what's going on here," I said. The kid wrinkled his eyes and shifted his weight nervously, slinking away.

"Benson," Alexis said. "No one wants to talk about this. Even Giuliani's trying to hide from this one, and he usually grabs the spotlight no matter how embarrassing the issue. This isn't a national emergency so much as a national disgrace."

"So what?"

"So someone should talk. Just so we have a chance at being heard."

Chico started a slow chant. "*Benson... Benson... Benson,*" and was joined by the rest of the gang.

"Damnit, Lex, I thought you were sweet on me. Why you

wanna put me through this shit?"

She kissed me on the cheek. "Because you're the best."

"...and I'm on the scene in Union Square, talking to Benson Lee, a grassroots activist who has dedicated himself to cleaning up the mess here in New York City. Benson, what can you tell us about your campaign?"

"It's not a campaign, ma'am. There's no goal in sight and no chance for personal gain. We're just trying to do what we can to survive."

"You said 'we.' Who else is involved in this endeavor?"

"There are a number of crews like mine, all over the city."

"Some people are calling you gangs. Is this true? I notice you all have your heads shaved."

"We spend our days with dead bodies, ma'am. You can't get that smell out of your hair."

That got her, and she didn't say anything.

"Listen," I said, "I saw the address Clinton gave today, and I just want to say that he's all kinds of wrong. The Bug started in Williamsburg eight months ago, and it's been spreading ever since. The press wouldn't cover it and Giuliani wouldn't acknowledge it officially, so we've been on our own. The only reason we're getting attention now is because the world is worried about their stocks, and the National Guard is just getting in the way. So please, air this message." I looked directly into the camera with the calm, dead look of Clint Eastwood at a high-noon shoot-out. "We need help. The death toll is in the millions and it's a big fucking mess."

I didn't know it was a live broadcast.

We called it a wash and scattered to parts of the city not yet infested by the National Lard. Alexis and I ended up in Queens, sweating and writhing, naked like snakes. Lying in bed, many hours later, she said that if I had kept my mouth clean I might have gotten to say more. I told her there simply wasn't a clean way to put it.

HELP

"And no sirens."

"Why not?"

"They're like a siren's song. Anyone with the Bug will run into the street. You turn on your siren and you'll be making new corpses. Besides, there isn't enough traffic anymore to warrant them, and there's no hurry."

"But if someone isn't dead yet—"

"You kill them."

"Excuse me?"

"Once someone has tried to kill himself, there's nothing you can do. They'll try again first chance they get. There's no cure for the Bug. Anyone with a self-inflicted wound should be shot on sight."

The Red Cross guy blanched at this one. We were at a folding table in a tent in Tompkins Square Park. They called it a debriefing. He had already spoken with Tim, Bernie, and Marlin, but insisted on talking with me because of my televised statement and the number of times the other guys had dropped my name.

"You've... killed people?"

"I've finished off remains. Once a person gets the Bug, all rights to personhood are lost."

"Mr. Lee." He took a deep breath. "What is 'the Bug?'"

"Fuck if I know. All I know is that it's irreversible. Some sneaky psychological trigger that induces suicide. A momentary loss of rational thought, an abandonment of realistic emotional reactions to the basic existential dilemma. You can see it in someone's eyes when they get the Bug. You can pinpoint the exact moment when it overtakes them. It's like—

it's like Bang-utot."

"I'm not familiar with—"

"When someone has a dream that they die, and they really die. If you don't wake up in time, you're dead."

"But suicide is a conscious choice."

"These people aren't aware of what they're doing. It's as if their soul flies right out the top of their head, and the body rushes out to destroy itself as quickly as possible. They're already gone. Why do you think all the suicides are so half-ass? It's the first available thing… no planning, no premeditation. If you happen to be in the subway, you lick the third rail. If you're at home, you drink Clorox. If you're on the street, you jump in front of a car. These aren't normal suicides. This is the Bug, and once you get it you'll take the first available exit—whatever can conceivably be used as a killing device."

"But what causes it?"

"I don't know. I don't know if it's the power of suggestion, or if it really is some kind of virus. There hasn't been time to get scientific about it—and I don't think it matters. What ever caused anyone to kill themselves? It's a prime directive, it's buried in our genetic makeup, preprogrammed cell death." I threw up my hands. "I don't have any answers for you, man. Ask the lemmings."

He shuffled his paperwork.

"Mr. Lee, have you always been this cold-hearted?"

I wasn't sure how to respond. The armor around me had become like a second skin; going out without it would be like leaving the house without pants. But something nagged at the back of my brain. This guy needed something from me before he would get on my side. If I could win him over we'd have resources we desperately needed at our disposal.

"I'm not. I'm already dead. My heart is broken, but I have to protect myself if I'm going to survive. You're thinking of me as a person, a civilian… some sort of regular guy. But I'm a soldier. It's war over here. You've seen this look before—you said you were in Bosnia. I've lost everyone, damn near everyone that mattered to me in this town. But there's no time for mourning. Not now. Now is for cleaning up the mess and rallying the survivors. There'll be time to cry later."

The man had seen worse. It wasn't as if we had an actual war on our hands; there were no mortar shells or air raids, and the infrastructure was essentially intact. There was nothing stopping the return to normalcy but the epidemic itself, and the Red Cross dealt with it like any other epidemic.

FEMA finally showed up, and brought in experts from every field of emergency services. They brought in administrators to oversee the reestablishment of city planning and organization. They sat Giuliani down with his few remaining bureaucrats and mobilized the survivors of the city government, appointing others to take the place of those who were dead or missing or presumed deserters. FEMA resurrected the Office of Emergency Management, and new positions were invented to deal with the rather bizarre status quo. The city was flooded with medics, firemen, and cops borrowed from other cities. Trucks came into the city again, bringing food and other essentials. Garbage men were brought in from Philly, D.C., Jersey and Connecticut to resume normal collection, since all New York's remaining garbage men had long since become full-time corpse collectors.

The National Guard became ubiquitous, acting as escorts to emergency vehicles, but Giuliani buckled under presidential pressure not to impose martial law. The New York Stock Exchange kept its doors open, and Alan Greenspan lied through his teeth and a global hysteria was deftly averted. The dollar actually gained a little strength against the pound and the yen; New Yorkers, and Americans in general, were seen as genuine badasses too stubborn to give up.

It was a census year, and the findings were staggering. The population of New York City was estimated at 5.6 million people—a third of the population could no longer be accounted for. It was a deceiving figure, as citizens who had left New York without notice were impossible to locate. Regardless, the effect of this pronouncement on the global community was heartwrenching, and aid, in the form of funds, medical supplies and food, poured in from all over America and all over the world.

Phil took a full-time job in the Disaster Accounts Division, which was a team of accountants, statisticians, and other number crunchers who worked in close association with the Disaster Legal Force and the Disaster Notification Team. The three committees studied all available information to calculate death tolls, determine legal rights to abandoned properties, and notify surviving family members. Phil's job was largely what it had been but on a larger scale—he went through IDs and other documents that we had salvaged and compiled lists of the dead.

He also cross-referenced data with information from the Disaster Housing Committee, which did reconnaissance on empty homes and tried to locate missing residents, landlords or owners, and failing to do so passed the data on to the Legal Force. A ridiculous amount of real estate became property of the state due to "no remaining survivors" or the absence of valid last wills and testaments. Giuliani, in a rare show of courage and decency, passed a bill decreeing that such property would immediately be available for occupancy with a grace period on rent. Any New York State resident, and in some cases, even immigrants from other states, could move in, rent free, until "such time as the disaster in New York City stabilizes."

The strategy here was obvious: get people back into New York. And it worked. Deserters were notified that their apartments would become state property if they did not resume occupancy, and people started coming home.

Phil worked out of his new apartment, our first safe house, where he had tacked up a sign over his computer with a quote from Josef Stalin: "One death is a tragedy. A million deaths is a statistic."

Chico, Luz, Ty, and Alexis took jobs briefing divisions of the National Guard and Army platoons, sharing whatever secrets they had gleaned. It was funny to watch, especially with Chico, this young kid with a Mexican accent cussing every other word, a gang of uniformed Army men listening attentively. Luz was well-organized and articulate, and she hadn't lost her looks; those poor soldiers listened to her with both ears and lusted after her with both eyes. New crews were formed, doing the same tasks that we had, but with greater organization in a systematic sweep of the entire city. Crews became a mixed bag of civilians and military employees, led in tandem by a National Guard official and a local. Any killing of walking remains was left to "real" soldiers, which helped the local morale immensely. Some of our better crew members were targets of military recruitment, and some of them accepted. Once you become a soldier it's difficult to return to a "normal" life. Any veteran will tell you that.

Tim, Marlin, Bernie, and Miles did what they had always done but with fancier job titles, an army of underlings, and a paycheck. They felt that we had achieved a kind of radical victory. Los Hombres was basically dissolved.

I turned down every job offer. First I was asked to train crews with Chico and the others, then I was offered administrative positions, overseeing various departments and task forces. I kept saying no. I stayed in Williamsburg and kept myself busy from day to day, pitching in with whatever needed to be done. I felt stronger about trying to return to a degree of normalcy. I had gained a considerable amount of notoriety, and I was recognized often. People on the street— and there were increasingly more of them—talked to me and asked me questions: how do we get this, do you know anything about that. I became a kind of one-man information center. I knew most of the bureaucrats. I could get higher-ups in the Red Cross on the phone, and between Phil and Bernie and Tim, I could get just about any information I wanted. People asked me about their friends, and I tried to find out their status. And more often than not, the powers that be called me. I was an informal consultant. I got asked to do a lot of TV and radio interviews, including that 20/20 special that was so heavily hyped. I tried to sound positive and upbeat, like everything would be okay.

And for the most part, it was. The Bug slowly burned itself out. As strangely and subtly as it had popped up in the first place, it kept dropping steadily until suicides became uncommon and we could walk the streets without being tensed up like springs. The suicide rate of the newcomers— the emergency workers and everyone else—was negligible, and the return of deserters seemed to act as a panacea, further slowing the rate of infection.

But there were so many bodies. It would be a long time before we would recover completely.

DISTANCE

With most of my friends we have a policy of the pop-in. Phones are suspect; it's better just to drop by. If the person's not home, you leave a note. Notes are personal. They prove that a human hand actually knocked on your door, a hand attached to an arm, attached to a body with another arm, arms that would have hugged you had you been home.

But I was expecting a call, so I answered. It was Olive.

I felt as if I were talking to someone in a faraway country, or to someone standing not far away in space but two or three years in the past. You were in different times, and could never connect.

She told me about how she had gotten on with her life out in California, until the day her mom called her out of the shower to hear Clinton's address on TV. She was terrified by the news that the Bug had spread to Manhattan, and she cried all afternoon and confessed to her mother why she had really left New York. That evening, Dan Rather took the reins of a detailed report, and cut to a local correspondent interviewing a young man with a shaved head, a bandaged arm, and a galaxy of powder burns on his face. It took her a while to realize it was me.

She might as have been be speaking Sanscrit. Somewhere, buried deep in my akashic records, I had always understood that words are merely wisps of wind stolen from the world, and all of us blabbermouths are nothing more than common thieves. I didn't know what to say so I resorted to small talk.

"Our landlord came by the other day."

"He did?"

"Yeah. He's not dead. He just ditched when the weirdness started. But he's back now. He won't charge me rent for a while yet, so that's okay. It was good to see him."

"I thought you didn't like him."

"I don't."

"Then why were you glad to see him?"

"Because he's alive. I'm always glad to see anyone that's alive."

"Oh." A gargantuan pause threatened.

"Are you still at your mom's?"

"Yes."

"How is everybody?"

"Everybody's great. We all watched you on *20/20*. My brother said—I shouldn't say it."

"No, go ahead."

I could almost see her screw up her nose. "He said you looked like a Holocaust survivor."

I laughed. "I am, Liv, I fucking am. Tell your brother he's right on the money."

"So what are you going to do?"

"I don't know yet. Up until now, just trying to live seemed like enough."

She seemed to loosen up. "You really are okay, aren't you?"

"I'm as good as can be expected. Better, probably." She didn't say anything. "What is it? What's up?"

"Benson… I… I'm scared to say this. But I want to come home."

"I thought you were home."

"I want to come back to New York."

"Oh." I had to catch myself. "Let me know. If you really want to, I can get you a sweet pad. I'm tight with everybody. It's a lot cheaper here now than it was, and there are jobs all over the place."

"I thought I would stay with you."

"Oh."

"You don't want me to come back?"

"It's not that I don't want you to come back. I'd love to see you. I just—I don't think you should live here with me. It's not a good idea."

"Are you seeing someone else?"

I chuckled. "Liv… come on. I have sex now and then, but sex is just another commodity here. It's not like that."

"Are you in love with someone else?"

"It's not that either. I—" I stopped and took a deep breath. "Liv. I love you. I always have and I always will. But I'm in love with everybody. Everybody who's alive. I can't explain it to you—that's why I don't think we should live together right now. You don't know how it got. You weren't here. You don't even know who I am anymore. You might not like me. If you want to come out here I'd love to see you but it's going to take awhile. You caught a glimpse, but I've been all the way down."

"Are you mad at me for leaving?"

"I don't blame you for a second. I probably should have left too, but I just couldn't."

"I'm glad you're not mad."

"Liv." I faltered. There wasn't anything else I could say to her. "It's nice to hear from you."

"Take care of yourself."

"I will."

EPILOGUE: REMAINS

It is a beautiful sunny day in May, and Phil and I are sitting up on my roof drinking beers. The view is stunning: a clear picture of the majestic Williamsburg Bridge reaching out to the island of Manhattan, the twin towers of the World Trade Center just beyond; the strange and mystical Byzantine church north of us with its green-onion dome, and the church just down the street reaching to the heavens in all its Catholic glory, its spire seemingly inches from the towering needle of the Empire State Building. It's a little hazy out, and large, full, pregnant clouds drift over us against a pale-blue backdrop, shaft lighting hinting at rain.

It is just before dusk, and the homing pigeons down on North 4th perform their daily wheeling ritual, chasing each other in a twister of wings and beaks, a mesmerizing spiral flashing white and pink in the dimming glow of the sun. We sit for a long time and sip slowly and look at it all, not saying a word. Phil still hasn't spoken since Toni's death, and I have taken up the habit of not speaking when he and I are alone together. It's become comforting to me to sit with him in silence. It's as if the vibrations of the universe have become enough for us; it is no longer necessary to impose our own upon it. We have become pawns in a larger struggle, and it is sufficient that we have chosen to fight on the side of the living. The universe knows this, and has apparently allowed us to live.

I'm gazing up, watching a floatplane circling around above us like he's looking for a place to set down. How wonderful it would be to have a plane like that, to have the freedom to fly anywhere, knowing that all I needed to land was a patch of water big enough to set her down. How amazing it would be to fly over Manhattan, just to glide in and set right down on the East River, get out and walk on home.

Phil seems to be watching it as well, and a mischievous smile plays across the corners of his lips. He jumps up and hurls his half-empty beer at the big white building just west of us, drops of beer spinning out of the neck, the bottle shattering with a crash against the side of the building, sending shards into the Chinese man's garden next door. Even before the glass shower is over Phil begins to scream, a bloodcurdling, transcendent scream of rank liminality, his larynx gurgling and scratching from disuse, his voice cracking and jumping octaves like a teenager's, and suddenly it's not just a scream, not just a violent shout-out to the world at large, but it becomes an intelligible chant, a single phrase repeated until his lungs empty themselves.

"I LOOOOOOVE NEEEEEEEW YOOOOOORRRK! I LOOOVE NEEEWW YOOORRRK! I LOVE NEW YORK I LOVE NEW YORK I LOVE NEW YOOOORK!" He runs out of air and almost squeaks as his diaphragm recoils and his lungs fill back up. He does a mad little spin and falls down on his back, looking up at the sky and panting.

I stand up and hurl my beer after his, with a little less force, and the bottle glances off the building across the garden and falls down into the bushes and still does not break. I lie on the roof next to Phil.

For a long time we don't say anything.

"Feel good?"

There's a long pause as he scratches his beard. His hair has grown out almost to a respectable length, and he's in bad need of a shave.

"That... felt... really good."

A cloud the size of Massachusetts drifts over us, in no particular hurry. "I was beginning to think you would never talk again."

He raises his hips slightly and something in his spine

cracks. "Just didn't see the need, really."

"I understand completely."

"Hey, man."

I look at him. He looks at me steadily through his glasses. He hasn't put his contacts in since this whole mess started. His eyes shimmer behind them, and I know what he's feeling, and I hope to whatever tired, puny god there is left that he doesn't start crying. I know if he does I'll never be able to stop.

"What is it?"

"Thanks. Thanks for pulling me back."

"Any time. I know you'd do the same for me."

The cloud above us decides to stay, and the light about us dims. I can now see the grey sheen over the East River, and I know the rain is heading our way.

"I mean it. You were great. You were really great."

"Thanks. You were pretty badass yourself, book man."

Phil laughs, a tired, spent little laugh that starts somewhere deep inside him and only barely manages to bubble to the surface.

"Hey, Phil. I think it's about to rain."

We can hear it creeping down the streets from the river… a steady pitter patter of heavenly love—a soft, early-summer rain that caresses the rooftops and kisses the sidewalks. The syncopated sound gets louder, and I see the rain spattering the edge of the roof, moving closer to us, and now we are lying down in a shower, the cool droplets soaking into our clothes, wetting our faces, smearing Phil's glasses, getting us drenched.

We don't move.

Now we start to laugh. It begins as a giggle and rises to a crescendo of belly laughs and chortles and chuckles, and still neither of us will stand up, we just lie there and laugh.

"We're gonna be all right, aren't we?" Phil says, talking over the rain and pushing the words past his laughter.

"We're gonna be all right."

"Are you going to leave?"

I look at him and laugh all the harder. "Leave now? Fuck. I'm with you."

And we both scream "I love New York" again and again and again, screaming out into the rain like a couple of madmen, screaming and shouting in a yogic chant of certainty, stubborn and indestructible, heroes of a war that was never fought, a disaster that history will try to forget. Both of us are soaked to the bone and neither of us gives a damn.

If there were a camera, it would pan out, and we would be seen as squirming inconsequential worms on a roof among an infinite number of other rooftops, all of them indiscriminately pelted with rain. And there would be a voice-over, by some famous actor with a solid-gold voice, and he would slowly intone over the tearful sounds of the rain, solemnly yet joyfully reciting my prayer:

Let the future unfold however it will. Let the universe expand to its greatest desires and maintain its own ignorance of destiny. Let the symmetry of perception match the spontaneity of motion. Let the chaos engulf itself. Let the people dance, the hyenas laugh, the ants labor. Let the sky be blue, the roots gnarled. Let the city override the nightmare, and watch nature take her toll on the soul of the world.

Let the sky be blue.

ACKNOWLEDGEMENTS

Thanks to Robert Lee for the layout, Meghan Carey for the cover, and Mike DeCapite for priceless editorial advice. Thanks also to Lee Anderson, Rebecca DeRosa, Steve Kosloff, and Matthew D'Abate. Thanks always to Ronit for keeping me together.

Special thanks to Thomas McCarthy, NYCHS general secretary and NYC DOC director of historical services, who clued me in to Hart Island. Credit to Desley Whisson, University of California, Davis, for the online information about rat poisons. Marlin's passage about the effects of a bullet wound comes from Ken Newgard, M.D.: "The Physiological Effects of Handgun Bullets: The Mechanisms of Wounding and Incapacitation," *Wound Ballistics Review*, 1(3): 12-17; 1992. The history of Williamsburg is taken largely from *Brooklynonline.com.*

My statistics on suicide rates were collected from sources provided by the American Association of Suicidology and the Office of Vital Statistics, New York City Department of Health, and compared to population and death rate data from the U.S. Census Bureau. For more information on the study of or prevention of suicide, go to *Suicidology.org.* If you are in crisis and need immediate help, call 1-800-273-TALK (8255).

Epigraph note: Harold Wobber's last words have also been reported as, "This is as far as I go."

Thanks to Axis Global (now SunGard) and Core Staffing for the job that allowed me to research this book. Thanks always to the Abbey bartenders for looking after me.

Many thanks to all those who, either willingly or unwittingly, served as inspiration for fictional characters, and especially those who suggested means of demise. Thank you Doug Parry; Will Kenton; "Rear Gang" regulars Robert Lee, David Sheehan, Amy Garrett, Kelly Starbuck, Sarah Katherine Gillespie, Karina Clark, and Stony Allen & Maciek

(R.I.P.); Williamsburg professionals Al the Bartender, Trippy the Bartender, Steve the barfly, Mario from Season's (now Acqua Santa), Tony from the Driggs Trattoria, Neil from the Driggs Luncheonette (now closed), George and the kid from Anna Maria's Pizza, and Ben Toro from Joe's Busy; James Mason; Sean O'Dea; Thomas Dwan; Tania Friedel, Angela Fratterola, Ilana Simmons, Henning Bierman (R.I.P.), and Aaron Hertzmann from NYU; Gabriel Faure-Brac, Susanna Harris, Craig Robillard, and the rest of the 1999–2000 crew of a certain lighting company; Roxanne Trimm; Andrea Goldfein; and the woman who convinced me to move to New York. And, of course, Rudy Giuliani, Bill Clinton, Al Roker, and Oprah.

—Bradley Spinelli
Brooklyn, 2013

©Kimberlee Hewitt

Bradley Spinelli was born in North Dakota. His play *Elusive* was presented by the National New Playwrights Network, Denver, and by 13th Street Repertory, NYC; *Pretty Mouth* was produced at the Duplex, NYC. He was a semifinalist for the Pirate's Alley Faulkner Competition. His short fiction has appeared in *The Sparkle Street Social and Athletic Club* and *Le Chat Noir*. An excerpt of this novel appeared in *Sensitive Skin*. Spinelli is currently working on a novel set in Bangkok. He lives with his wife in Brooklyn.

54893624R00157

Made in the USA
Columbia, SC
09 April 2019